A PERFECT MATCH

Bayshore (Keegan family) #1

EMBER LEIGH

Published by Ember Leigh, 2025

EmberLeighAuthor@gmail.com

Cover art: Qamber Designs

Editing: Elisabeth R. Nelson

contents

DEDICATION

This book is dedicated to Jorge: my personal chef, my baby daddy, and my 10/10 Zaddy. This book was made possible due to all of the excellent sammies my husband made for me, even when I reassured him I didn't need one (even though I secretly wanted one).

CHAPTER ONE

PIPER

"Good morning, Mr. Beverly!"

The wizened man watering his nearly-dead petunias is the first thing I see as I step out onto the front deck of my second-story apartment. Past his small bungalow, the sparkling waters of Briggs Bay shine in the early morning sun. It's seven thirty on this mid-September morning. That doesn't stop Mr. Beverly from tending his summer plants, which are ready to give their last gasp.

He lifts a hand, a big grin crossing his face. "Morning, Piper! Don't spend too much time on the commute, okay?"

His guffaw rings through the air, prompting my own giggle.

We've been trading these words for two years now, as long as I've lived in the apartment above my marshmallow and confectionary shop, Cloud Nine Confections. How cute is that? My commute is twenty seconds—thirty if I'm feeling sluggish—but I love the transition from cozy nested home space to carefully curated work space.

My footsteps pound down the worn wooden staircase hugging the back of the building. The last step feels like it might give out, but that's a landlord problem, one that I've been trying to get on Mrs. Decker's radar for the past several months. It's hard to get her attention when it comes to upkeep on the building—she's roughly two hundred years old and quite possibly lives in her native Germany—but occasionally she writes me an email with a promise to have one of her contentious sons look into repairs, so that's nice.

My keys clang against the metal back door. I'm grinning already. I love my business; I love inhabiting the space above my shop like some sort of weird marshmallow gremlin; I love everything about my cute little lakeside hometown and all the marshmallow-hungry fiends I call my customers and friends. It's my dream life.

Mostly.

I take a deep breath of the sweet scent of the back room, propping open the door to let some of that cool lake air drift in. I breeze through the shop, turning on lights, warming up the espresso machine, lighting ovens. It's all second nature to me—I could do this with my eyes closed *and* asleep. Once all the lights are on, the cute confection-core theme of my shop is all I can see. I've curated every last inch of this space to be an *experience.* One entire wall is a living moss backdrop (thanks, online instruction videos!); I installed a very small waterfall off to one side, which took me thirteen times as long as it would a professional, but dammit, I did it myself. Bulbous, cottony clouds hang by invisible wire from the ceiling. There are various spots along the moss wall where customers can sit at reclaimed wood tables, each one unique and paired with interesting chairs in a variety of bright colors. Illustrated marshmallows, cupcakes, suckers and more adorn the walls by way of framed pictures, neon lights, and wall decals. The entire place is a feast for the eyes, and there is an overwhelming amount of *pink*.

Just as I prefer it.

I've unlocked the front door and just poured my first latte for the day, the soothing notes of today's playlist pumping through the shop speakers—island reggae—when I spot someone darting across the sidewalk outside my shop. Thanks to her dark hair smoothed back into a low bun and crisply pressed white blouse set against high-waisted black slacks, I don't need to see her face to know who it is. This woman is a local celebrity.

Hazel Daly.

She pushes into my shop, the bells jingling against the glass as she glides in. Hazel is Bayshore's number one realtor, but she doesn't make a habit of being a doorbuster at Cloud Nine Confections. She tosses me a bright grin, but it fades quickly. Something dark tugs at the edges of her features, and I immediately get a knot in my stomach.

"Why do you look like you aren't here for s'mores and coffee?" I ask.

"Piper." Hazel walks up to me, her heels clicking against the wood flooring. "I don't love that I'm starting your day this way, but…"

"But?" I already have a high pitch to my voice. Hazel and I grew close after I catered her and Grayson's wedding with a late-night s'mores station and other marshmallow infused treats. I'm not afraid to go screechy in front of her.

"I just found out something you need to know." Her gaze drops to the countertop between us, and then she squares her shoulders. "This building has been sold in a secret sale. The deed was transferred yesterday."

I blink once. Then again. I don't even know how to make sense of her words. "*Sold?*"

"Yes."

"I didn't even know it was for sale," I sputter.

"Me neither. I think we both would have been very interested in that information," Hazel says with a sigh.

"Mrs. Decker never said anything to me." I don't add more when I realize she doesn't usually say much to me anyway.

"From what I heard," Hazel goes on, "the secrecy was a way to avoid some sort of family meltdown."

I frown, finally feeling able to take a sip of my latte. It immediately churns in my gut. "That sounds about right. Her sons are not exactly what I would call easy to get along with. They fight over everything. But why didn't she say anything to me?"

"I wish I knew."

"Do you know who bought it or...what they plan to do with it?" I can hardly utter the last part of that sentence. A new owner of the building could mean a lot of things. And most of them aren't great.

"All I could find out was that it's an out-of-towner," she says. "Their primary plans center around developing the empty side of the building."

That tidbit feels like a kernel of hope. The empty side of the building—that's all they want. I've always wondered about that unused storefront and distantly hoped to perhaps someday expand into it...if I ever gather the courage to expand my business beyond these four walls.

"So not kicking me out," I said slowly.

"Let's hope not," Hazel says in a firm voice. "I think you'll be fine—you have a lease in place, right? That, at the very least, will ensure you have time to get your ducks in a row. If you even need to. You might be facing a change of ownership, but I think they would be stupid to uproot a successful business that will essentially be paying their mortgage."

Something in her voice feels like a balm. Cool, collected Hazel is right. New owners don't have to mean I'll be kicked to the curb and forced to sell my business, move out of Bayshore, and stop selling marshmallows across all fifty United States per some ridiculous new legal agreement that somehow appeared out of thin air. That's ludicrous, even though I'd been secretly thinking that as a doomsday possibility.

"Thanks for letting me know," I finally say.

Hazel reaches across the countertop, squeezing my wrist. "You're welcome. Wanted you to know ASAP. Let me know what else you find out and if there's anything I can do, okay?" She winks and offers a reassuring smile. "I gotta run to a meeting, but I'll swing by later this week."

I watch her go, feeling both scared and oddly calm. This could either be completely fine or the beginning of an unimaginable nightmare. Who knows? Certainly not me.

Regulars begin to file in, either looking for their favorite coffees en route to the job or ready to settle in for a morning of remote work. Things are bustling for the first hour—one of my busiest times of day—and the hubbub helps me forget a little bit about the looming questions. Being forced to be on for my customers—bright smile at the ready, scripts on hand to describe today's specials—helps me forget about the anxiety gnawing at my gut.

But the second business lulls, the questions are back.

Who bought the building, if not one of Mrs. Decker's outrageously unappetizing sons? How did this mysterious new owner even find out it was for sale? What might they put in the other half of the building? Before I can even stop myself, I'm imagining the types of businesses that would want this lakeside proximity. A pool supply store. A yoga studio! Perhaps a boutique of some sort?

There are so many innocuous things it could be. Changing ownership doesn't have to be dire. Surely Hazel will return next week and we'll have a good laugh about how screechy I was for no reason at all.

I'm determined to not spend my day festering in uncertainty, so I move my attention to other aspects of my life. Between customers, I work on prepping more goodies for the rest of the week. I schedule a few posts on social media. I fantasize about a new business I'd like to start, even though the thought of sharing my hopes about this with anyone—especially my brothers—makes me feel sick. I reflect on the earth-shattering orgasms I had with a guy I met in a Cleveland club last month.

Oh, wait. I'm not supposed to be thinking about *that* either.

I look around the shop, curious if anyone noticed that my mind had gone down such a naughty route. All of the customers here are either staring at their laptops or absorbed in conversation. *Phew.*

I annoy myself with how much I still think about that guy. We spent eighteen hours of bliss in a swanky hotel room, yet I never got his real name. I'm not in a phase of life that has room for dating or falling in love, so I'm not eager to find him again. But at the same time, I'm dying to find him again.

He'd be a lot easier to forget if he hadn't dicked me down so good. Also if the only name he'd given me wasn't *Uncle Lobster.* That one night in Cleveland had been a pressure release valve for me, up to and including the amazing sex we experienced for hours and hours on top of all available surfaces in his hotel room. He'd slipped me his number—no legal name, unless his parents really did put Uncle Lobster on his birth certificate—but I let it float into the trash can at home the next day, even as a part of me was screaming not to let him disappear.

Do I regret ghosting Uncle Lobster? Absolutely. But that night had only been about releasing the pressure. Having a boyfriend is a non-option with my overprotective older brothers. I got Uncle Lobster out of my system—now I could continue with my regular life.

Except nothing feels very regular anymore with a mysterious new owner lurking next door.

I while the day away amid low-grade anxiety and sips of hot cocoa. It's early September, so technically still summer, but I'm ushering in the fall specials here at Cloud Nine. S'mores and hot cocoa are my jam—and my cash cows—and I'll be working overtime the next few weeks trying to get everyone stocked and ready for sweater weather.

Around two p.m., an unnaturally large cargo van pulls into the parking lot, followed by a few other vehicles. I only notice it because the van spends a lot of time backing into one spot, only to pull out, choose another spot, park again...and finally pull out and drive right up next to the sidewalk, completely blocking the sidewalk egress to the parking lot.

I'm not sure what's going on, other than an extremely indecisive driver. I keep an eye on the scene beyond my huge front windows while also replenishing that day's specialty marshmallows: caramel pumpkin. As I slice the block of marshmallow into small cubes, I notice a group of men standing on the sidewalk in front of the open side door of the van. A knot in my gut tells me this has to be related to the new owner.

These men don't look like they're here for s'mores and a latte. The equipment bursting out of the van tells me they're here to work.

The man with his back to the building suddenly turns and walks down the sidewalk, leading to the empty half of the building. The trendy angles of his haircut snag my attention first: short on the sides with longer layers on top that catch the afternoon light. Then my gaze drops to the broad, muscled planes of his shoulders stretching a thin black T-shirt that's seen better days. He moves with a distinct stride—somewhere between the confident swagger of someone who owns the place and the distracted urgency of a man with too much on his mind.

The closer he gets to the building the more details I begin to recognize. Chestnut hair that I already know how it feels to run my fingers through. A barrel chest that tapers to a lean waist, the kind of build you'd find on a linebacker who also happens to spend his days lifting heavy pans and hauling fifty-pound sacks of flour. His forearms are a roadmap of thin scars—some precise as knife cuts, others jagged from kitchen mishaps. Understanding begins a slow, uncomfortable prickle through my gut.

He removes his sunglasses as he strides past the front door of Cloud Nine, heading for the shop next door. The movement exposes his bicep and the chaotic lobster tattoo there—all claws and curves in black ink that I remember tracing with my tongue.

I know this man. Not just his body, but the way he felt inside me. Including how many orgasms he gave me.

This is the man who told me with a wink: *Do you like raisins? How about a date?*

The man I haven't been able to stop thinking about.

Uncle Lobster.

And if the way he's pulling open the door of the shop next to me means anything, he might be my new landlord.

CHAPTER TWO

KRU

"This is gonna clean up real nice." Dan the real estate agent smiles over at me, his high wattage grin reminding me of the huge billboard of his face over I-90 in Cleveland. That's where I've been living the past two years, and that's where I found his face—I mean services.

"Shouldn't be too much work to get it in condition to open." I lean against a countertop along the front wall. I wonder if Dan can hear how hard my heart is pounding. Being here, next to him, the camera crew and producers waiting outside, has the reality of the situation hitting me hard.

I did it. I am the new owner of this damn-near-lakeside building, which will not only be my newest business, it will be my *new home*.

But the work is only beginning.

This place has been empty for god knows how long, but the bones are good. That's what I keep telling myself, at least, as I launch myself into the wild unknown of financial risk. Because the reality is that I just sank every last penny I'd saved over the past five years into this place. Sure, I'd done extensive market research, pored over business plans and menu concepts. All signs pointed to this restaurant, here in Bayshore.

But it meant a big loan, a reality TV show to help offset some of the costs, and selling my share of the business Maverick Daly and I started in Cleveland.

This fucking needs to work out, because I don't have a Plan B.

"I saw you on that food truck show," Dan says, stuffing his hands into his pockets. "You did awesome. I love how you came back to help Maverick's food truck at the end, too."

"It's what you do for your brothers." I cross my arms, barely able to think back to the wild months of that food truck reality show. It had launched this exciting new chapter of my life, that's for sure—taking the leap to leave my native Wisconsin, move to Cleveland with Mav and build out our food truck concept together. The past few years have been a dream come true.

And now I'm ready for bigger dreams.

"I'm sure you'll drum up a bunch of interest with that camera crew outside." Dan tips his head toward the front of the building. "Bayshore is a solid little place. You should do well here."

I'm worried that I'll just fumble and fail, but I hope once I see the restaurant coming together, I'll start to feel more confident about this crazy ass scheme. I remind myself that I felt the same way in the weeks leading up to opening our Fork & Claw food truck in Cleveland. *This is part of the process.* I should get that tattooed somewhere on my body.

"It'll turn out great," I say.

"I'm sure you're ready for these." Dan reaches into his pocket, producing the keys. They jingle regally, somehow, the bell signaling my new life. We've already finished paperwork, so all that's left is this—giving me the keys to my own damn property.

As soon as I clasp them in my hand, Dan lifts a finger. "A couple extra details. You might have noticed the barn across the end of the parking lot. That *is* included with the purchase, the previous owner confirmed. She hasn't been inside it for at least a decade so there's no telling what's there. Apparently it was an old coach house from the family of the previous owner's husband that they never bothered to tear down. That's this key here." He points out a smaller padlock key on the ring.

"Cool. Surprise barn," I say with a laugh as I turn over the keys. There's only three, and if there's a surprise barn in the mix, there should be more. "And the other two?"

He points to each key in turn. "Rear entry, which goes into Cloud Nine. Front door on your side. Now, minor detail: I don't have the keys to the apartment upstairs. Turns out, the former landlord was renting it to the business owner next door."

I blink. "Well, that's new information."

"To me as well. But I'm sure you can clear that up. I don't think there was a rental agreement for the apartment upstairs, so it shouldn't be hard to get her out. She's got a lease for the shop though."

"And I don't plan on touching that," I say. The income from the other side of the shop is the bulk of my loan payment each month. But it doesn't cover all of it. So this restaurant that doesn't exist quite yet needs to generate some cash, *and fast.*

We share a chuckle. Dan looks toward the door, and I follow his gaze. The camera crew is unloading onto the sidewalk out front. It's time to get things going.

"I'll let you guys get to it." Dan offers a hand, which I shake firmly.

"Thanks for all your help."

"You let me know when you're ready to buy the next one, okay?" He shoots me that billboard smile again, and with a wave, he's out the door.

I watch the door shut behind him, and then let out a long breath.

This place is officially mine.

This barren, 1970s-looking, wood-paneled mess is mine.

I'll celebrate later. Right now, I have a camera crew to receive.

I breeze out of the front door, a few different emotions clamoring for space behind my ribs. But I don't have time to think about those, either. Leaving behind the business that Mav and I built is one thing. Moving to a brand new city is a whole extra level of newness. But hell if I'm not also mourning something I shouldn't even be thinking twice about...that girl I met in Cleveland last month.

The strawberry blonde goddess had shown up in the club, bought me three shots, and then rocked my world in every way imaginable...before ghosting me.

Moving to Bayshore is officially the end of *that* chapter as well. I'm tired of thinking about her. Tired of heading to that club on the off chance she'll show up again. I never got her name and she never called me, even though I gave her my number. I should really take that as my sign.

So this new venture in Bayshore needs to be clean slate.

No more pining over a woman I barely know.

I only have room for what's ahead. New horizons. New ventures. All that exciting next-chapter shit.

"All good to go in?" The producer of the reality TV show, Pat, shields his eyes from the afternoon glare as he looks over at me.

"Green light, buddies."

Pat is overseeing the show alongside a three-dude crew. We've met a couple times before this, going over the logistics, the show plans, what filming a renovation process will actually look like. This is part of a new reality TV series that follows small business owners through various stages of their business plans. For my episodes, the attraction will be coming into this dusty, forgotten space and turning it into a gourmet restaurant. Pat is sure that my previous stint on the food truck challenge will bring in a lot of viewers. I'm just happy to have a little extra financial padding as I dive headfirst into this exciting but scary chapter. I sure need it, because the mere thought of what happens if I miss a loan payment has had my palms sweating since we closed the deal on the building.

The parking lot is chaotic as the camera crew unloads and other patrons arrive, presumably for the store next to mine. I gave my neighbor's shop a quick check during my visit last month, but it was closed the day I came. I'd seen all I needed to that day—coffee, marshmallows, and desserts. Not direct competition, so nothing I needed to worry about. Probably some kooky old lady known as the go-to spot for kid's cakes. I'm looking forward to a quiet and innocuous relationship with my new neighbor, who I plan on introducing myself to as the next item on my to-do list.

My phone buzzes—it's a Cleveland number. It takes me a moment to place it, but when I do, I swear under my breath. It's the bank.

"Hello?"

"Mr. Krueger. Do you have a moment?"

It's rare that someone actually calls me by my full last name. Friends from high school and college firmly labeled me as *Kru*. Barely anybody calls me by my first name, Herman, because I don't like to admit that's my first name. It's much snappier to go by Kru.

"I do." I brace myself for bad news of some sort. Getting the loan was hard enough; maybe they've had second thoughts and need all the money back. "What can I do for you?"

The bank rep goes on to inform me in her calm customer-service tone that there was a problem issuing my debit cards for the bank accounts I recently opened. Relief threads through me. So I don't need to return all the hundreds of thousands of dollars—excellent. We can continue as planned.

Before I can even swipe out of the call, a sharp voice pierces the air.

"Hey! What are you guys doing out here?"

The voice sounds feminine. Possibly enraged. And it's coming from directly behind me. I pocket the phone and turn, finding a short, tightly packed strawberry-blonde bombshell staring straight at me, closed fists propped on her hips.

I blink once, then again. I'm not able to comprehend what I'm looking at.

Because the woman in front of me is the woman I haven't been able to stop thinking about since she ghosted me last month in Cleveland.

I open my mouth to say something, but I'm at a loss. She can't be my elderly bakery neighbor...can she?

"Your van is blocking the entrance for my customers," she says, leaning in with narrowed eyes. "My customer can't make it up the curb cut. You guys have been parked here for almost half an hour."

I still can't process who I'm seeing. I smile in spite of myself—she recognizes me, right? Did I imagine her? Or is this her identical twin?

"It's not funny," she snaps.

"Do you—" I cut myself off. She clearly doesn't remember me, which is fucking awkward, and not a great testament to my *skills*. The longer I stand here staring and not saying anything, the angrier she's getting. I can practically see her annoyance coming off her in comic book curlicues from the top of her head.

"You need to move that vehicle." Her voice is practically a slap across the cheek. She gestures to the back of the van. "Barb just had hip surgery. If she falls, you're getting the medical bill."

Fuck. I feel bad. Beyond the end of the van, I see someone assisting an elderly woman using a walker. They're attempting to step up onto the grassy divide that separates the parking lot from the storefront sidewalks. My brain rumbles back to life.

"I will assist Barb myself," I tell her. "We're unloading here, and the van will be moved as soon as we're done."

"You've been hogging the entryway for a full half hour," she reminds me. "There are about two hundred other places for you to park in this lot, but you chose the one spot that would ensure my customers can't enter safely."

"It was a mistake," I begin. Because it was. I'm definitely not the type of guy to be an asshole to people, much less paying customers.

"Furthermore, there's a time limit. So now you need to leave."

The sass in her tone prompts a laugh from me. "I won't be leaving. This is my property."

Her brows form a straight line and her chin dips. "So you're the new owner, huh?"

"Sorry, I didn't catch your name." I step closer, analyzing all of the details I can before she zips away. Her green eyes. The creamy skin I'd kissed every square inch of. I stick out my hand and she eyes it for just a moment too long before shaking it.

"Piper." Her smooth hand in mine sparks. The undercurrent is there, even if she's acting like she doesn't recognize me. She pulls away quickly and starts backing up, narrowing her eyes. "Hopefully you're a bit more considerate moving forward."

She zooms back toward the shop, brightly greeting Barb and her assistant who have since reached the front of the store via the grass. Piper looks over her shoulder at me, her bright smile falling only slightly as she narrows her eyes at me before disappearing into her shop. I still can't fully comprehend what just happened.

Pat comes up to me, saying in a low voice, "We got the whole thing recorded. That was epic. We'll be sure to get her to sign the release so we can use it for tension. Angry neighbors play so well on TV."

I heft with a small laugh. "And in real life?"

"That's for you two to hammer out once we're done filming," Pat said, nudging me in the side. "In the meantime, the thornier the better. You haven't even told her she needs to vacate the apartment yet, have you?"

My stomach turns into a knot and plummets to the bottom of my feet. *Fuck.* I'd forgotten about that small detail in facing down the woman who'd been haunting my memories for the past month. At least now I had a name, but along with that I had almost one hundred percent certainty that she either did not recognize me or was no longer interested in me. Did she not remember the four orgasms I'd given her?

"I sure haven't." I heave a sigh, rubbing at my forehead. First things first: I need to move this van. And after that?

I somehow had to find the courage to inform that little spitfire that not only am I her new landlord, I'm also kicking her out of her home.

CHAPTER THREE

PIPER

"Piper, do you want these in the walk-in or out front?"

The voice of my employee, Jerrica, jolts me out of concentration. I've been skulking near the front windows, tucking myself behind the mossy drapes, as I spy on the developments next door.

"Uh...walk-in's good." I toss her a bright smile, but she looks concerned as she heads for the back room with a tray of marshmallows. Jerrica has been helping me for the past year, once it became obvious that I couldn't open, close, prep for bulk orders *and* remember to feed myself while running this operation on my own.

Jerrica's in college and helps out super part time, which is about the extent of how much help I'll allow at this point. I barely let myself take on an employee until my mother reminded me a little sternly that it was normal for businesses to have employees and this wasn't a sign of my failing. That advice was in direct contrast to the loud chorus of opinions coming from my brothers, who have something to say about every single decision I do or don't make. Most times, I find it easier to just avoid certain situations at all costs. Until the decision to not hire someone started costing me my health. And even now, it makes me skittish.

The pleasant murmur of the Cloud Nine patrons settles over me, temporarily relaxing me. Until I spot Mr. New Landlord strutting out his front door, followed by a camera crew. I stiffen, a few sensations warring within me.

First of all, I'm disgruntled by the fact that he is so hot. The one-night-stand of my dreams seems to have bulked up since I last used his body as a playground. His biceps damn near doubled as a chin-up bar in Cleveland, and now? Whoo boy. I can't really think too long about it because I'm in public and someone is sure to ask me why my cheeks are pink.

And secondly, what in the actual fuck is happening over there? He's not just the new owner of the building, he has a camera crew. What sort of sociopath both blocks a curb cut *and* hires people to follow him around, documenting his every move? I never got narcissist vibes last month, but maybe I'd been too drunk to notice. I always thought I'd be able to sniff out a narcissist despite how many peanut butter and jelly shots I'd consumed.

"He's the guy from that reality TV show." A customer has materialized beside me—Mikey—jerking his chin toward my new neighbor as he addresses the cameras on the sidewalk. He's got a mic on, I notice now. I nod slowly.

"That explains the cord coming out of his pants," I mutter. Then I straighten, turning back toward the shop. So much for lurking in the moss drapes. "What show was he on?"

"That food truck show." Mikey stuffs his hands into his pockets, rattling change. "The one with the Daly kid."

"Oh, right." I straighten up the nearest table and chairs, fiddling with the centerpiece as though that's what I was intending to do all along. Really,

I'm just counseling myself to *not* stare out the window again. "I remember that show. I never watched it, but I heard about it."

"It was great. The Daly kid won, and he opened up his own food truck in Cleveland. With that guy, I think." Mikey's brows form a line and then he shuffles back to his table where he'd been sipping a hot cocoa and reading the newspaper. "Or maybe it was in Columbus."

"It was in Cleveland," another regular, Kaci, pipes up. She comes damn near five days a week for my homemade rice crispy treats.

"This is all very interesting." I try to sound bright and unaffected, but really I can't stop thinking about the way I'd felt in my new landlord's arms, the possessive way he'd bitten my neck that night, the way he'd tossed me around and filled me and—

"Piper, are you okay?" Jerrica touches my arm as I come around behind the front counter. "You're so flushed."

"Yeah, I'm—" *Horny. Unable to stop thinking about my new neighbor's dick. Remembering all the different places that man kissed me a month ago.* "Just thirsty. I need some water. I might be coming down with something."

Yeah, coming down with dickstalgia.

Nostalgia for that man's dick.

"I hope you're not getting sick! I saw your calendar back there—you've got a busy week of bulk orders."

"That I do." I draw a deep breath, some of the anxiety about the workload replacing my anxiety about the new neighbor.

"Do you want me to come in a few extra hours this weekend?"

"I think I'll be able to manage it," I tell her, though deep inside, I'm not sure I can. Still, I'm eager to prove to myself that I can be Superwoman. "I'll let you know if that changes."

Jerrica is going to close tonight so that I can escape a couple hours early. She's the closer on Wednesdays specifically so that I can attend my weekly family dinner. My mom, older brothers, and I have this family tradition where we get together on hump day as a mid-week check-in to eat together, play together, and laugh together. Instead of *Live, Laugh, Love* our family motto is *Eat, Laugh, Play Euchre.* My older brothers are absolute assholes when it comes to euchre, but it awakens the euchre asshole in me as well, so I'm powerless to resist.

This week, I'm gunning for first place. Brothers be damned.

"You better get going," Jerrica prompts. I check the wall clock—four p.m. She's right. She'll be closing up at six, when I'll be five cards deep into taking the throne in this week's euchre tourney.

"Thanks for your help, Jerrica." I untie my apron, my gaze sliding back toward the front windows, where I can just barely see one of the guys in the camera crew. "Let me know if anything crops up during closing. And those other marshmallows trays back there you can stick in the freezer. And all of the leftover brownies—"

"I know, plastic wrap and fridge." She's shooing me toward the back door. Separating me from my business is akin to separating a mother from her newborn—at least, I imagine it would be. I don't trust anyone to look after it or intuit its needs as well as I do. And it definitely needs milk every few hours.

I barely get out a *bye* before she pushes me out the back door with a quick, "Now go enjoy your time off!" I'm left waving at the closed steel door. For a moment I look around awkwardly. It always hurts to detach from my baby. But my mom will be mad if I don't make time for the family once a week, and I'm not trying to piss off my mom.

I run upstairs to my apartment, cooing *hello* to all my beautiful potted plants, fixing the throw blanket on the corner of the sofa, picking up my backpack for the bike ride to my mom's. I change out of my work leggings and into my leisure leggings. I'm a woman who likes leggings, dammit. After tossing on a nice slouchy sweater, I pop on my backpack and thump back down the exterior staircase. The early evening air is crisp. It's still warm enough to bike across town without a jacket, but I can feel the promise of true autumn in the air. I love it.

I unlock my bike from the bottom spire of the staircase railing and hop on. It's a quick ride to my mom's house across town, but I like to take the long way. I'm just one block from Briggs Bay and the boardwalk that traverses the width of the shoreline, and I need the scenic distraction today. I take in big gulps of freshwater air, listening to the caws of seagulls and the excited shouts of small children walking with their parents as I zoom down the path. Briggs Bay sparkles in the early-evening sunlight, and further out I can see where it opens up to Lake Erie. On the horizon, Kelley's Island glitters.

I smile into the warm sunlight, trying to quiet a small voice at the back of my head that keeps getting louder these days.

Everything feels perfectly fine...as long as I ignore the nagging sensation that I'm keeping myself in a box so that I don't rock the family boat.

I force those thoughts out of my head. I don't like entertaining anything less than wild satisfaction. Everything is great, dammit. I shouldn't want more than this. I have an amazing life. I'm a business owner at twenty-eight. I have a good relationship with all of my siblings. I love my mom. Having lost my father at a young age, I know the preciousness of life. I need to gulp it all down, take it all in, savor every second.

The nagging feeling like I'm missing something? Like somehow a romantic relationship might be a wise addition to my life? Like maybe I should take some risks and see if I can chew more than I've already bitten off? I don't have time for that.

I'm dating my marshmallow shop and men are perfectly good as siblings or friends, the end.

I zoom into the tree-shaded neighborhood where my brothers and I grew up. The leaves are just beginning to turn yellow and orange at the tips, but plenty of trees are still hanging on to summer green. In a few weeks this whole street will be ablaze with autumnal glory, and I cannot wait. By the time I pedal up to the garage door of my mom's house, I'm barely breaking a sweat. I pop the kickstand and leave my bike in front of my brother Jett's car. I can tell by the cars that everyone is here already, and I can already anticipate how *loud* it is inside.

The front door showcases Mom's new fall wreath—an excessive amount of fake leaves and a big burlap bow—and I push inside, the familiar scents of home washing over me, warm wood mixed with the lingering aroma of her lavender diffuser. The clamor of voices pulls me deeper into the house. Once I hit the dining room, it's Keegan time.

Everyone is here, and everyone turns to look at me all at once. I get varying levels of interest from my brothers, who are mostly focusing on some sporting event on the TV in the adjoining living room. My mom is the only one who lights up like she hasn't seen me in years.

"Hey, Pipe Cleaner," Asher says in his trademark grumble. He almost exclusively refers to me by my nickname. As the eldest, he stepped into that dad role once our father passed, so he treats me slightly more like a father would than the other male heathens I call my family.

"Hey, Asher. Hello, Griffin. Hello, Dane. Hello, *Jett.*" I drift around the table to give my mom a hug while my brothers jerk their chins in response. "Where's Lia?"

"Napping," Dane says without even looking at me. Lia is his three-year-old daughter. She's the one who makes this family complete, and I'm always ready for some niece snuggles.

"Fine, I'll impatiently wait for my favorite person to wake up." I sigh dramatically, sinking into the open chair beside Mom. It's my preferred space, but sometimes my brothers and I still fight for the honor of sitting next to mom. Thankfully, they're distracted enough by whatever is on the TV right now to not hassle me about it.

"You hungry?" Mom asks, squeezing my knee. Her dark blonde hair is pulled back into a low bun. She smiles warmly at me, and I spot signs of flour on her shirt. She runs the Bayshore Bakery downtown, one of the longest-running businesses in the area. She took it over from the former owner and has been keeping the tradition alive for the past twenty years.

"Sure am. What's on the menu for tonight?"

Suddenly, all of my brothers inhale sharply, eyes on the TV. Dane mutters under his breath and pounds the dining room table with his fist.

"Fucking Roberts did it again," Jett says.

"What are we watching?" I ask anyone who can hear. "It looks like there's a notable lack of ice."

Mom sighs. "Football."

"Oh, right. Football season."

We're a hockey family, thanks to Griffin's early and unnatural talent for the sport, but my brothers are still Midwestern men through and through, which means the occasional tailgate party and plenty of football season kick-offs—until hockey season starts, at least. Now that Griff is playing at the professional level, late September through early spring is usually dominated by hockey. This year will be different, though, because Griff got hurt; he's officially out on injured reserve until his ACL tear heals fully.

"Anything I can help with in the kitchen?" I twist to see what the status of dinner is. I can see the crockpot plugged in along the far wall, no doubt the source of the tantalizing smells. I pop to my feet just as my brothers all groan in unison.

"Fumble," Griffin confirms.

"You can get the plates out, honey." Mom drifts along behind me, heading for a fat loaf of sourdough bread. No doubt she brought it home from the shop. She reaches for a serrated knife and cuts big chunks off, arranging them on a plate.

We always eat first before we start playing euchre. It's a family tradition that came from my dad's side of the family that we keep up as an homage to him. It's also why we keep an hourglass on the mantle full of dad's ashes, so that he can participate in game night. One of the varied reasons why it's easier to not have a boyfriend. Explaining the family quirks would be…a lot.

I peek inside the crockpot—pork roast—and grab big plates to stack on the countertop.

Something else happens on the TV, and then Asher finally says, "There's no hope. I can't watch anymore."

"Turn it off," Dane agrees.

The TV clicks off, and I can feel my brothers' souls return to the present dimension. They begin filtering into the kitchen.

"Oh hey, Piper." Jett says. "When'd you get here?"

I side eye him. "You're not serious right? I said hello specifically to you like ten minutes ago."

Jett shrugs as he heads to the kitchen sink to wash his hands. "What can I say? I'm focused." A few grease streaks are still visible on his forearms, left over from his job as a mechanic.

I snort laugh just as Dane pulls me into a too-tight hug. "How's my baby sister this week?"

I open my mouth to give a breezy response but nothing comes out. Everyone notices my pause. Eyebrows lift.

"Piper?" Mom prompts as she serves big chunks of roast onto plates.

Griffin narrows his eyes at me as he steps up to our mom, reaching for the plate she holds out. "You good?"

The longer I fumble for words, the sharper the attention becomes, like a javelin ready to pop the flimsy balloon carrying my emotions. I hate showing weakness or indecision around my brothers. They prey upon it like it's fresh meat in a lion's cage.

My brothers aren't just relatives who happen to be a little older than me.

After our dad passed away when I was six, they became my caretakers. My protectors. My stand-in fathers, Asher more than the others. But as I've grown, they've all made it their mission to oversee my life.

"I'm fine," I say brightly, but it's too late. Asher is watching me suspiciously now too. This is the downside of being *too close* to your family. I can't even pause for too long around these people.

"Why do I not believe that?" Dane says with a smirk.

"I just got a little visit from Hazel Daly today—"

"Oh my god, don't tell me the building sold." My mom sets the ladle down and turns to me gravely. Now I'm actually anxious, because I can watch this conversation gathering steam to form a full-blown *situation*, and all I wanted to do was forget about my Uncle Lobster landlord for a few hours.

I struggle to find words to respond, because *how do moms immediately know?* "So you heard it was for sale?"

"The building sold?" Asher asks.

"I heard something about Mrs. Decker the other day—" my mom starts.

"Wait, doesn't she have like, a few surly sons that were planning on buying it?" Jett carries his plate over to the dining room table.

"Apparently her surly sons were kept out of the loop," I say, grabbing my own plate full of pork roast that my mother thrusts into my hands. "It sold and I met the new owner today."

My mom rolls her lips inward. "Who is it?"

"Nobody I know," I hurry to say. Maybe a little too quickly, like somehow the family closeness will also enable my brothers to read my mind and find out I slept with my landlord already on a drunken outing. They'd have a field day with that one. To them, I am not only their little sister, I am sacrosanct. Yet another reason why I find it easier to simply not have a love interest: I do not have the energy to bring someone new into this testosterone minefield.

"So not a local?" she prods.

"No, he's from Cleveland. Or somewhere else. I don't know."

"He's not gonna kick you out, right?" Asher says slowly, eyes narrowing.

"He better not." I carry my plate over to the table and settle into my usual spot, which is to the right of Griffin and the left of my mom.

"You have a lease, I'm assuming," Asher goes on.

"Of course I have a lease," I say, wracking my brain for the details. "It's got me locked in for another...I don't know...three years at least."

"Good," Jett says. "You're safe. For now."

Safe. From somebody kicking me out of my shop, maybe. But not from this little pulsating marshmallow of desire inside me.

It isn't long before little Lia joins us, sleepily rubbing her eyes and climbing up into her daddy's lap to watch us all in a post-nap daze and take the occasional bite of pork roast Dane offers her. Dad's hourglass looks out over the dining room from a ledge in the family room, where he'll participate in family game night in the only way he can. All is well. The pork roast is delicious. My brothers are happily ribbing each other about something I'm not paying attention to. And then suddenly the conversation returns to my shop.

"What's your new landlord's name?" Jett asks suddenly.

"Uh...I don't know yet." I won't admit I know his bizarre nickname. "But I almost called him by a name that starts with a d-i-c-k-wad today when he was blocking the entrance for my disabled customer." I try not to swear in front of my niece, even though it's a lost cause in this household. My brothers are as bad as sailors.

"I'll be stopping by to check him out," Griffin says with a harrumph. The chair groans underneath his enormous hockey build. The man must eat seven thousand calories a day. "Make sure he doesn't pull any shit."

"You don't have to do that," I say, but my voice withers under the boisterous voices of my brothers.

"Let's make sure he sees the lease with his own eyes, too," Asher says, leaning in closer to Griffin in that conspiratorial way that reminds me of every other thing my brothers have hijacked in my life.

"His own eyes and his asshole, even," Jett cackles.

"Jett," Mom starts, but I can tell she's smiling behind the admonishment.

"He better not fuck around with my little sister," Dane goes on. Lia pouts and looks up at him.

"Bad word, Daddy."

"Sorry, baby." He kisses the top of her head. "Don't repeat that."

"You guys," I say, thankful that nobody can tell how fast my heart is racing. "It'll be fine. I promise. He's fine. I'm fine. I have a lease. There's nothing wrong."

I'm babbling, because I know the truth. My brothers aren't hearing me. And they don't even know how far from *fine* I feel about the sexy one-night stand of my dreams becoming my new neighbor. Or the fact that I have a kernel of disappointment throbbing inside of me, because I had wanted that empty space for my own. I liked having the expanse of possibility beside me, on the off chance I grew some courage to expand my business in a way I haven't told a single soul about.

But it doesn't matter.

Because they'll never find out. The last thing I need is a love—or lobster—interest. I'm committed to my family. To my shop. To my life exactly how it is.

No matter how hot and muscled and intriguing my new landlord might be.

CHAPTER FOUR

KRU

Bayshore is awaking slowly the next morning. I'm drawing deep gulps of the fresh air as I make the short drive from my rental in a nearby neighborhood over to the new building. Satisfaction prickles through me as I cross the small, sleepy town.

Holy shit. I'm doing it.

I might be two hundred thousand dollars in debt, but I'm doing it.

I pull into the parking lot—safely away from the hotly contested curb cut—just as the first rays of dawn are creeping through the sky. I made it a point to get here extra early, because I need to have an uncomfortable conversation with Piper as soon as humanly possible.

I'm raw-dogging life right now, un-caffeinated and staring down a fourteen-hour day. But duty calls. I park my black pickup, and head around to the back of the building. Her shop is still dark, but I know she'll be awake—at least I hope she will be—since her shop is due to open in a little over an hour. In the back alley, I size up the rotted staircase leading up to the apartment. I hope it's not an indicator of what's up there. I never got a tour of the apartment, just was promised that it was functional and in need of only "light repairs in line with the primary business space."

So either a shit show awaits me or something extremely cute and bakery-esque like Piper's shop.

Either way, it's getting a face lift. While I've got the crew, I'm taking care of *everything*, no exceptions.

My footsteps go *thud thud thud* up the wooden staircase, and I'm worried the whole thing is going to break away as I knock on the door and wait.

I haven't exactly practiced what I'm going to say to Piper. I know the words will come to me when I need them. Besides, kicking my new tenant out of her home isn't a situation I can really ask any friends for guidance on. Per the advice of a lawyer I contacted, I made a formal written notice to kick off this awkward process. I scan the words on the sheet I brought along as I wait for her to show up.

There's a rustle behind the door, and then it swings open. Piper's head pokes out, her blonde hair damp and hanging heavy around her face. She's hiding her body behind the door. "Oh, it's you."

"Good morning," I say, wondering if I should smile. Be friendly. Buffer this bad news with a chat about the weather.

"What are you doing here?" Her scowl tells me to get to the point. That's when I notice the water droplets gathering in the hollow of her neck. They highlight the light freckles I'd loved and lavished attention on during our impossible night.

I can barely keep the words from escaping me. "Do you remember me?"

"Of course I remember you." Her brows nearly meet in the middle of her face. "You were blocking the sidewalk yesterday for like an entire year. What do you want?"

Everything inside me sighs heavily. She has to be lying. How could she not remember staying up to watch the sunrise on that hotel balcony? The thousands of kisses I'd given her, all over her chest, down her belly, between her legs. But now is *not* the time to get into it.

"I need to chat with you about a few things."

"And you think while I'm fresh out of the shower, about to open my shop for the day, is the best time to do this?"

"I don't know a better time," I shoot back.

"Why don't you schedule one?" she asks.

I swallow my annoyance. "Great. What would be a good time for you, Piper?"

"Well…" The expectant pause tells me she doesn't have a name to insert there.

"You don't know my name, do you?"

She sniffs, then shrugs.

"You can call me Kru."

"Kru?" she says, her face scrunching up. "Like…the cabin crew of an airplane?"

I tilt my head, watching as she becomes lost in thought.

"Or maybe it's like crew cut socks," she adds. "Crudité? Is it French? No, it must be short for something else. Cruesome? Like the word gruesome, but, you know, *you*."

I clear my throat, waiting until she's good and done with the guessing. But she's got more.

"Oh wait!" She snaps her fingers. "I know. You're a chef, right? Your name is Crouton. That's it. It's short for crouton. Very on brand, Kru."

"Are you done?" I ask. I'm amused, but I won't let her know that.

"Yeah, I guess. Just tell me if I'm right? I feel like one of those is bound to be right."

"You're not, though I'm sure it doesn't come as a surprise. Listen, I have something that needs to be discussed now." It should have been discussed yesterday, as a matter of fact. "There are some changes you need to be aware of."

She frowns, and the door opens slightly, revealing the cotton-candy pink towel she's clutching around her chest. I know what's under that towel. My fingers curl involuntarily as I try not to stare.

"Oh, great."

"I don't know how say this." My palms are actually sweating and I cross my arms, bolstering myself for the fall out. "There's no lease on this apartment here and I need it."

She blinks, nothing registering on her face. "What?"

"I own this apartment now."

"But I live here," she says slowly.

"It's getting renovated along with the space downstairs. It will become my primary residence. You have to move out."

She blinks a few more times. I feel like I just punched her in the face with this information, so I'm letting her take some time to absorb the blow.

"You can't kick me out," she starts.

"I'm not kicking you out. At least not yet." I offer the paper. "This is a formal written notice just so you know the eviction process will begin if you don't vacate within two weeks."

"Eviction process?" Her chest is flushing, along with her cheeks. She stares up at me with what I can only call a gaze full of loathing before she snatches the paper out of my hands. "And I'm sorry, did you say I have two weeks to find a new place to live and pack and...No. You have to be kidding me. You can't just kick somebody out of their house. I've been living here for *three years*—"

"Without a lease," I remind her.

"It was part of the arrangement," she hisses.

"Unless it's on paper, it's not an arrangement, it's a favor."

Her face falls, and that look turns into something more sinister. Something tells me I better start looking over my shoulder at night. "That is so fucking rude."

A little dose of reality can sting. Maybe this will be her lesson in getting *everything* on paper moving forward. "Listen. I'm sorry to be the bearer of bad news here, but whatever arrangement you had with the previous owner is null and void now. I'm the new owner, and this apartment is going to be renovated for me to occupy. They're starting downstairs first, but I can't knock them too far off schedule."

"Whatever happened to thirty days?" she demands.

"You can take thirty days if you want," I tell her, "but the construction crew is starting before that."

I'm the automatic jerk in this situation—I know it. But I need to treat this like the business situation it is, even if it hurts. I can't really think of anything else to add that won't make her hate me more, so I tear myself away from her cotton-candy deliciousness and thump down the staircase. Before I reach the ground, I hear her exasperated sigh of frustration, followed by the door slamming shut.

Well, that could not have possibly gone worse.

But I'm not sure there was a positive outcome for her in that scenario anyway.

My mind is on fire as I head around to the front of the building. My side of the building doesn't have a back entrance—yet—which is another thing Piper is absolutely going to hate once the construction crew starts bringing things up to code. Our sides of the building are going to have to meet in the back room, which means what is now her territory is officially going to become ours.

Can't wait for her to learn that little tidbit. But that's definitely for another day, because we need to let the smoke clear from the bomb I just dropped on her.

The camera crew is just arriving as I unlock the front door. Pat bounds up to me a moment later, looking too fresh for this hour. He's probably used to the insane schedule of reality TV shows. I'm used to the restaurant grind, which features late nights and not so many six a.m. wakeups, unless we sold out the night before. But the next month will be balls to the wall, especially with a full production and construction crew on site.

"Morning, Kru. Ready to get this party started?"

"As ready as a casserole at a family function." It's not my best food joke, but I'm a little distracted today. We step inside, the musty smell hitting me. It's almost hard to imagine what this place will look like after the refresh, but I can't wait.

"That reminds me, we need to make sure we get some of your one-liners today," Pat says. "You know so many food jokes, is that part of going to chef school?"

"Wasn't part of the curriculum," I say. "I've got food jokes for days though. I had a joke about pizza, but it was a little cheesy."

Pat snorts, pulling out his phone. "So let's make sure I'm up to speed on the schedule..."

"Interior reno crew will be arriving any minute. Pretty sure the plan is to start with dismantling the hideous wood paneling as top priority. Floors should be done by the end of the week with the kitchen equipment arriving next week."

"Yes, perfect." Pat is swiping through schedules on his phone. "And we will be on hand to catch it all! We should be rolling soon."

Kit, one of the camera guys, gives us a thumbs up. It's go time. I check my watch—almost eight. The windows are still covered with brown paper, but I swear I hear the rumble of heavy equipment outside. I push open the door and spot three commercial vans rolling into the lot, all with the same *Cookfield & Co.* branding emblazoned on the side.

"Here we go." I pop on a grin, striding outside. I can't help but glance over at Cloud Nine Confections. Piper is in the doorway, turning her hanging board sign to OPEN just as I walk out, and our gazes meet. Electricity sizzles through me all the way to my toes. Her strawberry blonde tresses are pulled up into a bun at the top of her head. She's got big dangly earrings, and those pouty lips are frowning.

Why won't she talk about the night in Cleveland?

The question is burning inside of me. I hate that she's playing some stupid game about it; then again, I didn't exactly show up in a very sexy light here in Bayshore.

"You must be Kru." A grinning man with a big belly and mischief in his eyes reaches for my hand. This is Mr. Cookfield himself, and as we exchange hellos and we introduce the construction team and the TV crew, I can feel Piper's gaze boring through me from her shop. The tops of my shoulders prickle, and I fight everything inside me, urging me to turn around and verify that I'm right.

I didn't come here to play games with a cute blonde with a bakery.

I came here to build my brand and my legacy.

I need to remember that, especially when the memories of Piper's kisses get too loud in my head. I've already learned my lesson when it comes to the type of attraction that makes you dizzy, upends you. It didn't just swallow me with my ex—it consumed me from the inside out. And I'm never going to let that happen again.

Focusing on the job isn't just a priority for my future. It's a priority for my reputation. Millions of people will be watching this show, watching *me*.

And I don't plan on making a fool of myself on national television.

CHAPTER FIVE

PIPER

Thump. Thump. Thump.

I draw in a deep breath through my nose, count to three, then slowly release.

It's my meditative exercise that I've been implementing around the clock, because if I don't? The construction noises coming from next door will drive me to murder. And believe me, I don't need much else to make me want to wring somebody's neck after my new landlord's unappetizing news.

My store is unnaturally empty today, and I can only assume that it's because everyone who's stopped in today realized the sawing and pounding was killing the vibe. I plan on invoicing Kruesome for the lost revenue. And for the ocular migraine I'll no doubt need to treat after two days of non-stop noise next door. On top of the new medications I'll undoubtedly seek due to excessive distress in having mere days to find and move into a new place to live. In fact, I'll just send him all the bills from my doctors to make my point.

Something that sounds like the highest-pitched sander in the world goes off. A shudder goes up my spine. I might perish in here. How many more days do I have to withstand this? I grind my jaw, focusing on the tray of marshmallows in front of me. I'm readying that day's Lakeside S'mores Packs orders, and roughly fifty bags are already stuffed with the requisite graham crackers, marshmallows and chocolate bars my clients have come to expect. Each bag is tied off with a pretty ribbon, branded with my store's name followed by a dreamy affirmation on the tag. I go the extra mile with the small details people love, which is why my store has gone viral a time or two on social media. One list of the top ten bakeries in the Midwest said that my shop was better than therapy.

Which I tend to agree with. Except for yesterday and today, when the construction noises combined with my new landlord are making this place worse than a nightmare.

The door opens and one of my regulars, Tammy, comes in. She's cringing, covering her ears immediately.

"I'm sorry," I say in lieu of a greeting, but my words are drowned out by the high-pitched whining. My shoulders slump. This is ridiculous, and it's barely noon. As soon as the noise breaks, Tammy orders, and I make quick work of ringing her up in the relative silence. My ears are ringing all through the break in construction noises.

"They're sure making a racket over there, huh?" she says with a small laugh as I prepare her coffee.

"Racket is an understatement. But it should be ending soon," I assure her with a big grin. Thankfully, she doesn't know that I'm fibbing. I intend to find out just how long the racket will last as soon as my shop empties out. One day was permissible. Two days of this is going to put me in the leading role of an episode of *Snapped*.

I pass Tammy her pumpkin latte so she can sip it while I get the rest of her order ready. She gifts her work clients a tray of packaged brownies each week, which I have sitting in the cooler in the back. But before I go back there, I grab the tray of extra marshmallows I'd been working on so that I can save the pre-cubed pieces for a different project. I'm humming to myself, enjoying the blessed quiet from next door. In the quiet, my thoughts are returning to me. I can actually hear myself think! Maybe now I can get back to thinking up fast alternate plans for somewhere to stay. I draw a deep sigh of relief, but just as I round the corner into the back room, *CRRRRAAAACK.*

The wall to my left begins to crumble, and I scream and jolt back. The tray in my hand goes flying. Drywall crumbles, and a massive hole is exposed in the back hallway.

A moment later, Kru's face peeks through at chest height.

He grins up at me, waving. "Hey there."

I'm sucking in big breaths of air, staring at him in disbelief. My heart is pounding and I might have peed my pants.

"What the fuck are you doing?" I demand.

He reaches for a piece of drywall and tugs at it, freeing it fully from the wall. After a few more punches to his side of the wall, he's created a landlord-sized hole, through which he steps. Suddenly, he's in the back of my shop, towering over me, his chestnut brown hair mussed and falling across his forehead, streaks of dirt on his arms.

"So...this door belongs to both of us," he says, pointing to the heavy steel back door.

"The hell it does," I spit. "There's always been a wall here, and I'd like it to return, thankyouverymuch."

He sniffs, propping his hands on his hips. He's broad and muscular, filling out his black tee in a way that makes my core ache. "Can't do that. Fire code requires an emergency egress point for both units."

I sigh, rubbing at my forehead. "How on earth can this be a problem when this wall has been here for probably thirty years?"

"Both units haven't been used in a long time," Kru says as he grabs the neckline of his shirt. He uses the collar to wipe at the sweat on his upper lip, which exposes a tantalizing glimpse of the flat planes of his lower belly, right above the belt that keeps his work jeans hugging his hips. Everything inside me cinches tight. *My lips have been there.* I study his face extra hard as I struggle to excise those thoughts. "So one condition for approval of my new restaurant is that I bring the building up to code. That's what I'm doing."

"And you didn't think a little warning was called for?" My voice is nearing shriek level. "Look, I just tossed this whole tray of marshmallows. Ruined product. Not to mention the fact that I thought I was about to be attacked by some sort of wall-punching ghost."

A smile flickers at his lips but then his gaze falls to my tray of marshmallows. "Shit. Sorry about that. I really didn't think the wall would break that easily. I was testing it on my own, and I punched through, and you were there. Totally wasn't my game plan."

"Well...make sure it doesn't happen again." Then I remember Tammy out front, waiting on me. "I have to go. I have customers, shockingly, even though your construction noise has driven almost all of my regulars away these past two days. Hard to work remotely from someplace you can't think."

"Is it loud over here?" he asks.

"Unfathomably," I tell him as I rustle in my cooler. When I have the small tray of wrapped brownies, I slam the cooler door shut and spin to face him. "How much longer is this nuisance going to last? It's affecting my business, and I didn't sign up for this."

Kru rubs at the back of his neck. "There's a lot left to do—"

"Oh good."

"—but the inconvenience will be worth it in the long run," he says with a pointed look. "The upgrades are necessary."

"Yeah. For *your* half of the building, including your brand new apartment." I flash him an extra-fake smile and head back to the front. Tammy has been waiting too long, and I'm so tired of the surprises from my lobster landlord.

My insides are drawn tight as I return to the counter, but I pop on a bright smile. "Sorry, just chatting with my new landlord."

"Is he going to take care of all the noise?" she asks.

"He's the one making it."

Tammy frowns. "What's going in over there?"

"Some sort of...questionable restaurant." Truth is, I know nothing about what he's planning to do, and I'm curious to find out. But I'll take that secret to the grave.

Tammy murmurs her condolences for the noise, then escapes with her brownies and latte. I'm left festering in my own discontent, gazing out at an empty store.

But not for long.

A bright-eyed man strides into the shop a moment later. I recognize him as a member of Kru's entourage.

"Welcome. Can I help you?"

The man breezes toward me. I can tell he's not from here. There's something a little too perfect about his face. His forehead is a little too plastic. "Hi, Piper. I'm Pat. It's a pleasure to meet you." He sticks out his hand, which I shake cautiously.

"Nice to meet you, Pat," I say slowly.

"I'm the producer for the reality TV show that's covering Kru's build next door." His smile widens slightly, and I can feel his hooks sink into me. "I've been meaning to come over here and chat with you. You have an *adorable* shop here, and I'm dying to see if you'd be interested in being featured on our show as well."

It takes a few moments for his words to sink in. "With Kru?"

"Not *with* him, but you might be featured in the same episode. Our specialty is following start-ups, small businesses, and entrepreneurs in all stages of growth. Kru's restaurant will definitely be a multi-episode affair, but your place is too cute to pass up. We don't make this offer to just anyone, but since we're in the plaza already, it's the perfect opportunity. Our viewers will *die* for this concept!" Pat's lilt tells me he comes from the West Coast somewhere, possibly LA. He reaches for my arm across the counter. "Honestly? This could be the number one confection shop in the entire *country*. People need to see this place."

I'm not sure if Pat is recruiting me or selling me something. Whatever it is, he's doing a good job. All I can see as he speaks is dollar signs. Lines of people. The exact opposite of whatever this *emptiness* is.

"I'm inclined to sign on the dotted line already," I admit with a little laugh, "but what's in it for me?"

Pat lowers his chin. "Exposure, honey. Tons of it. Hundreds of thousands of viewers who will become instant fans of Cloud Nine Confections. But I know exposure doesn't pay the bills. We pay out according to how much planned airtime you'll get. Your store would be something of a smaller segment, but we'll be cutting you a check if you agree to join the show."

"And what would I have to do?"

He shrugs noncommittally. "Nothing. Just be yourself. Make your marshmallows. Brew the coffee. We'll just grab some footage, capture you in your natural habitat, and see what comes up. Stuff like that."

I pretend to think about it, but I already know my answer. *Fuck yes.* I've been researching this show since the crew showed up, and they have a voracious fanbase. If I can convince even a fraction of those viewers to stop by my shop on their next trip to Ohio, I'll be further ahead than before.

Besides, it'll be a chance for me to make America love me more than they love Kru.

And I can't pass that up.

"It sounds great," I admit. "I'd love more eyes on my business."

"That's what we'll give you. In *spades*," Pat says. He winks at me before he turns for the door. "I'll get some paperwork to you shortly. They'll be filming over here by next week. Talk soon, Piper."

Pat pushes out of the shop, leaving me pensive and alone.

I mill around for the rest of the day, alternating between focus on custom orders and wondering what the hell I got myself into. Did I really just agree to be on a reality TV show? It seems a little extreme, but I also recognize it for what it is: a business move.

I've seen what viral success can do. It helped boost my business early on. It's why I'm as successful as I am, barely six years in, especially after the dumpster fire origin story of this place. Cloud Nine didn't start as *my* marshmallow shop; it began as a partnership between me and a former friend (emphasis on *former*) who wanted to run this place like a personal bank account while disputing every marketing idea I had. Our first year was a total nightmare, and when our sales barely equaled expenses and she was ready to jump ship, I jumped on the chance to push her out of the business altogether.

I'd gone into business with her in order to offset the scary investment required to launch a business like this. And to avoid having to ask my family for money. But I ended up crawling to my brothers for a loan to buy her out—and that whole debacle was imprinted in their mind as evidence that I have no idea what I'm doing and can never be trusted with business decisions ever again. Never mind the fact that I have long since paid them back.

And while this reality TV show might be a one-way ticket to the next level, I have a sneaking suspicion my brothers aren't going to see it that way.

Somehow I make it through the noisy, slow workday. When it's time to close down at six, my head is pounding. I can already envision all the zeroes my invoice to Kru will have for the damages related to surviving his construction-related racket. Once I'm in the shrouded sanctuary of my second-floor apartment, I feel some of the tension leave my shoulders, only to be replaced by a recurring donkey kick of realization.

I need to move ASAP.

Whatever tension I had from the work day has now multiplied. Kru sure knows how to ruin my day *and* my week. I sigh heavily, looking at the meager stash of boxes I've managed to assemble since he dropped the bomb on my cozy little above-shop life. I need help. Not just with packing, but finding somewhere to live.

My phone rings. I have a sinking feeling in my gut before I even look at the phone, and the name on the screen confirms my spidey sense.

It's Griff.

I answer hesitantly. "Hey, brother."

"Sup, Pipes?"

"Just getting home from work," I say, sinking into my green velvet love seat near the door. One of my most treasured thrift finds.

"Aren't you normally still at the shop?" he asks.

"Yeah, I've just got so much left to do," I say, then snap my mouth shut. I haven't told anyone in my family yet about the kicking-out. I feel it's best to drop one life-altering bomb at a time with my brothers, at a rate of about a month per piece of bad news. I've learned the hard way what it means to grow up with four hawkish, father-like older brothers. They can't find out about my needing to move until after it happens, since they're already incensed by the purchase of the building.

"What's going on?"

"Nothing."

A tense silence emerges. "Then what is there to do?"

"Nothing. I don't know. It's just a phrase."

"A phrase." The way Griffin repeats my words back to me tells me exactly how full of shit he thinks I am.

"Yeah. Like English."

His haughty chuckle begins slowly, but it quickly picks up steam. "You are so full of shit."

I bristle, glad that he can't see me, because he'd read my body language and know he was right. He's just two years older than me but sometimes I felt like we were twins growing up. "What did you call for?"

"Just wanted to check in on my little sis after the big news on Wednesday. That landlord still being a piece of shit?"

It takes everything in me to bite my tongue. But I can't hold it all back entirely. "Well, he burst through my back wall today…"

"What?"

"Something about fire code and the emergency egress." I sigh. "Our shops are going to be unified at the back. I'll be *conjoined twins* with him. Griff, this is a nightmare."

"Wait, he literally broke through your back wall?" he repeats.

"Yes! With a hammer or whatever." I remember the way his forearms flexed as he stepped through the hole in the wall and frown. The mischief and innocence in his smile will haunt me for longer than I want to admit.

"Oh my god. Let me talk to this guy."

"Don't. It's pointless. It's part of the fire code and it must be done—"

"Yeah, so he's telling *you*," Griff says. "Pipes, he's probably trying to run you out of there. You have a lease, right? Well, what's more convenient than an ending lease he doesn't renew? A suddenly vacant second half of the building for him to use however he wants!"

His words land harder than the hammer that broke through my back wall earlier today. I'd not considered this possibility. The idea makes me sick. "You think he's trying to push me out?"

"It sounds a little fucking suspicious, don't you think? Who needs to just burst through a wall? Next thing you know, he's gonna be reclaiming parts of your shop. Then suddenly you lose the whole back room. He probably plans to make it extra uncomfortable for you, so he can have the whole place to himself."

Lightbulbs are going off. "Oh my god. You're right! This makes so much more sense for why he'd want the apartment upstairs too—"

"Want what?"

I clamp my mouth shut, realizing I'd leaked the bad news without meaning to. I can hear my heart thumping in my chest. My entire face goes hot. *Fuck.*

"Say what now?" is all I can muster.

"It sounded like you said...he wants your apartment too?"

Silence throbs between us for a few beats. "I mean..."

"Jesus, Piper, you're doing it again! What the fuck is going on?"

I crumple against the couch. I can't keep this up any longer. I backed myself into a corner, and I need to face the big brother music. "Ugh, fine. He's kicking me out of the apartment."

"Excuse me?"

I groan. "Yes. I have five—no, three—more days to move. I've started packing. I'm leaving. He's renovating it and moving in—"

"Dude, Piper. I don't even know where to begin with everything you just said. Where the fuck are you going to go?"

The phone slips away from my face after that question. But it doesn't matter. Because I know he'll hear me as I shout my response. "I don't knoooow!"

I put the phone on speaker because I can't handle hearing his incredulity right next to my ear drum. "When the fuck were you going to mention this?"

"After I had found another apartment."

"Which would be when? After you spent a few weeks living on the sidewalk outside The Daily Grind? Jesus. This is insane. Why didn't you show him your rental contract?"

I drag my hands down my face, melting off the couch. This is the throbbing heart of the matter. The major fuck up that I, the youngest Keegan, am known for. The thing they all saw coming. The detail they'll hold over my head for the next four decades. "I didn't sign one."

Griff sighs.

Silence pounds all of his unspoken sentiments into me.

"So you've been living there for three years..." he begins.

"Without an agreement, *yes*," I clarify. "I never imagined Mr. Lobster would breeze in from Cleveland to start some reality restaurant, so you'll have to forgive me for not foreseeing this."

He sighs again, which just makes the disappointment burrow deeper.

"I really don't need to hear your well-meaning criticism right now," I start.

"That's not what I'm trying to do," he grumbles.

"Well, I know it's coming and you can save it," I snap. "I already feel like an idiot, I don't need you making me feel like more of one."

"You're not an idiot..."

"It sounded like you were about to add a 'but' there."

"But would it kill you to think about this shit next time?" he finishes.

I groan, snapping up the phone. "Okay, I'm done. Thank you for calling. Goodbye."

Before I can swipe the phone off, Griff says, "Wait, Piper. I'm really not trying to be an asshole. I have an idea."

My finger is a hair's breadth away from the End button. "What is it?"

"Move in with me."

I blink a few times, everything in my body rejecting this idea. "No."

"Why not?"

"Because you're my older brother, and I might be desperate but I'm not *that* desperate. I already lived with your stinky hockey pants once; I don't need to do it again."

"And I'm pro now, so I have people who take care of that for me, you know." A chuckle rumbles out of him. "It wouldn't be so bad living with me. It can be temporary. I just can't stomach the thought of you having nowhere to go."

My gaze drops to the old brown carpet of my living room. It's truly an eyesore and needed replaced probably twenty years ago. "I don't know, Griff."

"You'd rather be homeless than live with me? Wow..."

"It's not that," I hurry to add. "I just...I can do things on my own, okay? I don't need you or the others to come swooping in—"

"We're not controlling jerks," he snipes.

"I didn't say you were a controlling jerk," I hiss. "Even if you're using the exact words a controlling jerk would use. I'm saying I'd like to do this on my own."

As soon as the words leave my mouth, I know how foolish I am to pass up an opportunity like this. I have a soft landing pad. A way to ride out the storm.

Griff must be able to read my thoughts due to our twin-like nature because he says, "You like making things hard on yourself. I know. But listen. Living rent-free with your big brother for a month or two isn't the end of the world. Besides, I'm barely here. I might be injured this season, but I still go to practices and games. You work full-time. It's not like we'll be up each other's asses. Maybe you could do *me* a favor and just say yes because then I wouldn't worry about you freezing your ass off on the sidewalk once the cold weather really hits."

I can't fight the smile. I roll my eyes, even though he can't see me. "So now I'm doing *you* a favor."

"Yes. Relieving me of my big brother worry. Listen, I'll even go a step further and not tell Dane, Jett, or Asher the real reason you're moving in with me."

I swallow hard. That's a pretty sweet deal. "What about Mom?"

He tuts. "You know I gotta tell her. But I'll swear her to secrecy."

I weigh the offer. He makes sense—of course he does. All of my big brothers know best, which is exactly the problem. "You promise you won't let the rest of them find out?"

"Swear."

The last of my reservations float away. This is a huge weight off my shoulders, and the deepest parts of me are so relieved. "Deal."

I can hear the smile in his voice as he says, "I'll bring over some boxes tomorrow morning and I'll get you packed up...*roomie*."

CHAPTER SIX

KRU

I'm pretty sure Piper has been cursing my name since our encounter outside her front door last week. I swear I can hear her grumbling right before I drift off to sleep, like she's whispering her complaints about me into the voodoo doll she's no doubt created in my likeness. I'm trying not to let it bother me, even though every time I happen to cross paths with her in the back of the building, I get an icy stare. I don't think she's said one word to me since she moved the last of her things out of the apartment upstairs. Not unless you count the things she's said to the voodoo doll.

"Kru? Truck's here."

Pat tips his head toward the front of the restaurant. Progress has been zooming along since we started a week ago. The brand new flooring—vinyl planking in a rustic wood design—is enough to completely makeover the space, but we're not stopping there. The walls enclosing the kitchen are complete, and the crew is updating the interior walls right now. Everything is getting a rustic tinge—gourmet restaurant meets hipster barn. I think it's going to come together nicely, and I'm assessing everything for the hundredth time this week as I head toward the front of the restaurant.

As soon as I step outside, I tip my head up to check out the new sign that was installed. *Ray's.* I chose a scrawl-like font, something that almost resembles the handwriting of the man this place is named after—my father. It looks so damn good, and makes the whole thing feel much more real.

My smile fades when I notice the box truck is idling in front of the infamous curb cut. Shit. I hope Piper doesn't see. Or maybe I do, because then she'll say something to me for once. I can't lie, I don't hate it when she gets shrieky.

I jog toward the truck, waving. The passenger side window rolls down, and two incredibly large men greet me from inside. They're here to drop off the patio furniture I ordered. I point out the area the furniture will go—my brand new brick patio, laid on Monday morning. It's turning the dead space between the front of the building and the parking lot into a vibrant extension of the restaurant. A landscaping crew will arrive tomorrow to make things pretty and plant some privacy hedges. It's coming together faster than I could imagine, in part because I've only been sleeping four hours a night. I'm nearly a zombie a week in, and we're just getting started.

"Ooof. This one's a heavy guy." The huge driver and his even huger helper let out deep grunts as they unload six circular wooden tables along the sidewalk. I secretly name them Hans and Frans. I can't tell if they really think the tables are heavy or if it's a show they're putting on since I'm a customer, since they each carry a table by themselves without breaking a sweat.

The chairs come next. Twenty all together. Soon my patio—and the sidewalk I share with Piper—is a chaotic maze of furniture. I begin moving things into place while they unload, but I don't get too far on my own. Because that's when I realize they vastly undersold the weight of this outdoor patio furniture.

I'm not sure how Hans or Frans moved a table without the help of the other, because this shit isn't just heavy, it's made out of dark matter. I need someone from inside to help...or maybe a crane. The delivery guys wrap things up by depositing approximately eight huge, closed umbrellas along the last available slice of space on the sidewalk. *Great.*

"All righty. You have a good day." The driver tips his hat to me and clambers back inside the truck, his helper slamming the passenger door before I can even croak a thank you. The truck has barely rumbled out of the parking lot when another car pulls in.

Someone for Piper's shop.

Fuck.

What took them twenty minutes might take me a full week on my own. But hey. I'm young, I'm strong, and I'm delusionally inspired as a small business owner. I can fucking do this. I'm lugging all the chairs onto my new patio, watching for the customer in case there are any issues. An older lady sheepishly steps around my furniture mess, looking over at me with drawn brows.

"Sorry, just had a delivery." I wave to her as she continues her consternated creep toward Cloud Nine. Once she's inside the shop, my shoulders relax. See? No problem with entry. No medical mishap or broken bones from using the grass. I can rest easy.

Ten minutes pass in an increasingly sweaty patio workout. I've got two tables moved by sheer force of what amounts to hump-pushing them across the bricks. The camera crew is lurking near the front door, lenses aimed this way, so of course they're catching it all. Pat emerges a moment later, then helpfully shouts, "Take your shirt off for the next shots, okay?"

I straighten, shielding my eyes against the mid-day glare. "Seriously?"

"We've got an angle here and we're running with it," he shouts back.

I prop my hands on my hips, analyzing the bricks as I contemplate my next move. Taking my shirt off seems gratuitous. But this show *is* footing my loan payments for almost the first year of business so I suppose I can show a little skin for my reality-TV benefactors.

It might not be OnlyFans, but it could be OnlyPatioChairs for now.

"Nobody in there wants to help me, huh?" I finally ask before tearing my shirt off. I stuff it through my belt near my hip. Pat cheers as I flex for the camera.

"They're all busy in there," he calls out. "Besides, this is what we call ratings, baby! You got this, Kru."

If every piece of furniture here didn't weigh three thousand pounds, this would be easier. I use every ounce of brawn I've got to get these things into place. There's a lot of grunting involved. A few guttural roars. When I glance toward the building to see if I should keep going, Pat is all smiles. Along the wall of windows fronting Piper's shop, I see five different faces pressed to the glass. All women.

Maybe they like what they see. No harm there.

I'm just annoyed that a part of me wishes Piper did too—like she did last month.

"I hope you're getting the content you need," I force out as I begin to push one of the tables. Pat's looking at the digital screen of the camera, nodding.

"We definitely need this," he says. "Your abs play so well on camera."

I grunt out a laugh. I'm not sorry for the workout. With these long days, it's hard to get to the gym. I haven't even started the hunt for one in Bayshore yet, and most days I just crank out a bunch of push-ups right after I wake up.

Once all the chairs are moved and only two tables remain in the sidewalk, I need a break. Sweat prickles across the tops of my shoulders. The sun is out but the breeze is chilly, so I'm not too hot, but a breather sounds nice. I hop up onto one of the tables and draw a few deep breaths, looking out over the parking lot. I can imagine all the cars that will be filling it, the regional food bloggers coming to try my specials, my family from Wisconsin driving down for a long weekend. I can almost hear my mom's excited gasp, the way she'd say "Your dad would be so proud..."

It's no secret that I do what I do in honor of my father. He passed away from cancer five years ago, and it still feels like it happened yesterday. I was an adult when he passed—a fresh twenty-five—but I wasn't ready or remotely prepared, even though we knew it was coming. He was a fiend in the kitchen, and he'd be proud as hell of the business Mav and I built together. Prouder still of this one. Fuck, I wish he was around to see it all.

I'm lost in my feels, which means I need to get back to work or I'm going to start getting snot nosed and teary eyed here in the middle of the damn sidewalk. I hop off the table and reach for an umbrella. It swings around easily in my arms, and I'm still thinking about my dad when I pop it open to see how it looks expanded.

"Oh my god!"

There's a shriek.

"The muffins!"

I spin on my heels to see what the hell is going on. But my shoe connects with something first—a spongy muffin. Thoughts are forming a logjam in my brain—why am I stepping on a muffin? Whose muffin is this? Why was someone screaming? But before I can begin to answer any of these questions for myself, Piper is in front of me.

"Are you done here?" she hisses.

"Depends on what you're talking about," I offer, but the way her brows draw even tighter together tells me that was the wrong response. My gaze slides over this Cloud Nine cutie—who's somehow even more attractive when she's mad at me. A frilly white apron covers her clothes, and a big white box in her hands has an open lid—with a suspicious number of muffins on the ground around her. "What the hell happened?"

"*You* happened."

"I'm just minding my own business."

"Sure, if that's what you want to call it. I came out here to politely ask you to clear the way for my customer, and you nearly beheaded me with that umbrella. Now I have to go bake another dozen muffins on the fly for her order."

"Good thing you're a baker and know how to do that." As soon as the words leave my mouth, I know that was another wrong response. "Why were you carrying her muffins out here anyway?"

"She's in the car, waiting for me to hand them over," she seethes, slamming the lid of the box down. "She just had hip surgery. It would sure be nice if I wasn't battling my *landlord* every step of the way these days. It's like you're purposefully making things harder."

I blink from sheer surprise. She couldn't be farther from the truth. "Are you serious right now? I'm one hundred percent focused on my lane. Not sure if you can tell, but I'm in the middle of renovating a building that I purchased. With my money. To open *my* restaurant. I'm focused on myself. I promise you."

"Oh?" Something devilish lights up her eyes, and she takes a step closer. "Maybe that's exactly the problem, *Kru*. You've been blocking the sidewalk for an hour. Putting on this ridiculous display of—" she sputters for a word for a moment "—physical fortitude for some non-existent audience. And now you've completely ruined my customer's bulk order because you're *so focused on yourself*. Seriously, Kru. I know it might be hard to fathom, but I still have my business here too."

Her words are irritating. Actually, they're hurtful. And now I'm getting mad.

"I know you'd love to believe that my entire world revolves around you," I tell her, stepping closer as well, "but the fact of the matter is that things will work best if you do you, and I do me. This is a temporary inconvenience, but you're acting like it's the end of the world. Once the construction is done and the patio furniture is in place, you'll never be inconvenienced like this again."

"Until you think of something else to bother me with," she spits.

"Do you think I'm making it my life's work to bother you?"

"I think you have a financial interest in trying to get me out of my shop, yes. You already got me out of the apartment. I'm sure you could use an extra six hundred square feet for your neo-hipster chain restaurant small plates menu or whatever you're going to serve in there. Shit, you probably need a bar to dance on too—don't you take your shirt off and dance hourly? Isn't that part of the gimmick at Ray's? Lucky for you Cloud Nine already has a bar ready for you to strip on."

I cock my head, equal parts annoyed and amused. "You're just writing my business plan on the fly, aren't you? Keep it coming." I pull my phone out of my back pocket, opening the Notes app. "Go on. Tell me my next move. I'm writing it all down."

She rolls her eyes. "Not surprised this aligns with your goals. But be honest with me—just admit you're trying to drive me out of here. Because then maybe you'll stop with these dumb games."

"Whoa. Hang on." I lift a palm and jam my fingers onto it to form a T. "Time out, champ. You're jumping to a lot of conclusions and this ain't a track meet."

She rolls her eyes. "Ha ha, so funny."

"You've done nothing but throw muffins *and* accusations at me since you stepped out of your angry cloud over there. So you've got two options right now—go back inside your shop, take a breath, and try again, or just keep walking and let me finish what I'm working on."

She purses her lips. "I don't like those options."

"Not my problem."

She reaches into her muffin box and grabs one, throwing it at me. It bounces dully off my chest and joins its squished friend at my feet.

Again, not sure if I'm more upset or amused. A laugh escapes me.

"Option three: throw a muffin at me," I say.

"I don't like being told what to do," she hisses.

"Clearly."

She scowls at me, then spins on her heel to leave. I can't help myself. I pick up the muffin and lob it at her tightly packed ass. I can see the ricochet jiggle through her leggings and yes, it makes me smile. She gasps, turning to me with a look of shock.

"Did you just muffin my ass?"

"You muffined my chest!"

Her jaw drops further. For a moment, I'm not sure if she's going to burst into laughter or march over here and slap me. "You deserved it."

"So did you," I inform her, "for all the untrue things you just said."

She lets out a little squeak of indignation and reaches for the muffin. It's looking a little worse for wear but still has its form. She hauls her arm back and throws it—surprisingly hard—but I'm able to step aside in time. It misses me entirely.

But then her eyes go wide just as I hear a distinct *thwap*.

A timid voice interrupts us.

"Um, Piper?"

Piper covers her mouth, mortified, just as I turn. A very sheepish man stands at the curb cut, behind one of my very heavy tables, his gaze darting between her and me. A squashed muffin lies at his feet.

"Oh my god, Will, I'm so sorry!" She presses a hand to her forehead, cheeks flushed. "I meant to hit him, not you. What, uh...what can I do for you?"

He clears his throat, offering me a small smile. "I came out here to chat with you and, well, whoever is in charge of Ray's."

I wave at him, realizing how absurd this looks. I'm shirtless. There are cameras. Not to mention the muffins littering the sidewalk. I reach for my shirt, still hanging from my belt. But the damage is done. Putting the shirt on now would just prove to everyone that I should have been wearing it all along.

"That would be me." I offer a hand and my most winning smile, as if this might somehow distract him from the fact that I'm bare chested at noon at a local business. "I'm Kru. Head chef and owner of Ray's."

Will shakes my hand firmly. "It's great to meet you. I have something that will interest you."

He offers me a postcard from his other hand. He hands one to Piper as well.

"The Bayshore Chamber of Commerce is hosting a friendly Best of Bayshore competition. I thought you both would be interested in joining. We're looking to highlight the best specials from local eateries."

"That sounds amazing," Piper gushes.

"I'd love to join," I say.

"People will vote on the entries for the most beloved Bayshore dish." A smile flickers at Will's lips, but he still looks suspicious. "The sign-up information is there; feel free to reach out if you have any questions."

"Oh, I definitely will," Piper assures him.

"This will be a great way to launch my restaurant," I add.

"And a great way to test my new dessert special that I've been working on," she says. "Which will surely be considered one of the best things in Bayshore."

Will smiles wanly. "Great. I'm looking forward to it. I'll leave you two to...whatever you were doing before." He shuffles back into the parking lot and toward his car. He's barely ten steps away when Piper is in my face, her nose scrunched.

"I'm gonna win this," she tells me. The fire in her eyes has me inclined to believe her. But I'm nothing if not up for a good challenge.

"You'll win second place," I clarify.

She harrumphs and stalks away, leaving a trail of squished muffins. I try not to stare as she walks away, so I force my gaze over to Pat. He's got a big grin on his face, giving me a double thumbs up.

"So good it's like you planned it in advance!" he calls out.

Maybe it seems that way to him.

But becoming the landlord and neighbor to the one-night stand of my fantasies was never something I could have planned. The pricklier Piper becomes, the more desperate I am to tap into the *why*.

She melted like sugar in coffee when I met her in Cleveland. And now she's harder to crack than a frozen marshmallow.

I know I should let it go. I don't have the time or energy to pursue the answer to a question I shouldn't even be asking.

But I can't let it go.

I'm not just going to find out why.

I'm going to take first place in the competition while I figure it out.

CHAPTER SEVEN

PIPER

"And your challenge for today..." The dramatic reality show host voice booms out of the TV. "...the recipe must include *chutney*."

The camera switches between each contestant's reaction. Kru's face suddenly fills the screen, and something hot zips through me. I've been holed up in Griffin's living room since yesterday evening after work, binge watching the food truck reality show competition that featured Maverick Daly and Kru, among others. Maverick's girlfriend—or maybe she's a wife now?—Scarlett is featured on the show as well, another Bayshore native. It's wild to see people from my hometown on the big screen. It's even wilder to see a younger Kru here—flat-billed ballcaps galore, long hair on one side, shaved underneath. Every inch a punk chef.

This reality TV show was filmed maybe three years ago, and the Kru I met in that club—and now conduct business beside—seems so different from this kid on the screen. Now that I see this punk chef on the show, I understand the wiliness in his gaze. I'm connecting the dots about why he promised I'd come in second place.

All of it just makes me want to know more about him...and see what would happen if we found ourselves alone again in a hotel room for a night.

I reach for the bowl of popcorn at my side. I need to distract myself from those thoughts.

I couldn't possibly make a return to sexy time with that man after all the frustrating incidents accumulating between us.

But I can't possibly forget about the chemistry we shared, either.

I've settled in nicely to Griff's house, I must say. He's a neat freak and keeps a cozy home. Combined with the fact that he's not often home, this might be a more ideal situation that I wanted to acknowledge. I snuggle deeper into the black and rust red Cleveland Crushers throw blanket. Most of my household things are boxed up in his garage, but all my essentials have been unpacked into the spare bedroom—so this feels like half vacation, half temporary housing.

My attention snaps back to the television once the story returns to Kru. He's telling the camera how unfamiliar he is with chutney, but he's relying on Google and vibes for this challenge. I fight back a smile as he winks. The man is too charming for his own good.

"Piper?"

The deep voice of my older brother shocks me out of my skin. I am too stunned to even gasp. All I can think of is the fact that I'm watching Kru on his big screen TV, and I absolutely must hide this evidence before Griff catches me.

"Griffin?" I squeak. I dive for the remote, but I lose it in the fluffy folds of the blanket.

"Whatcha doing?" His voice grows nearer, as do the thuds of his footsteps through the kitchen.

"Just watching some TV." I struggle to keep my voice calm. Where the hell is this damn remote? "Are you back early?"

"Early?" He laughs as he towers over the back of the couch. "Do you even know what time it is?"

"Of course." My voice is pinched as I lift up the blanket, fanning it out. No remote. And worse yet, I'm realizing I lost track of time in a huge way. "It's...the evening."

His gaze slides to the TV just as something pops and fizzes on screen. Then there's a booming, "Holy shit, Kru! You exploded the chutney!"

Griffin squints at the screen. "Is that your *landlord*?"

The panic zipping through me turns to heavy resignation. I give up looking for the remote. "...Yes."

"Why are you watching him on *television*?" The disgust in Griffin's voice is unmistakable.

"I was just flipping through—"

"Is this related to the email notification I got yesterday that my account had been used to purchase a show?" Griffin's confusion is now turning into suspicion. He quirks a brow, a muscle in his square jaw ticking. I can just imagine the pieces falling into place inside his head, and it makes me panic.

"Well...you see..." The familiar cold dread of *needing to explain myself* snakes through my veins. Not just explain, but prove. Show Griffin, and my brothers in general, that I know what I'm doing. But the words form a logjam inside me. I can't squeak out anything, much less a perfectly acceptable "I wanted to watch it."

Instead, I'm clotheslined by the weight of my needs: to make sure none of my brothers find out I'm intensely attracted to Kru, and to maintain the image that I am a cool, confident, capable younger sister who needs no man.

"I don't know how you can stand to see his face all day and then also watch him on TV," Griff mutters. I've resorted to plunging my hands in between the couch cushions in a desperate bid to find the remote. Has it been that long since I turned the TV on or adjusted the volume? I finally make contact with it on the cushion seam beneath my butt. I hurry to click the TV off and take a deep breath.

Maybe now I can start thinking straight.

"I've been trying to get an idea of my competition," I finally say.

"Competition?" Griff sinks onto the far end of the couch, wincing a bit as he avoids overusing his injured leg.

"Bayshore is hosting a 'best of' food competition. I'm going to enter a dessert, of course. But Kru was there when Will from the Chamber came by and so he's entering too. He's determined to win."

Griff scoffs. "Fat chance of that."

"So I need to know as much as possible about my competition." I gesture toward the dark TV, content that I've finally explained myself. "If I'm going to beat him, I must understand him." My heart races as I wait for Griff's reaction.

He tips his head from side to side as he contemplates the dark screen. "We know where he plans to live. Where he works. I could always orchestrate an untimely refrigeration failure. Maybe he wakes up with one broken ulna."

"Ulna? Griff, I'm not talking sabotage *or* a back-alley beatdown here. Besides, do you really want to risk your career? You're the one rich Keegan—your poor entrepreneur siblings need you."

"Fair point. I'll send Jett. He'll pull some weird shit and never get caught."

I snort laugh. "I appreciate your willingness to fuck a dude up for me. But that's not what I'm after. I just want to see what he might be planning. This is the third food business he's opened. He's already been on a reality TV show." I don't want to say the next words, but they're ricocheting around my chest: *He's also been in my pants.*

I can already *feel* the shock and disappointment that such a confession would elicit from Griffin and the rest of my father-brothers. They can never find out. It would just be the final nail in a coffin I never wanted them to put me in.

"He might have been on a reality TV show, but that doesn't mean shit. *You* have the cutest marshmallow shop in the country, and that's a fact." Griffin jabs his finger in my direction as if this seals the deal. His words warm me, but I also see them for what they are: a proud big brother who is slightly blind to reason when it comes to my shop's reputation.

Griff wanders off into the kitchen. As he rummages around for snacks, I sigh and pull myself to standing. I suppose it's time to do something other than rot on the couch. I do some light stretching and finally opt for some fresh air, since I may have spent my entire day off sealed in the living room—-*oops*.

I step through Griff's sliding glass door leading out to a small cement patio. It's already dark and I take a deep breath of the chilly night air. I love the air in Bayshore in the fall—so crisp and clean. After a good lungful, I feel like I can conquer the world, not to mention win the Best of Bayshore competition. In between Kru-binging, I've been planning out my entry for the competition. I've settled on a strawberry and s'mores torte, which has been one of the most requested items from customers since the shop opened. I knew saving it for a special time would come in handy. That special time is *now*.

As my thoughts become more grounded, I begin to take notice of the neighbors. Specifically, the house directly behind Griff's backyard.

There's music. Voices. Laughter. Nothing terribly loud, but it piques my interest. I step barefoot over the patchy grass of his backyard—professional hockey players barely have time to keep a yard seeded, apparently—drifting closer to where the sound is coming from.

Deep male laughter booms through the night as bass-heavy music thumps in the distance. A thinning barrier of honeysuckle and roses divides the back of Griffin's lot from his neighbor's, along with a chain link fence. Somehow, he can't keep grass alive, but the roses are looking excellent.

Like the Nosy Nancy I am, I push aside some of the honeysuckle and peer through the greenery. A similar bungalow style home is in the lot behind Griff's. The backyard is a postage stamp, but unlike Griff's, it has a stone patio, a fire pit, and a whole crew of large, beefy men standing around, drinking beers and grilling.

Something warm churns to life inside me. The skin on my forearms prickles.

I'm looking into a stranger's backyard, but it feels familiar.

The faces. The wafting smell of cooking meat. That unmistakable laugh I'd just heard coming out of the TV speakers…

I straighten as the realization begins churning through my limbs. A broad-shouldered man wearing a gray tee and dark jeans is at the grill. He's wearing a flat-billed ballcap backwards, chestnut hair peeking out from the sides. Tattoos cover his forearms. He's regaling his audience with a story in his rich, bass voice.

I'm looking at Kru.

And the man at his side, in black pants and a tight black tee? Maverick Daly.

A moment later, a woman with a dark, silky high ponytail joins Maverick, sliding her arm around his waist. It's Scarlett. She nuzzles into him.

Holy shit. I just spent at least twelve hours watching them on TV, and now here I am, lurking in the honeysuckle while watching them in *real life.*

Have I accidentally taken a hit of a bong and am just imagining this on Griff's television? This is the height of parasocial weirdness, but I can't look away. They're having a house party of some sort, but I can't piece together why Kru is at the house directly behind Griffin's. Maybe Scarlett lives there? I don't know much about her; she's from Bayshore, but she was a few grades ahead of me in school, and we didn't cross paths much. Other people stream in and out of the house as Kru cooks, continuing his story. I can't hear what he's saying, but I'm dying to know the punchline.

Grayson Daly joins Maverick after a bit. Hazel's husband in the flesh. Good lord, the Daly brothers are good-looking. Maverick and Grayson share smiles, nodding and chatting about something. But then the star of the show closes the lid of the grill, turning to face the Daly brothers. My gaze solders onto those biceps. I can remember how his forearms flexed when he hoisted me, seemingly effortlessly. Like I weighed nothing. Memories slide through me, sticky sweet. I bite my bottom lip.

"Piper?"

Griffin's voice breaks through my voyeuristic daydreaming. I jolt, turning to shush him. I don't want his neighbors to realize what's going on.

"Keep it down!"

"What are you doing?" He looks genuinely confused, standing there on the cement patio.

I carefully remove myself from the honeysuckle and hurry toward him. "I'm spying," I whisper. "You won't believe who's back here."

His brows arch, and I beckon him to the honeysuckle with me. He begrudgingly follows, though I can practically hear all the doubts and sanity checks he's not saying out loud.

"Piper..." he begins as I part the greenery for him.

"Shh. Just look."

Griffin bends his enormous athlete body to peer through the bushes. I'm looking through my own honeysuckle window, immediately seeking out Kru. He's brushing something on the meat with a silicone brush. Maverick is clapping as he does it. Damn, I wish I were over there.

"Is that..." Griff finally starts.

"Kru, my landlord."

"I still can't believe Kru is his name." Griff's incredulity is a little too loud for the backyard peeping so I shush him. "What does it mean?" he asks in a slightly lower voice.

"It's his nickname, I guess. I don't know. I asked him, but he wouldn't tell me."

"Most sociopaths don't want you to know their real identities," Griff mutters.

"He's not a sociopath," I shoot back.

He turns to look at me. "He kicked you out of your apartment and gave you less than a month to find a new place."

"Right—"

"He axed through your back wall without any warning," he adds.

"Yes," I concede, "but—"

Griff huffs. "I don't really know what I'm supposed to be looking at other than a bunch of guys having a party, one of whom I'd really like to punch right now."

"*Griff,*" I hiss. "Don't you find it interesting that all of these people are at the property behind you?"

"Yeah. One more notch on the sociopath column, if you ask me. Koopa wasn't satisfied with taking your home, I guess, now he's following you to mine. That's some crime documentary behavior if you ask me."

I shake my head, the familiar sense of defeat threading through me. My brothers can't ever just be normal human beings. They always have to escalate everything to the nth degree of danger when it comes to me. Maybe it was a bad idea to move in with my brother, even temporarily.

"His name is Kru, not Koopa."

Griffin grumbles as he extracts himself from the honeysuckle. "This is weird, Piper. I'm gonna go back inside now."

I wait until the back door shuts behind him before I return to the honeysuckle. He might think Kru is a sociopath, but me? I'm just curious.

Perhaps *too* curious. I'll admit the Daly brothers are something like local celebrities now, after Maverick was on the show and Hazel and Grayson got married, not to mention their older brother Dominic opening up a heart clinic downtown that specifically serves low income patients. They're great guys—and if Maverick is in this backyard with Kru right now, that means Kru must be great, too. Right?

Grayson brings out a new round of beers; everyone clinks bottles before drinking. I spy until I, too, begin to feel weird. I need to lay this post-coital obsession to rest. Kru is my landlord now. Potentially my neighbor as well, and definitely my *usurper*. Resuming the behaviors from our first night together would not be wise, because it would make everything intolerably messy. Not just for me, but also with my family.

No way in hell would *any* of my brothers let me date the man who kicked me out of my own apartment.

So this is it. You've thrown muffins at his bare chest. You've binge watched his reality TV show. You've spied on him during a cookout. Can this be done now?

I turn to extract myself for the last time from the honeysuckle but my T-shirt snags. Damn, it's the rose bush. I twist to find where exactly I'm snagged, but my fingertips meet the sharp point of the rose thorn. I yelp, bringing the wounded fingertip to my mouth.

It's too dark back here along the fence line, so everything is a struggle. Not to mention, I really don't want to mess up the perfect roses I'd spotted, so I'm trying to dodge those as well. The leaves rustle as I twist and bend and grope for release. Does this rose bush have claws? Has it grown fingers and made a fist around my T-shirt? Frustration grows as I continue my battle with the foliage.

"Can I help you?"

A rough voice interrupts my struggle. I look up, finding Kru along the fence line, looking down at me with a smug smile.

"Uh...no. I'm fine, thanks."

He tips his head, and I can feel his gaze coursing over me, even in the low light of the backyard. "Damn, Piper. You just can't get enough of me, can you?"

The grit of his voice scrapes through me, leaving goosebumps in its wake. I'm embarrassed to notice that my panties are damp now. Still, I scoff, even though internally I'm agreeing with him. "Please. I just came out to enjoy the night air. I had no intention of finding you here."

"Finding me is one thing. Staying is another."

Fuck. Heat floods my cheeks, and I'm glad it's dark so he can't see proof of my embarrassment. Maybe he's been watching me for longer than I realized, which is another source of embarrassment altogether.

"I've only stayed long enough to notice you don't have your camera crew following your every move. I wasn't aware you were able to survive without that level of documentation."

"Just like you can't survive without keeping tabs on me." He delivers his rebuttal so coolly, effortlessly, that I want to stomp my foot. This was the same type of energy that hooked me the night we first met. And I'll be damned if it's going to get me a second time.

"I have zero interest in keeping tabs on you," I tell him. "Meanwhile, it seems you are obsessed with following me everywhere. Even to my brother's house."

"Me?" A small laugh escapes him. "I didn't even know your name until last week, how could I have possibly followed you to your brother's house?"

"There are ways," I tell him, though I don't care to expand on what they are. "Fact is, my brother has been living here for longer than you've even known Bayshore existed, so I don't want to hear anything that suggests I'm in the wrong here."

His head tips to the side. "I found you creeping along the fence line, staring at my party like an underfed orphan from a Dickens novel, and somehow that's my fault?"

The Dickens novel reference stops me, so all I can do is blurt, "Yes."

He laughs. Genuine belly laughter. It dissolves every last ounce of friction inside me and suddenly I'm glad the rose bush has its death claws in me.

I'd like to stay here.

"It's not funny," I tell him when his laughter dies down. "Stalking is a serious thing."

"Stalking. Right." He drifts closer, leaning his forearms against the chain link fence. I wish it were lighter back here so I could see how close he truly is. Maybe I'd catch the flecks of amber in his eyes like I did in Cleveland. Get lost in the map created by the tiny freckles on his cheeks.

"Piper, I have one question for you." The rough scrape of his voice straightens my spine. "Do you remember me from last month?"

He's added "from last month" to his question because he remembers how I answered this question last time. Damn him. The question, combined with the fact that I can feel the heat radiating off him, catches me off guard. I lace my fingers into the chain link fence for stability while I grope for my answer in the darkness.

"I guess I should take your silence as my answer, huh?" His voice is a little softer now. I can hear the hurt threaded through his words. I squeeze my eyes shut. I wish emotions had an off button. But there's no stopping the tidal wave of desire that courses through my body whenever I'm near this man. Especially this close.

"Maybe I just need a reminder," I blurt. My throat is dry and I swallow hard. Did I really say that? I tip my head back, and Kru fills my vision. My belly presses against the fence between us, and my knuckles brush against the solid heat behind his gray tee. Everything else shrinks to a blip around us. All I can see is his handsome face bathed in shadows, those brown eyes drinking me in, his lips curling at the corners.

"Oh yeah? What kind?"

I push up on my tiptoes, hoping my meaning will become clear as our noses touch. I don't remember in what moment we erased the space between us, but I'm glad we did. The hard planes of his chest press against me. He wants it. I want it. Anticipation bloats between us, heavy and seductive.

I don't know who moves first, but the air whooshes out of my lungs and suddenly my lips are against his. The scent of wood smoke fills my senses, mixed with the manly tang of his cologne that takes me straight back to the intimate cocoon we created in Cleveland. One kiss turns into two, then his lips are parting, inviting me to do the same. His tongue presses into my mouth, searching for mine. I whimper as his hand finds the back of my neck. His touch sends electricity skating through my limbs and I push higher onto my tiptoes, begging for more.

He lets out a soft grunt as our kisses go from tentative to unrestrained. Heat pools between my legs. Yes, I remember this. I remember it so well, and I don't just want more of it, *I need it.*

"Does that remind you?" His voice sounds drugged as he breaks away. His rough fingers are buried in the hair at the nape of my neck, sending tingles down my spine.

I can see the haze of arousal in his eyes; maybe I'd feel it pressed against my hip if it weren't for this damn fence in the way. Suddenly, none of the awkwardness or bitterness about recent events matters. I just want this man between my legs again. Face buried in the V of my thighs like it was in Cleveland, sending me to heights of pleasure that I hadn't even known existed.

"Mmmm," I begin, my eyes fluttering shut.

"You need another reminder, huh?"

I nod, and he tugs on my hair before dipping back down. His lips consume mine, and we're fucking each other's tongues when Griffin's voice pierces the air.

"Piper?"

Fuck. I disconnect from Kru with a gasp, like I've just come up from the bottom of the ocean. And in a way, that's what this is. My attraction to Kru submerges me to a dangerous level—I need to stay up where there's air. Clarity. Logic.

"I need to go," I bite out, ripping myself away from him. Except those kisses erased the rest of the thoughts in my brain. I forgot about the snag. About the rose bush and the death grip of the thorns. My shirt is still snagged as I begin sidling out of the foliage.

"Piper," Kru starts.

"Sorry. I need to leave."

My head is cloudy. My limbs are desperate to stay near Kru. But my brain knows Griffin can't find out I just kissed the man responsible for making me homeless, so I plow toward the house.

Rrrrrrrip.

I stumble a few steps away, still kiss-drunk. I feel the breeze across my belly before I notice I'm no longer wearing a shirt. Just my bra. My T-shirt dangles from the thorny claw of the rose bush. Kru just smirks at me, and I hurry toward the house.

"Don't ask," I warn Griffin as I speed past him into the house.

"A few questions come to mind," he says, but I don't let him ask a thing before I'm shut in my bedroom.

I need some time—and space—to myself after what just happened in the backyard. My heart is pounding and all I can think about is *more.*

More of that sweet pause. More kisses. More *Kru.*

But everything in my life right now is telling me I should have as little Kru as possible.

CHAPTER EIGHT

KRU

I may be a chef on various reality TV shows, but I'm starting to think my true calling is as a fence enthusiast.

Because holy shit, what happened at my rental home's fence line last night has been playing on repeat in my brain all fucking morning.

Piper Keegan kissed me. Well, technically I kissed her, but she was the one who leaned in first, who made those soft little noises in the back of her throat that drove me absolutely insane. The same noises she made back in Cleveland when we—

"Kru, you with me?" Pat, the producer, snaps his fingers in front of my face. "We need to finalize the shot list for today."

"Yeah. Sorry." I run a hand through my hair, trying to focus. "Where were we?"

"Final walk-through. We'll get some B-roll of you checking out the final details in each area of the building and then on the patio." Pat gestures broadly as he speaks, visualizing the shots. "I want to have a nice sit-down in the kitchen too. Something emotional. You're good at waxing poetic about ingredients."

I snort laugh. I've offered up plenty of impassioned monologues about garlic and gastropubs and all manner of food service since we started filming. I'm one rant away from starting my own podcast.

"Just say the word, and I'll give you a thirty-minute ode to your food item of choice. Plus a food joke as a bonus."

Pat snorts. "The food jokes will play well with the audience, I can already tell. You got a new one for today?"

I think, accessing the compendium within me. "Which potato makes the best detective?" After Pat shrugs, I say, "The one whose eyes are peeled."

There are a couple groans, which only make me laugh.

"If we're lucky, your feisty neighbor will make an appearance," he adds with a smirk. "She sure acts different when you're not around, I've noticed. It's like night and day when we're filming over there."

Pat has roped in a new part-time camera crew to begin capturing footage over at Piper's shop. I'm glad that she's getting a slice of the pie too—even if her spot will end up more of a footnote than a feature like mine—because I still feel bad for ousting her from the apartment. Maybe I view it as my secret olive branch, because she certainly doesn't give me a chance to explain myself.

But she'll take the time to suck your face off.

Fuck. Those kisses. A shiver runs down my spine, and I'm half-hard from the memory. Not great when I'm running through the day's shooting plan with Pat.

I clear my throat. "Yeah, she's not exactly a superfan of Ray's."

Though maybe that'll change after last night. Even though nobody but us knows what happened across the fence.

We go through the rest of the shot list, but my mind keeps drifting to that strawberry blonde caught in the rose bush, to soft lips and eager moans, to the way she'd melted against me like she's been dying for it since Cleveland just as much as I have.

And her radio silence this morning? Annoying, but not unexpected.

As soon as Pat leaves to address something with the crew outside, I decide I need coffee.

I'm going straight to Cloud Nine.

The bell on Piper's shop door jingles when I push it open. The smell hits me immediately—sugar and vanilla and something distinctly her. Her shop is busy with the mid-morning crowd, perfect lighting streaming through the windows, illuminating the selfie wall with its impossibly photogenic marshmallow and moss display. Everyone's got their phones out. I can just imagine the social media tags flying, the shares, the filters enhancing the photos being uploaded.

She's got a winning combo in here, and she knows it.

Piper is behind the counter in a crisp white apron, her strawberry blonde hair swept up into a messy bun that somehow looks completely intentional. She doesn't even glance my way. She's too busy piping something onto a tray of marshmallows, her steady hands betraying years of practiced precision.

"Good morning," I say, sliding up to the counter.

She jolts like I've shocked her, nearly ruining whatever design she was creating. "Oh my—*Crouton*. It's you." Her cheeks flush a shade of pink that matches some of her more colorful confections. "What do you want?"

"Coffee. Black." I pause. "Do you greet all your customers like this?"

"No. Just the ones who kick me out of my apartment and habitually block access to my main source of revenue."

So we're back to that. "Can we talk about what happened last night?"

Her eyes dart to her customers, then back to me. "There are people here, Kru."

"So?"

"So I'm not discussing my personal life in front of paying customers."

"When would you prefer to discuss it?"

She rolls her eyes and busies herself with pouring my coffee. "I've been working. Some of us can't just wander around whenever we feel like it."

"I'm working too."

"Seems more like you're annoying me." She slides the coffee across the counter. "Four dollars."

I hand her a ten and don't bother collecting the change. "You know, most people who spend the night with their tongues down each other's throats don't pretend it didn't happen the next day."

The old lady behind me gasps. Piper's face goes from pink to crimson in half a second.

"Oh my god. Can you please—" She lowers her voice to a hiss. "Can you please just go back to your side of the building?"

"Fine." I take a sip of the coffee. It's good—better than whatever we've been brewing in our kitchen. "But we should talk about this."

"There's nothing to talk about."

I lean in, dropping my voice low enough that only she can hear. "If you want to take this back to the fence, just say the word. Nobody has to know."

Her mouth falls open, and I can see the exact moment her brain short-circuits. It's delicious. She looks like she wants to leap over the counter and either slap me or rip my clothes off. Maybe both.

"You're impossible," she finally manages.

"But I could make something else possible if you want."

"Go. Away."

"Thanks for the coffee, Piper." I give her a wink and turn to leave, but not before I see her reach for a nearby tray. I imagine she's weighing whether throwing it at my head would be worth the mess. I escape unscathed—and still as horny as she left me last night.

Back at my restaurant, Pat is still reviewing the day's plan with the camera crew. I duck into the kitchen, away from their lenses for a moment of peace. My brain is still buzzing with Piper—the curve of her lips, the flush on her cheeks. She wants me. I know she does. This push and pull between us is just foreplay, and we both know how that story ends. I just can't figure out why she's still insistent on acting like last month in Cleveland never happened, and it's driving me fucking nuts.

Truth is, I shouldn't care. I don't have time for this. I've got a restaurant to open, a show to film, a reputation to build. The last time I let a woman get under my skin, I nearly lost everything I'd worked for. I still haven't fully recovered from that tailspin.

And yet.

There's something about Piper Keegan that makes me want to throw caution to the wind. The memory of those two nights in Cleveland, when neither of us knew each other's names but somehow understood each other perfectly, haunts me harder than a Victorian ghost in a dilapidated mansion. Or maybe it's because she's the first woman since Vanessa who's made me feel like there might be someone worth risking my heart for again.

I'm still contemplating this when my phone buzzes in my pocket. It's a text from Maverick, checking in on me.

MAVERICK: *Cameras are getting good stuff? Producer called me for a cameo.*

KRU: *Everything's chill today. Getting final shots before we open.*

MAVERICK: *Glad to hear.*

KRU: *I did visit my neighbor...*

Three dots appear immediately.

MAVERICK: *Trouble in paradise? Or maybe just pure paradise...*

I laugh out loud at that. He heard all about what happened at the fence last night. He and Scarlett are rooting for this match, but I'm not sure it's the wisest thing. I want Piper, but part of me thinks I should be smart...and single.

KRU: If paradise includes a hostile marshmallow maven.

MAVERICK: That could be a cool new restaurant concept...

I laugh again and shove the phone back in my pocket without answering.

He's getting me back on track, even if he doesn't realize it. I can't afford to get sidetracked, not when I'm this close to everything I've worked for. The restaurant, the show, my name on the map—it's all happening. A girl with killer curves and a talent for marshmallows is not part of the plan.

Even if she kisses like she was made for me.

Even if I can't stop thinking about her.

Even if I haven't felt this alive in years.

Pat comes barreling into the kitchen with the camera crew, interrupting my doomed train of thought. It's time to get back to work.

We spend some time with me inspecting the gleaming corners of the freshly installed kitchen—pointing out equipment, opening cabinets, entering the walk-in fridge. We move into the front of house, inspecting the wooden chairs, pointing out the grain on the tabletops, highlighting the pieces of art and why I contracted Wisconsin artists. After a few stints on the patio and some retakes along the way, we've got our content for the day.

Now comes the next item on my to-do list: interviewing potential new staff.

This is the part that makes me anxious. Like *really* anxious. I need a good crew, and I need to train them up right. Finding good help is no small feat, so I'm spending a lot of time with each applicant who steps through my door that afternoon. Some are clear no's, like the one guy who admitted halfway through the interview that he'd thought this was for a position as a taste tester. Some are maybes—part timers who seem enthusiastic—and then I've got a few stand-out applicants who would be an immediate yes except I need to take my time and weigh my options.

After a few grueling hours of interviewing strangers in front of cameras, I'm whooped. It's almost dinner time, and my stomach is growling. I convince Pat to wrap early—I need a proper evening of rest, dammit—and retire to the kitchen.

My sanctuary.

There isn't much in here in the way of food yet, but I do have a few staples that I picked up at the local wholesale place just to start toying with ideas. It felt like a braised short rib taco sort of night when I was at the store earlier, so I check on the meat simmering on the stovetop. It's been going for almost three hours, and I'm dying to test my first official meal in the new place. I crank the hood, pleased with how it sucks out the rising steam from the pot. This kitchen is fucking awesome—and frighteningly expensive. I've done the mental math on how many steaks I need to sell to pay it off, and my calculations tell me it'll take at least three years.

The smells coming from the pot already tell me this is going to be a banger. I replace the lid and wander to my stock room to grab some cleaning rags. While I'm back there, I hear a voice.

Specifically, Piper's voice. Singing what sounds like some kind of made-up tune. I pause, straining to hear better.

"My name is Piper and I'm doing piping," she croons in a surprisingly melodic voice. " Making tiny roses that are oh-so-striking..."

Oh my God. Does she sing this every time she works? This is too cute and I must hear more. I move quietly through the storage room to the portal between our shops, the still-jagged but human-sized opening leading to her back room. Through the opening, I can see Piper with her back to me, piping something onto a tray of marshmallows, completely in her own world as she continues her song.

"Squeeze the bag and twist around, make each petal tight. Ten trillion more trays to go before I sleep tonight..."

I can't help myself. I step through the hole and clear my throat. "Grammy-worthy."

Piper screams—like, actually screams—at the same time she squeezes the piping bag. It squirts and hits the wall, leaving a trail of pink buttercream sliding down the clean surface. Her eyes are wide, hand clutching her chest like she's having a heart attack.

"*What the actual fuck?*"

I burst out laughing, which only makes her angrier. Her face turns the exact shade of the buttercream now oozing down her wall.

"You!" She grabs the nearest thing—a kitchen towel—and throws it at my face. I catch it easily. She's breathing hard, like she's run a mile. "God, I hate when people do that."

"Do what? Walk through doorways?"

"Startle me." She runs her hands through her hair, messing up the bun. "My brothers used to hide around corners just to hear me scream. Assholes thought it was hilarious."

I lean against the remnants of the wall. "Well, it *was* kinda funny."

Her eyes narrow. "I'm glad my trauma amuses you."

"Trauma?"

"Four older brothers, Kru. Four. Do you know what it's like to constantly be on edge because at any moment, someone might leap out at you?"

"No, but I'm beginning to understand why you're so tense all the time."

She crosses her arms. "I am not tense."

I give her a pointed look, and she sighs, shoulders dropping slightly.

"Fine. Maybe a little. But it's not just the startle factor. It's..." She gestures vaguely around her shop. "Everything. Building a business from scratch isn't exactly relaxing."

"Tell me about it." I drink her in from head to toe, appreciating the smear of buttercream on her cheek, the wispy fly-aways escaping her cute messy bun. "Though I noticed you managed to keep your shirt on for the entire work day. That counts for something."

"Unlike you," she counters.

"I took mine off willingly. Yours was ripped off by a bush."

Her cheeks flush, and she looks away. "That was...unfortunate."

"I wouldn't say that."

Her eyes snap back to mine, and for a second I think she might throw something else at me. But then the corner of her mouth quirks up. There's something she wants to say. She jerks her gaze away, and it feels like a cold breeze blows between us.

I step further into her space, taking in the organized chaos of her work area. "So tell me about your day. Stressful?"

She sighs and turns back to her ruined piping work. "Just busy. I've been taking on a lot of extra orders to save up for a security deposit."

"For a new apartment?"

"Yeah." She grabs a spatula and starts scraping the pink cream off the wall. "Living with Griffin is...fine. But it's just temporary. I need my own place."

"Found anything yet?"

"No. And rents in Bayshore are insane right now. It's the tail end of tourist season still."

I watch her clean for a moment. "What about buying?"

She snorts. "Yeah, because I just have a down payment sitting around." She tosses the soiled spatula into the sink. "Between running this place and trying to figure out how to expand my business, I barely have time to sleep, let alone house hunt."

That catches my attention. "Expand your business?"

She freezes, like she's said more than she meant to. "Just...something I've been thinking about. I don't want to talk about the details too much yet, but...I want to build out an event-facing side of the business."

"Smart move. Expand your revenue streams."

She eyes me suspiciously. "Why do you sound impressed? Aren't you supposed to be hoping I fail so you can take over my side of the building too?"

I narrow my eyes. "Contrary to what you might think, I don't actually want you to fail. You renting this side of the building is part of my business plan. Besides, our businesses complement each other."

"Will you still be saying that when I win Best of Bayshore?" she challenges, but there's less bite in her tone than before.

"Of course. But those aren't the words I'll be practicing in the mirror. I'm ready to take first place, Madam Marshmallow."

She groans, but there's laughter behind it. "Seriously? Madam Marshmallow?"

"Would you prefer Cookie? Cupcake? Sugar Plum?"

"I'd prefer my actual name."

"Piper is so legal, though."

"Says the man named after the ground crew of the Cleveland airport." She smirks.

"Are you opposed to using nicknames?"

"Not when they make sense," she shoots back.

"Madam Marshmallow makes perfect sense for you. And if you're talking about my name, it's short for Krueger. In case you were wondering but were too stubborn to ask."

She raises an eyebrow. "Like Freddy?"

"Yeah. My parents were such fans of horror movies they legally changed their last name when they got married in honor of Freddy Krueger."

Her eyes grow wide, but the grin overtaking my face tells her just how full of shit that was.

"Stop it." She laughs—a genuine laugh—and the sound does something weird to my chest. Makes it tight and warm at the same time.

"All right, the origin story is a total lie, but that *is* my last name," I say. A lull emerges, the natural space that would give either of us a chance to exit and continue on with our respective days. But the warmth pulsing between us is too seductive. I'm not ready to let it go.

"You should come see the progress on my side." I swallow hard, wondering if she realizes this is my attempt to steal more time with her. "It's basically done."

Her eyes narrow. "Why would I want to see that?"

"Because it's impressive. And maybe you'd be less of a grump if you saw what I'm trying to build."

"I'm not grumpy," she snaps. A beat passes. "But it's gotta be quick."

I lead her through the shared back room into my space. I wasn't gone for too long, but seeing everything with fresh eyes wows me again. *Damn, this place is amazing.* I can't hide my smile as I begin pointing things out.

"This is the kitchen, obviously." I lead her across the gleaming tile.

"Cooking already?"

"Just something for dinner."

She takes a long inhale, and her eyes flutter shut. "Whatcha making?"

"Braised short rib tacos. You want some?"

Her throat bobs. "No, I was just curious."

I don't buy it, but now's not the time to needle her about dinner when it's not even ready. I point out the prep station, the walk-in fridge, the dish-washing station. Then I lead her through the swinging doors.

"And here's the dining room."

She's quiet for a moment, but I can see her wide eyes taking it all in. "Wow."

"Did you see it before we started working?"

"No. Mrs. Decker never even talked about this side of the building. As far as I was concerned, it didn't exist. But now..." She lets out a low whistle, beginning a slow walk across the room. She drags a finger over a tabletop as she passes, her gaze bouncing from exposed beam to framed art to sconce light. "This is incredible. Even without a 'before'."

"Thank you."

"And this bar." She pauses in front of the bar spanning the far wall of the building. It's a huge wooden slab, topped with gleaming pennies, and then covered in resin. "How much money did you sink into this bar, literally?"

"Eleven thousand pennies."

"What a deal." She looks back at me with a mischievous smile.

I shove my hands into my pockets, watching her admire the place. Seeing her take in all the details sends warmth through my limbs. I don't know why, but I feel like I've known Piper for way longer than I actually have.

"I probably don't have to show you the patio. Unless you brought muffins you'd like to throw at me again." She sends me a long look that has me biting back a satisfied grin. "So you approve?"

"I guess all the loud-ass knocking was worth it," she admits reluctantly. Then something in her stiffens. I can almost see the prickliness sliding back into place. "But you're probably just showing me all this to mine me for ideas so you can win the competition."

I laugh. "I don't need your help to win."

"Is that right?" The competitive spark in her eyes is back.

"Yeah. And I'll prove it to you while we brainstorm ideas over dinner." I gesture to the kitchen. I wonder if she can tell how hard my heart is pounding right now.

She looks toward the kitchen doors, drawing a long inhale. "I need to get back." But she doesn't sound convinced.

"Come on. You have to eat."

"You're right. But I've got dinner plans."

We start walking toward the kitchen. I'm disappointed but trying not to let it show. I want the kisses from last night—and last month—to continue.

I'm drawn to Piper, no matter how much she intends to keep her distance from me.

"Will you at least try my braised short ribs?" I check the pan; things have progressed nicely during the tour. I snap the heat off.

Her gaze is stuck to the pan. Silence bloats between us as I heat a different skillet then toss a corn tortilla on. She might not have told me *yes* in words, but she's certainly telling me yes with her attention. Once the tortilla is ready, I use the tongs to add the incredibly juicy short ribs, followed by sliced red onion, the mango slaw I made and marinated in the morning, and a final sprinkle of cilantro. When I look her way, I can tell she wants to say no out of principle. But I'm ready for it.

"I'll put it in a to-go box. Then you try it and let me know what you think." I deftly prepare the takeout box for her, handing it over before she can reject it.

She blinks up at me. "Thanks."

"Consider it a peace offering. Or maybe just an assurance that you won't abuse me with muffins again."

She takes the box, her fingers brushing mine. "No promises on that last part."

"Fair enough."

"And this doesn't mean that I'm going to let you win the competition."

"I wouldn't dream of it."

I watch her go, a small smile playing on my lips. It's not much, but it feels like everything.

CHAPTER NINE

PIPER

It's Wednesday game night, and I'm feeling more skittish than normal.

Usually, this is my chance to recalibrate and reconnect with my family. But right now, I have a few things I don't want them knowing about. So I need to focus on the priorities: eating dinner as uneventfully as possible then demolishing them all in euchre.

Mom's house is buzzing with the usual Wednesday evening chaos—Asher's deep laugh rumbling through the living room, Jett and Dane arguing about some call in yesterday's hockey game, Griffin stealing bites of dinner before it's ready while Mom swats him away as Lia dances underfoot. Mom's weekly vase of fresh flowers sits proudly on the counter—this week, it's white roses and pink lilies. She's always got fresh, gorgeous blooms somewhere in the house, whether from buying herself a bouquet or one of us kids surprising her. The smell of Mom's lasagna fills the air, yet all I can think about is how damn delicious Kru's mango slaw and braised short rib taco was two days ago.

The one-off weekend in Cleveland would almost be passable; but the fact that my usurper has now *fed me*? That's a hop, skip, and a jump away from a dinner date, and I feel like my brothers would never see the logic in that. Now I must spend the rest of my life making sure they never find out. *Great.*

Once we've all tucked away the lasagna and opened up a bottle of wine to share, I'm ready to get this show on the road. I start clearing plates.

"Jeez, impatient much?" Griff whines.

"You've had enough," I tell him. "Three helpings, Griff. Where do you even put it?"

"I have high caloric needs," he snaps as I carry off his last few bites of lasagna. "Besides, I'm not on the active roster this season, so I have to take advantage of being able to eat whatever I want."

I sigh, bringing the plate back to him. He forks the last couple of bites into his mouth and sits back contentedly.

"Thanks, Pipe Cleaner."

"So do you guys have dinner together every night?" Asher asks us with a warm, fatherly smile.

"We don't eat together much," Griffin says. "I'm usually gone; she's always working. And then sometimes she brings dinner for herself and forgets all about me, like she did a couple nights ago."

My chest tightens. I don't want to venture anywhere near that story, so I pivot. "I'm your roommate, not your personal chef. Besides, I don't have enough money to provide the amount of food your organism requires."

Dane snorts. "Organism."

Lia looks up at her daddy. "What's orgamins?"

"It's just another word for body, honey." He presses a kiss to the top of her head. "Your uncle Griff eats a lot of food."

"So cohabitation is going well?" Mom asks as I circle back to the table to get the rest of the empty plates.

"Of course," I say cheerily. "What could be better than living with my big brother?"

"I'm surprised you wanted to move in with him," Asher says in his typical musing drawl. "You loved your apartment. And it was so convenient to your shop."

My heart rate picks up again. This definitely falls on the list of things I do not want to talk about tonight. "I know. I just wanted...more space. A backyard."

Shit. That word reminds me of Kru and the fence and all those kisses that I absolutely must forget about.

Griffin keeps up his end of the deal when he adds, "I might have sweet-talked her into it a bit. I told her I wanted someone to help keep an eye on my house during the season."

"I'll do anything for family," I add with an over-the-top smile. Griff laughs but rolls his eyes. "Until Griff gets a girlfriend. Then I'm definitely moving out."

"What about if you get a boyfriend?" Mom asks slyly.

"Not happening," I quickly say, and my brothers are quick to reaffirm why.

"No chance he'd make it through my front door," Griffin says.

"I'm pretty sure we already learned what happens when Piper has a boyfriend," Jett adds.

I groan, thankful that I'm focused on loading the dishwasher. They're talking about the time in ninth grade when I tried to take poor Marcus Smith to Homecoming. My brothers spooked him so badly at the front door that he took off running back into his Mom's car. I ended up going to Homecoming with my besties, nary a Marcus in sight.

"If I were dumb enough to try to have a boyfriend around this family, I can assure you I'd never bring him to the front door." I slam the dishwasher shut with more force than I intended. It doesn't dissuade my brothers.

"You can have a boyfriend," Asher says. "He just needs to be vetted."

"Vetted, cleared, and approved," Jett adds.

"With a full mental-health evaluation," Griffin pipes up.

"And a minimum of ten references," Dane says.

"No, twenty," Asher butts in.

"And one evening alone with me and the rest of your brothers just so we can perform our own tests on him." Jett's devious smile grows wider.

"Tests?" I squeak.

"Yeah. With our fists," Griffin finishes for him, and all my brothers burst into laughter.

Mom snickers, which I don't understand. These men would never let her date anyone either, which is probably why she's never tried since my dad passed away.

"Thank you all for reminding me of the process. You bunch of heathens." I grab the deck of cards on my way back to the table, eager to get this show on the road. My heart is thumping. "Can we start playing now?"

I team up with Mom, while Griff and Asher pair up against us. Dane and Lia migrate closer to the television at Lia's request for a princess show, while Jett hovers over Asher's shoulder, nodding while he assesses his cards.

"Let's go," I snap.

Jett squints over at me. "What's got you in such a hurry?"

I'm not about to admit that my head is full of Kru—his hands, his mouth, the way he looked at me as he handed over the best taco I'd ever eaten. Nope. That's staying locked in the vault. It has to, because my brothers have just confirmed they'd either send him into a bureaucratic sinkhole *or* beat him to a pulp for daring to date me.

But you're not trying to date him, I remind myself. *So this is completely irrelevant.*

"Nothing," I lie. "Just ready to win."

We play the first hand in relative peace. Mom and I win, which earns the expected chorus of groans. I point at the hourglass, so Dad knows that win is for him. Jett deals the next round while Mom taps out to watch TV with Lia, and the conversation drifts to local gossip.

"So the side street we're on is closed for construction," Jett says.

"Oh shit." Griff deftly deals out the next hand. "How's that working for customers?"

"They've got some back entrance set up, but nobody knows about it," Jett grumbles. "It's just pure chaos all the time. I swear we get twenty calls a day asking how to find us now."

"That sucks," I add. "I've been having annoying traffic flow interruptions too but nothing like a street being cut off."

"What's cutting off your traffic?" Asher muses as he assesses his hand.

"Just my new *landlord*," I say with a sigh. "Always blocking the curb cut for some new reason. We had a whole showdown the other day when he completely blocked the sidewalk with all his heavy ass patio furniture for *hours*." I can hear Kru in my head correcting me that it wasn't *hours* but rather a *half hour*, and I tell imaginary Kru to shut up because I'm busy reassuring my brothers I don't have feelings for my landlord.

"Oh my god, this guy," Griffin groans as he lays down a card. "Piper, I'm gonna go talk to him."

"Absolutely not," I say, and then toss my card into the middle. "Not unless you want the altercation to be captured by the camera crew, and used as evidence in your inevitable harassment charge."

He snorts. "Camera crew?"

Oh god. I forgot that they don't know he's filming a reality TV show.

"Yeah," I say slowly, focusing extra hard on the cards my brothers are laying down. "He's doing another reality TV show with the buildout of his restaurant."

Silence stretches across the table for an unsettling amount of time. I can see my brothers glancing at each other, as though silently questioning how to handle this piece of information. Mom drifts back into the kitchen.

"Did you say they're filming a reality TV show?" Mom asks, eyebrows raised.

"Yeah. Capturing the renovation process or whatever," I say, clearing the table after I take the trick. I lay down another card to start the next round.

"All right. So I'll lure him into your back room and confront him there, where the cameras aren't watching," Griffin says. His attempt to avoid a filmed altercation is cute, but it doesn't work as he intended.

Now I'm in a sticky spot.

"Well, the cameras are sometimes on my side too," I begin.

"Why are they bothering you?" Griffin presses, because of course he does.

I clear my throat. "They're not *bothering* me. They're just..." All of the attention is on me now, which makes my brain short circuit. "The producers thought it would be, you know, a good idea if I was...involved."

"Involved how?" Asher's stern voice comes out, the one that makes me feel like he's my dad.

"Just as the neighboring business owner. I guess for filler." Asher plays a card, and we win the round again. "You go, Asher."

But nobody's paying attention to the game anymore. All eyes are on me.

"Wait. Let me get this straight," Jett says slowly. "You're on a reality show with the guy who's trying to kick you out of your building?"

"He's not trying to kick me out," I mutter, but Jett and my other brothers still don't know the truth: that he actually did kick me out of my apartment.

"It's safe to assume he's trying to drive you out of there," Asher says. "Did you sign a contract to be on the show?"

I swallow hard. "I did."

All four brothers sigh tersely. Now I feel like I'm in trouble and don't know why.

"You guys should be happy," I say. "I'm getting paid *and* getting tons of exposure."

"Or getting tons of conflict," Griffin says, his dark brows drawing together. "These shows thrive on drama. They're going to make you look like the villain or the victim, neither of which is good for business."

"That's not necessarily true," I argue, feeling a familiar defensive heat rising in my chest. "It's a huge amount of advertising for Cloud Nine. Do you know how many Instagram followers those shows pull in?"

"Life is more than Instagram followers," Asher says dismissively.

"Sometimes Instagram followers pay the bills," I snap. "How do you think I built my business in the first place? Social media is how I get ninety percent of my customers."

"It's different," Dane jumps in. "You control your own social media brand. This show? They control the narrative."

"I know what I'm doing," I insist, but my voice sounds weaker than I'd like. I look to Mom for support, but she just gives me one of those noncommittal mom looks, the ones that say "I'm staying out of this" without actually saying it.

"Great," I mutter. "So you all think I'm an idiot."

"We didn't say that," Dane says quickly.

"You didn't have to."

The familiar feeling washes over me—being the baby sister, the one who's never quite trusted to make her own decisions. The one who needs four surrogate fathers checking her every move.

"Piper," Griffin starts, his voice softening. "We're just concerned—"

"I'm twenty-eight years old," I cut him off. "I run a successful business. I make my own decisions."

"Of course you do, sweetheart," Mom finally chimes in. "Your brothers are just being protective, as usual."

"We've seen these shows," Jett argues. "They're trash. They make everyone look bad."

"Well, I guess you'll just have to tune in and see," I say, trying for nonchalance but landing somewhere in the territory of petulant child. "Can we please just play cards now?"

The game resumes, but the air is thick with unspoken tension. I win again, but it doesn't feel good this time. It's not the victory I really wanted.

Three hands later, I bow out, claiming a headache. It's not entirely untrue—my temples are throbbing from the effort of holding back my frustration.

"I'm going to head home," I say, slipping on my coat. "Early day tomorrow."

Mom walks me to the door. "Don't be too hard on them," she says softly. "They love you."

"I know," I sigh. "But loving me and respecting me as an adult are two different things."

She kisses my cheek. "For what it's worth, I think you're more than capable of handling a reality show. And if this new landlord tries anything fishy, you'll put him in his place."

I smile weakly. "Thanks, Mom."

The ride back to Griffin's house is exactly what I need—cool lake air in my face, the physical exertion of pedaling, the quiet of the tree-lined residential streets. By the time I arrive, some of my anger has subsided, replaced by a nagging doubt.

Maybe they're right...which is exactly what I've been avoiding my entire life. What if I did make a stupid decision? What if the producer is just going to paint me as some annoying little pest for conflict, and I'm going to end up looking like an idiot on national television?

I store my bike in the garage, shut the door, and head inside. Griffin won't be home for at least another hour, which means I have the place to myself.

I should shower. I should call my cousin Bella to talk through this quagmire I've found myself in. I should go over the week's orders on my tablet.

But I don't want to do any of those things.

Instead, I find myself wandering into the backyard. I know what I want...and it's the one thing I shouldn't go after. As soon as I'm outside, I can smell something cooking, unique and savory, such a blend of smells that I can't quite place a single ingredient.

Anticipation scorches through me. Through the thinning bushes and the gaps in the chain link fence, I can see movement in the yard behind Griffin's. A familiar silhouette stands at a grill, spatula in hand. The glow of the flames highlights the sharp angles of his jaw, the broad span of his shoulders. He's in a simple T-shirt and jeans, looking unfairly hot for someone just casually grilling on a Wednesday night.

Kru.

Hunger cracks open inside me, but not for food. I can't stop thinking about the conversation we had in his restaurant.

I should go inside. I really should.

But my feet carry me closer to the fence, like there's some kind of magnetic pull between us. I'm trying to get a better view when my foot catches on something—probably the roots of that rose bush coming to claim my pants this time—and I stumble, grabbing the fence for support.

The fence jangles loudly.

Kru's head snaps up, eyes scanning the darkness until they land on me. A slow, knowing smile spreads across his face.

"Well, well, well," he calls out, "if it isn't my favorite marshmallow maven."

Heat crawls up my neck. "I was just—" I scramble for an excuse. "Looking for my golf ball."

"A golf ball?" He raises an eyebrow as he shuts the grill. He slowly approaches the fence. "In the dark?"

"Yes," I say firmly. "I golf. I was practicing my swing."

"In this tiny backyard? With a fence in the way?"

I'm glad it's dark and he can't see my cheeks flaming. "It was a chip shot."

"Uh-huh." He's standing right at the fence now, close enough that I can smell the savory aroma of whatever he's cooking. "And does your brother know you play golf in his yard after dark?"

"He doesn't care. He supports all sports, especially mine."

Kru's smile widens. "I still don't believe you. Just admit it: you want to come over and help me test these recipes."

I should say no. "What are you making?"

"Lobster tail with a brown butter sauce." He nods back toward the patio. "It's almost done. I'm trying to decide if it needs something else."

My mouth waters involuntarily. "Smells amazing."

"You wanna try?" He tips his head toward the grill. "There's plenty."

Again, I should say no. But I step closer to the fence without even realizing it. It jangles again as I thread my fingers through the links.

"I probably shouldn't go farther than this," I tell him. It makes sense in my head. If I don't cross the fence, then this isn't real, whatever this big, throbbing potential is between us.

If we can keep to the fence line, I'm safe.

Kru watches me with those intense eyes of his, and I fight the urge to smooth my hair, to check if I look okay. Which is ridiculous—he saw every last inch of me in Cleveland, there's almost nothing left to hide from him at this point.

Except for the fact that this pesky attraction will *not* go away, no matter how much I ignore it.

"Give me a second. I'll bring you a sample." He heads to the grill, arranges some food on a waiting plate, brushes something over top of it all, and then takes some time to cut things up. He grabs a fork and comes back with the most gorgeous plate I've ever seen come out of a basic backyard grill.

The lobster tail is glistening with butter sauce. There's asparagus, too, and what looks like some kind of risotto.

"And you did all this just for a casual Wednesday solo dinner?" I ask.

"Recipe testing," he says with a shrug. "Have to make sure everything works before I put it on the menu."

He picks up a fork, stabs a small piece of lobster, and holds it out to me. "Try it."

I should take the fork from him, but something makes me lean forward instead, letting him feed me. The moment his eyes meet mine as my lips close around the fork, I know I've made a tactical error.

But then the flavor hits, and I don't care.

"Oh my god," I moan, eyes fluttering shut. I keep them shut as I savor and chew. I'm already craving more, even though I'm not hungry in the slightest.

When I open my eyes, Kru is watching me with an expression that makes my insides melt faster than the butter sauce. "Good?"

"Good doesn't begin to cover it." I'm not even exaggerating. The lobster is tender, the sauce rich with hints of herbs I can't identify. "What's in this sauce?"

"Secret recipe." He grins, forking another piece. "Have some more. I want to hear that moan again."

I clamp my mouth shut, cheeks flaming.

"Don't act shy," he chides. "A reaction like that is the highest compliment you can pay a chef."

When he offers the fork again, I let him feed me. This time, I'm prepared for the flavor explosion, but it still makes me groan with pleasure.

He nods, his gaze drifting to the plate. "I'm definitely going to win Best of Bayshore with this."

And just like that, the spell is broken.

"In your dreams," I retort. "My strawberry s'mores torte is going to blow your lobster out of the water. Besides, your lobster is missing something." I struggle to come up with something that could possibly improve what he's already done here. "It needs a marshmallow to win."

"Is that right?" He steps closer, and suddenly the air between us feels charged. "Care to make a friendly wager on that?"

"What kind of wager?" I shouldn't be engaging. I should walk away. But I can't help myself around him.

"If I win, you admit on camera that I'm the best."

"And if I win?"

His eyes glint with challenge. "Name your terms, Maven."

"If I win, you have to..." I think for a moment. "You have to let me redesign your restaurant's dessert menu. With marshmallows. Lots and lots of marshmallows."

He laughs. "You can't be serious."

"Deal or no deal, Lobster Man?"

"Deal."

I hold out my hand to shake on it. His grip is firm, and when I pull back, he doesn't let go right away. The darkness disorients me, and I stumble forward. Somehow—I swear it's an accident—my face ends up inches from his.

And then, because my body is a traitor to my better judgment, my lips are on his.

The kiss is electric, sending sparks down my spine, pooling low in my belly. His mouth is warm and tastes faintly of butter and herbs, and when his tongue slides against mine, I make an embarrassing noise in the back of my throat.

His free hand comes up to cup my face, then slides into my hair, angling my head to deepen the kiss. I've already got one hand fisted in his shirt, the other one clinging to the chain link fence like it's somehow anchoring me to the world.

He breaks the kiss first, eyes dark with desire. "You should come over. Cross the fence. It's safe, I promise."

I'm still trying to catch my breath. "That's a bad idea."

"I promise you, it will be *so good*." His thumb swipes along my cheek, and his gaze is so intense I can barely keep eye contact. "Just like you remember, Maven."

I'm shaking my head, hoping it will knock some common sense back into me. "Nope. You've already roped me into a reality TV show. What's next, marriage?" I joke, but my heart is racing at the mere suggestion.

"One step at a time." The fact that he doesn't balk at that word is somehow even hotter. "First comes reality show, then backyard lobster tasting, and then..."

"You forgot kicking me out of my apartment as the first step," I correct him.

"Mm. Right." The intensity wavers. "Sorry."

Something about his words reminds me of my family's reaction earlier, and I step back, the moment broken.

"What's wrong?" he asks.

"Nothing." I take another step back. For safety and clarity of mind. "I should go."

"Piper." His use of my actual name stops me. "Talk to me."

I hesitate, then sigh. "My family thinks I'm an idiot for agreeing to be a part of the show."

His eyebrows shoot up. "Why?"

"They think it's going to make me look bad. That it's bad for business." I wrap my arms around myself. "That I'm being manipulated."

"By me?" He looks genuinely surprised.

I don't want to confirm that, so I say, "By the situation."

He shakes his head. "That's ridiculous. Pat and the crew are not out to start drama. Did they watch the food truck show? Because this is a totally different vibe and you know it. Besides, you're one of the smartest businesswomen I've ever met. Why would they doubt you?"

I blink at him. "You've known me for less than a month. If you can say that, you haven't met many businesswomen."

"I don't need long to recognize talent." His voice is sincere, his eyes locked on mine. "Look at what you've built. Cloud Nine is a marketing masterpiece. Your product is unique, your branding is on point. You know exactly what you're doing."

Something warm unfurls in my chest at his words. "You noticed all that?"

"Of course I did. You've got a line out the door most mornings. People taking pictures with your products, tagging you on social media. The show is lucky to have you, not the other way around."

I swallow hard, oddly touched by his assessment. "I've seen your show too, you know. The food truck one."

"Yeah?" A smile tugs at his lips.

"You were good." I shrug, trying to play it casual. "Ok, you were great. I was really happy when you came back to help Maverick at the end."

He's about to say something else when Griffin's voice carries from the back door of his house.

"Piper? You out here?"

Shit.

"I have to go," I whisper, already backing toward the house.

"Meet me at the fence tomorrow night?" Kru calls softly after me.

I don't answer. I'm too busy hurrying toward the house, pretending I was just getting some air.

But as I slip through the back door, I can't stop thinking about Kru's words, about the way he sees me—not as the baby sister who needs guidance from brothers who know better, but as a capable businesswoman who knows her worth.

It's dangerously addictive, that kind of recognition.

Almost as addictive as his kisses.

But I'm not going to be some backyard railbird with my rival. Kisses are temporary—what I'm building with my business? That lasts a lifetime. I need to stay focused, so that was the last time with Kru. It has to be.

Even if every cell in my body is already anticipating tomorrow night.

CHAPTER TEN

KRU

The next two days are intense. Early mornings, grueling days, and by the time I get home, I'm looking forward to only one thing.

The marshmallow maven...who was a no-show both nights.

I'm not proud to admit that I hung around my backyard like a hungry dog waiting for a scrap of food.

I'm trying not to let her absence bother me. And I'm sure as hell not sniffing around her marshmallow shop like I want to. I've already confronted her once in the daylight about the chemistry she clearly knows we have. I know she's resistant, and I've got a good idea of the *why*. But that chemistry should overrule everything else. Right?

Maybe I'm just thinking with my cock. No, scratch that. I'm absolutely thinking with my cock. Because my cock knows how juicy Piper is, inside and out.

Thankfully I have plenty to keep me busy, like this entirely new staff I've hired, and this brand-new restaurant vibrating on the cusp of opening. When Friday rolls around, I'm ready for the health department. This is the final inspection to clear us before open—and once we get the green light, I'm doing a soft launch for lunch. I've got the braised short ribs tender and waiting in the kitchen, with my new sous-chef Brady overseeing the progress.

I've been teasing this soft launch on social media all week. Word has been spreading around Bayshore about an up-and-coming restaurant with a reality TV crew, and I see the rubberneckers daily to prove it. Everything is coming together nicely.

Perfectly, almost.

I wonder if I should be suspicious.

"Mr. Krueger?" A very tall and lanky man enters the dining room at nine on the dot. I can tell by the clipboard and his scrutinizing gaze that he's from the health department.

"Hey, Jerome! Great to finally meet you." I hurry his way, wiping my hands on my black apron before I offer to shake. My heart starts racing as I run over the map of the restaurant in my mind's eye. I'm accustomed to health department inspections after operating Fork & Claw with Mav for so long, even though I know firsthand how crossing all your t's and dotting every last i doesn't exempt you from a surprise health code violation.

But I've got this one in the bag. I've been working my ass off, and I'm minutes away from the finish line.

"You too," Jerome says, shaking my hand firmly. But his voice is devoid of emotion, and I can tell he's not here for chit-chat. "I'll let you know if I have any questions about what I see."

"Sure, yeah." I gesture around. "Have at it."

I glance back at Pat and the camera crew, who aren't filming during the inspection. My two lunchtime servers, Jackie and Tina, linger near the front wall of windows. Tension crackles in the air as I try to busy myself straightening up the dining room, while keeping an eye on Jerome's movements. He's immediately making notes on his clipboard, and I don't like that one bit. Then he disappears into the kitchen, and I wonder if I should follow him.

"It'll be great," Pat assures me, as though he can sense my mounting worry.

"Yeah. We're more than prepared." But my words feel hollow for some reason. "He's gonna go check out my sexy walk-in and say, 'You know what? I've seen all I need to see. Ready to open.'"

Jackie and Tina snicker.

I migrate to the kitchen doors, peering through the plastic windows at the top. I can see Jerome temping the freezer in the back while Brady looks sufficiently occupied. "He'll probably just want to live in the kitchen, it's so nice."

"It's one of the cleanest ones I've ever seen," Tina says brightly.

"And it'll stay that way. Didn't I tell you, Tina? We have mandatory four-hour deep cleans every night." She sends me a scared look, and I crack up laughing. "Sorry. Not a good boss joke on opening day."

The three of us shoot the shit while Jerome remains in the kitchen. I'm doing my best to distract myself by cracking food jokes and quizzing Jackie and Tina about the soft launch menu. They're holding their own as I pepper them with questions about the types of cheese we use and where our buns come from. They even manage to laugh at my best food joke of the day: *Why did the diner on the moon get bad reviews? No atmosphere.*

It's an agonizing, eternal wait for Jerome to emerge—but when he finally does, three thousand minutes after he first entered my kitchen, he looks grim.

"Okay, I've seen all I need to see." He comes to a stop in front of me, scribbling something on his clipboard. "I've made a note of all the violations I spotted—"

"Violations?" I can't believe my ears.

He looks up at me, annoyance flashing across his face. "Yes. Here in Bayshore we take our food service code very seriously."

"And so do I," I hurry to add. "What issues did you find?"

"Your sani-rag was outside of the bucket. It must be immersed in the sanitization liquid at all times. Your prep table fridge registered a temp of forty-two degrees, which is in the danger zone. It must be below forty-one degrees."

"The rag is easy, we can pop it right in that bucket. And I think I know why the prep fridge is clocking high. Brady was probably rustling around in there right as you came in. Can you re-temp?"

He sends me a long look. "Additionally, your dining room is over capacity. This building is cleared for max fifty occupants but you have seating here for sixty."

"Easy fix, I'll throw three of my tables in the trash right now. Was there anything else?"

His eyes narrow. My jokes aren't landing with this one.

"I'll be sending you a copy of your report. Please sign here." He pushes the clipboard my way. "Then we can set a time for a re-inspection."

Once again, the words aren't computing. "Uh, Jerome, we're set to open in an hour..."

"Not without clearance you aren't."

I swallow hard, realizing I need to tread lightly. "You're right. And I want to point out the issues you found are relatively, well, minor."

"The health and safety of Bayshore is no minor issue," he snaps.

"You're right." I do my best to form a well-meaning smile and not let out a grunt of annoyance like I want to. "The rag situation is an easy fix. I can avoid using that prep table, and I'll block off three whole tables in the dining room so we don't go over capacity..."

He sniffs, looking around. "I think those remedies would be adequate to approve you for a *provisional* license for take-out only."

Take-out only.

Fuuuuuuck.

I'm grinding my teeth as I sign on the dotted line. Jerome nods my way and quietly leaves the restaurant. Once the door swings shut behind him, I release the groan that's been building in my chest.

"Fucking take-out! On our soft launch day! What the fuck!"

Pat motions for the cameras to start filming.

"He might not come back to check," Jackie suggests. "Maybe we can just...seat them anyway."

I rake a hand through my hair. This is the worst news I could have gotten today. I shake my head. "No. We can't risk that. If word gets out that we violated his decision on day one, that doesn't bode well for the future. We've gotta pivot. *Fuck.*"

My mind is working on overdrive trying to formulate a new plan on the fly. I stride to the kitchen, pushing past the doors.

"Brady," I say. "Change of plans. We're not doing sit-down service today."

Brady blinks from over top a fresh batch of braised short ribs, our soft launch feature. "Uh, we're not?"

"Nope." I check my watch. "Jerome approved us for takeout only. Got about two hours to prep for orders. At least we won't have to worry about dishes today."

He stares at me for a beat, then nods. "Right. I'll go count to-go boxes."

I knew I liked this kid.

"Let me know how many we have, then I'll send Jackie or Tina to the store to buy more. And bags. We're gonna need bags." I head back to the front to begin doling out orders.

"Who here is great at handwriting?"

Jackie and Tina share a confused look.

"Whoever is better at handwriting needs to work on the chalkboard sign. The other one is going shopping with a list from Brady of what we need." I reach into my apron pocket and pull out my scratch pad, which I always keep on me in the kitchen for noting flavors, ratios, and ingredients. I scribble out a quick message, tear it off, and slam it onto the table. "This is what the sign should say. It just needs to look...a lot better than this."

Tina nods, picking it up. "That's me. I've got you, boss."

"Thank you. Jackie, you'll head out as soon as Brady has that list. You'll both be handling the takeout orders once we open. I know this isn't ideal and cuts into our ability to upsell alcohol and get those tips, but I promise I'll make up for it."

What I didn't mention was my ability to begin wowing customers for the Best of Bayshore competition, which officially began yesterday. Votes have been pouring in for the dishes each business submitted to the contest. My entry: the buttered lobster tail with morel and asparagus risotto. It was a tough call between that and the braised short rib taco, but I based my decision strictly on how loudly Piper moaned when she tried the lobster.

But that means that if I can't get people to try my lobster tail, they won't vote for me. Few people trust a lobster tail to take out. I'm not one of them. Buttered lobster tail is a dine-in experience, and I've crafted the entire meal around that setup. I'm more annoyed with Jerome than I can express right now. But I know that now is *not* the time to lick my wounds inflicted by the health department.

While my team is working on their to-do lists, I'm turning to social media. I need to start managing expectations. I craft a quick update to our page along with some pictures I snapped earlier of the prep process. It gets reactions within seconds. Apparently Bayshore is foaming at the mouth for my food...which I'm totally fucking here for.

The next couple hours fly by as I oversee the take-out pivot. Our chalkboard sign is completed, showcasing a cutesy but apologetic message about why we're take-out only. Needed supplies have been acquired. About twenty minutes before open, a curious thing happens.

A line starts forming.

By 10:59 a.m., it's halfway across the lot.

Panic settles deep in my gut. My limbs are electrified—this is the type of stress that activates me. After years working in food trucks, I know how to handle this.

I give Jackie and Tina the signal to open the door and I slip into the kitchen. Even from back here I can feel the hum of energy crackling through the dining room as customers wait in line. Brady and I handle the food, and orders begin pouring in. My focus narrows in on the slips of paper pumping out of the kitchen printer.

Tacos. Tacos. Tacos. Lobster.

Brady responds well to my gruff instructions as I help navigate us through a bona fide lunch rush. I make sure we stay ahead of the curve while we pump out orders, sliding them into boxes with their names scribbled on top in Sharpie. Brady stays with me, though we occasionally need to rope in Jackie or Tina to help run supplies so we can focus on the line. I'm distantly aware that Pat and the cameras are lurking somewhere in the vicinity, though I couldn't even say if they're in the kitchen with me.

I wish I could see what's happening out front. Pat will catch me up later. All I know is that this launch is far from soft. The tickets don't stop, and it's about an hour into the lunch rush when I realize it's happening. We're doing it. I grin through my order assembly, imagining all the rave reviews that are about to begin pouring in.

Fuck yeah, hard-ass soft launch.

"Kru."

Piper's voice cuts through my focus like a paring knife. The confusion of why I'm hearing her voice in my kitchen during the lunch rush causes me to abandon my order and swivel.

She's a vision in pastel—pink shirt covered by a frilly, daffodil-colored apron—arms crossed and eyes ablaze. I recognize the spark in her gaze immediately.

But I don't have time for this shit.

"What's wrong?" I wipe my forearm across my cheek, watching her expectantly.

"My entrance is completely blocked. Again."

I sigh, shaking my head. I turn back to my station, trying to focus again on the ticket I was prepping. "We're takeout only today. We had a wrench thrown into our soft launch. Nobody's allowed inside per the health department."

There's an unnerving silence behind me. Then she's at my side, looking up at me.

"Are you fucking serious?"

"Piper, I'm not in a joking mood right now." I gesture to the tickets pumping out of the kitchen printer. "Now is there something I can help you with or are you just here to give me shit on my soft launch?"

"You didn't tell me you were soft launching today," she hisses.

"You didn't give me a chance to, you never showed up the last two nights," I remind her.

She recoils slightly. "How long is this going on?"

"Till we sell out. Or till you call the fire marshal."

She doesn't laugh. I didn't expect her to. Not when she's in Put-Out Piper mode.

Her eyes flick back to me, and something in her expression shifts. It's not just frustration anymore. There's heat. Tension. Maybe even hurt. And suddenly I realize what this is really about.

"I'm not trying to sabotage your shop," I say firmly. "I didn't expect this crowd. Now I'm doing everything I can to stay out of the weeds back here on opening day. I need to focus on the food. That's what this is about for me, Piper. I don't know what to do with the line. Go tell them to fuck themselves. I don't know. I can't set foot outside of this kitchen until that line is gone."

Before she can respond, Brady rushes up. "Uh, chef? We're out of aioli."

"Fuck. We already plowed through the reserves in the walk-in?" I ask.

"All gone. I thought there was another jar back there but I made a mistake."

Brady looks nervous. The tickets are twenty deep and I know the stress he's feeling at being new in a high-tension kitchen with an unexpected crowd beating down the doors.

"You handle these orders, and I'll go prep more."

"Wait," Piper blurts. "Let me help. My employee is here for the morning so I can do something if you need me to."

I could kiss her. And I would if I wasn't stress-focused on aioli.

"Go into the walk-in and get six bunches of cilantro. Take them to the prep table over there and start chopping, leaving out the stems. It's already rinsed."

"Got it." She zips off, leaving me smiling to myself. She should have said *yes chef*, but I'll teach her about that later. I get back to cranking through the orders. Jackie and Tina pop in and out of the kitchen, checking on us while whisking away the prepped orders.

Piper is fast. I try not to look too impressed when she comes back for more instructions and takes them without a peep. Once I've walked her through the aioli prep without missing a beat on my own station, she proudly hands the pan to Brady.

"Good luck with the rest of your lunch," she tells me as she walks by. Before she's made it too far, she turns and adds, "By the way, I had an idea while I was chopping cilantro. I'm going to go give your entire line free samples of my dessert...with a QR code that leads to my Best of Bayshore voting page."

She's gone before I can protest, much less formulate a reaction. I'm too caught up in the tickets before me. But one thing is certain.

I like a little bite in my competition. And Piper is the spice I never planned on including...but also the one that makes the whole dish better.

CHAPTER ELEVEN

PIPER

It's Sunday morning.

I wake up at a leisurely nine a.m. Well rested and ready for my delightful day off.

I stretch and yawn in the big comfy queen bed I've been calling my own here at Griffin's house. Barely ten seconds pass before my brain gloms onto the one thing I spend every day trying to avoid thinking about: *Kru*.

I roll over and groan into my pillow. Just when I think I'm making progress—*not* meeting him at the fence, *not* sucking his face off on a nightly basis, *not* losing yet another item from my wardrobe to an overzealous rose bush—I remember the way I found him during his soft launch. Not just the way his biceps strain at the sleeves of his black work tees or the adorable tousle of his hair, but his attention to his job. Hyper-focused, in control of the chaos, moving around his kitchen like he's been doing it for years.

Hot guys are a dime a dozen, but hot entrepreneurs? Hot *chefs*? They have a little something extra. At least for me.

And now my fantasies of what Kru might sound like ordering me around the kitchen will haunt me for the rest of my life.

I smash my pillow over my face as though this will somehow quiet my thoughts. Spoiler alert, it doesn't work. All I can see in my mind's eye is Kru popping me up onto the edge of that prep table after hours, filling the space between my legs with his body, kissing me so hard my lips go numb.

I'm dying to see him again.

But since I know what's best for me, I won't let myself dip even a toe into those waters.

So what's the smartest idea for my day off? Distraction. I force myself out of bed and into the bathroom. My cousin Bella is arriving in Bayshore today with her brand-new, honest-to-god *famous rock star* boyfriend, Jackson Bedd. Nobody in the Keegan family has met this man yet, but today is the big day. We're all excited, but Mom has been tittering the most about this. She's going to flip when a rock god plays euchre with her on Wednesday night. I freshen up in the bathroom, change into a fresh set of clothes, and wander down the hallway.

It takes me a few moments to understand what I'm seeing. Maybe I'm still waking up, but Griffin is mopping the kitchen floor like he's on a timed game show.

I blink a few times. "Morning."

He looks up at me, and jerks his chin. His breath comes out in quick bursts of air. "Morning."

No mention of working that mop like it might double as a hockey stick.

"Why are you so, uh...vigorous right now?" I gingerly step past him, making sure to stick to the already-dry areas of the floor. I can't stop looking at his mop technique though. Amazing how you can know someone for your entire life and still not know *this* is how they mop a floor. "And have you always mopped a floor like this?"

He pauses, straightening slightly, chest heaving. "Like what?"

So he doesn't realize he looks like he's bailing water out of a sinking ship. "Nothing."

He grunts and returns to his maniacal mopping. "Kay."

I begin brewing some coffee, glancing back at his full-body mopping. "Like, are you specifically trying to burn calories?"

He stops mopping, standing up straight. "Do you have a problem with the way I mop?"

"No. No mop problems." I tuck my hair behind my ear. I file away this tidbit for when I really need it around my other brothers. "You absolutely mop like a normal person."

He narrows his eyes at me and continues. *Thwump, thwump, thwump,* goes the mop against the kitchen floor. He's even got a booty wiggle involved. I'm about to make another comment about how he apparently learned how to mop by watching aliens give it their best guess without ever having seen a mop, but my phone buzzes on the countertop and distracts me.

BELLA: WE'RE ON OUR WAY!!!! ETA 3 hours!

I gasp. Then a squeal escapes me. Griffin pauses, leaning against the handle of the mop.

"What is it?"

"Bella texted! She'll be here in three hours!" Bella is my cousin, but she might as well be my sister. She lost her parents at a young age and came to live with my family from about eleven onward. So my mom is basically her mom now. This is the first time she's been home since a whirlwind work trip led her straight into the arms of America's most famous rock star.

Griffin's face falls. "Shit. There's so much more to do."

The pieces begin clicking together. "Is that why you're mopping like you've been possessed by a disgruntled 1950s housewife?"

His brows draw together. "Piper, the floor is dirty. I'm cleaning it. I don't know how else you'd rather I do it."

"You're using, like, 300% body strength when you only need 5%."

He huffs. "I don't have time for your bullshit. Bella is gonna be here soon and the house is not ready."

"Not ready?" I laugh as I look out over his sparkling house. "Griff, this could be a model home."

"I haven't even touched the baseboards."

"Do you *need* to...?"

His death stare helps me understand. I nod slowly. "Okay. This is important to you. I can help. Even if I don't understand how you were ever able to set foot in my apartment with these cleanliness standards, I can help. Also, please don't go into my bedroom at any point while we're living together because you may have a heart attack." I live in what I like to call organized chaos, which is the opposite of how Griffin operates.

While he finishes mopping, I prep my coffee, take a fortifying gulp, and get to work. To my eye, there isn't much that needs done, but I try to see things from his perspective. I head to the shoe rack and toe a few pair of shoes into alignment. I fluff the jackets hanging on the hooks on the wall, making sure the pockets are facing outward. I tweak the collar on Griffin's team coat.

"Piper what are you doing?"

"I'm helping."

Griff sighs and rolls his eyes. Thankfully he's finished mopping so I don't have to watch him punch morse code into the linoleum any more. I drift to the couch, gathering the throw blanket. I try draping it in an aesthetic way over the back of the couch, but that seems messy if I'm looking at it from Griff's perspective. I wrap it into a tight little roll and stuff it behind the couch cushions. Griffin raises an eyebrow at me from across the living room.

"What? Is there a better place to stash it?"

"Pretty much anywhere other than behind the cushion." He heads to the bookshelves and begins dusting off his various trophies and awards. "That makes it look like contraband."

"This is faster," I argue. "Time is of the essence. And they're not going to be inspecting your couch cushions."

"You don't know that." Griffin's gaze darts my way before he begins dusting the television screen. "Bella's engaged to a rock star now. He probably has people who check for, I don't know, listening devices or something."

I snort. "In Bayshore? Who's spying on them here, the seagulls? Let's be real though—are you nervous about meeting Jackson Bedd?"

"Well, I'd like to make a good impression," he stammers, which tells me all I need to know.

"Griff, seriously. Relax." I grab the dusting wand from him before he can start on the shelves for the third time. "Bella's still Bella, and she has assured me that Jackson is normal. Yes, he might be the resident American heart throb and all over the radios right now, but he's a small-town guy with a big talent, just like you. They don't care if your throw pillows are perfectly fluffed."

What he doesn't know is that I'm just as nervous. Life has changed a lot for Bella. She's the first one to have a serious partner out of all of us. And she's the youngest of the Keegan clan...so maybe that's a little embarrassing for the rest of us.

Asher's in his mid-thirties and still hasn't even had a whiff of a girlfriend, though I suspect that's because he's secretly in love with his assistant. And even Dane, the only one with a child, didn't date Lia's mom before they had her, since Lia was the product of a one-night stand. And while I'm pretty sure Jett fucks his way through the female population, I don't think he's ever called a single girl twice.

As for Griff, I've caught him chatting to a couple girls on his phone before, but he's never brought anyone home and never talks about his dating life. And since I'm not allowed to even think about a boyfriend according to my father-brothers, I don't think any of us Keegans have a shot at significant others.

Griffin disappears into the kitchen, presumably to sanitize the refrigerator or alphabetize his spice rack. I drift toward the glass sliding back door, straining to see through the foliage into Kru's backyard. It's Sunday, so he's probably home. Maybe I could slip outside and trim back the rose bush. Deadhead some of the plants so Jackson Bedd doesn't see what secret heathens we are. Hell, it might be a good time to seed that patchy backyard before company arrives...

"Griff, you want me to clean up your patio?" I offer. If he tells me to do it, then it's not me deciding to go snoop on Kru.

"Do the front porch instead," he instructs.

Dammit. I sigh and head to the front porch. The crisp morning air is a beautiful refresh as I soak in the fall sun and sweep the leaves off the front porch. About halfway through my porch-cleaning project, I wonder about the Best of Bayshore results. Seeing the voting results in real-time is not the most helpful thing for my peace of mind, but I can't help myself. I have the webpage bookmarked, and I quickly pull it up. There are about fifty entrants in the competition, a wide range of interesting dishes and offerings from all sorts of Bayshore eateries. I sink into one of the porch chairs as I scroll through the results. I'm number five. Not great. But what's an unexpected relief is that Kru's restaurant is currently number ten.

Phew.

I'm at least beating *him*.

Now I need to beat dishes one through four and hold the lead.

The front door swings open. Griff sticks his head out and frowns.

"Piper! You're supposed to be cleaning!"

I huff and get to my feet. "I needed a break to check the Best of Bayshore results."

His eyes light up. "Are you number one yet?"

"Number four. But that's better than yesterday, when I was at six."

"I vote every day and you know the rest of the fam does too. We just gotta get more people on board. I'll tell the team tomorrow at practice. Oh, I know, I'll get my assistant to make a post on my public page about the contest too."

"Griff—"

"Piper, you're gonna be number one. Don't you worry. I'll take care of it."

I offer him a small smile, biting my tongue. He means well. I'd rather say nothing than get into the pulsating heart of the matter, which has my heart racing and my chest tight: *nobody trusts me to be able to do a damn thing.*

I tuck the feelings away deep inside. I don't have time for them right now. It's easier to march forward with the day, to clean, to prepare for Bella and think about Kru in the periphery. I get back to my subpar cleaning assistance: porch tidying, hallway sprucing, a quick bathroom clean. We share an easy lunch of deli meat sandwiches, during which I try not to think about all the ways Kru would have made them exceptional, and then I head to my room to get changed. While I'm pulling on leggings, Griffin shouts from the living room,

"They're here!"

I rush to the door, taking a deep breath before pulling it open. A shiny black car is parked in the driveway, right behind Griff's. I see Bella in the passenger seat, and I squeal.

I barrel toward the car, shrieking in lieu of a calm greeting. Bella turns and watches me with a bright smile through the passenger window. I am distantly aware of Jackson Bedd's confusion in the driver's seat as I arrive at the passenger door and begin knocking on the glass.

"Bella! Open up!" I demand.

She peers up at me through the window, acting like she can't hear me.

"Oh, stop it right now," I tell her.

She shrugs, looking over at Jackson like she has no idea who I am. I groan loudly, pulling at the car door. It doesn't budge. I can see her cackling from inside the car.

"Come onnn," I whine, knocking on the glass.

She continues taunting me from inside. I huff, crossing my arms.

"You're mean," I inform her, and then I stomp away.

The car door clicks open before I reach the porch, and I spin to look at her. "*Finally.*"

Bella leans against her car door, her warm, familiar smile erasing all of my annoyance. It's like no time has passed at all as she holds out her arms for a hug. I zip back over to her, and we hug for a solid ten seconds. I don't care that her boyfriend is a famous rock musician and is probably wondering what the hell is wrong with this woman's family. I need my Bella hug.

"I missed you, Pipe Cleaner," she says.

"I missed you too, Sweet Pea." I pull back and smile at her. And then I notice the towering, long-haired hunk just past her shoulder. I straighten, feeling my cheeks heat up.

There is a frickin' celebrity in the driveway right now.

"Time for introductions," Bella starts, just as Jackson comes up to her side. "Jackson—"

"Jackson Bedd. Yes, I know." I hold out my hand, but quickly recoil it. "Do we shake hands? Or—"

"Can we hug?" Jackson offers in the same voice he uses to woo millions of women on the radio every day.

"Oh my god, *let's hug*." I throw my arms around Jackson. He feels solid and real, like a regular human, even though he's also capable of playing to crowds of eight thousand people at once. "You're family now."

Bella laughs. "That escalated quickly."

"Excuse me?" Griffin's booming voice breaks through the reunion. We all turn to look at him. "You bring a famous rock star to my driveway and don't even honk to let me know you're here?"

I know he's just giving them shit, since he's been on Bella-and-Jackson patrol since nine a.m. He strides out to the driveway, pulling Bella into a hug. He and Jackson exchange hellos—and more hugs. I'm sure Jackson has more than realized by now that the Keegans are huggers.

"You're a third of the way inducted into the family," Bella informs her boyfriend.

"Not fully inducted until you meet the rest of the family," I add.

"Is there anyone I should be concerned about?" Jackson asks, looking between me and Griffin.

"Well, my brothers are all kind of brutes," I say.

"Hey." Griffin elbows me.

"Sweet brutes," I hurry to add. "Jett might be the wild card."

"Is he the one I have to win over?" Jackson asks. "I can set up a private concert if needed..."

Griffin squeezes Jackson's shoulder. "I'm suddenly very hard to win over. I want in on this private concert."

"How about we go inside?" Bella suggests, glancing at Jackson, who's watching some slowed cars on the street. "I've been dying to see how the house looks now that you two are roommates."

"Significantly messier," Griffin grumbles as we all walk toward the door.

"Listen, I'm running a business," I snap. "I don't have time to organize the shoe rack or whatever it is you wish I'd do every day instead of making marshmallows."

Griffin holds the door open, and we all file inside. "I don't need the shoe rack organized. I just need the *shoes* on the *rack*."

I sigh dramatically, looking back at Jackson. "Never move in with your older brother, Jackson. It only spells trouble." I elbow Griff so he knows I'm just poking at him. He knocks my chin and sends me a lopsided smile.

"Trust me, I wouldn't dream of it. Though I did temporarily move in *next* to my brother, and that seemed to work out okay." Jackson grins as he looks around the cozy bungalow. I'm sure he's thinking how crazy Griffin is to call me messy, since this place is *spotless*.

Griffin leads us into the living room. Jackson and Bella sink into the couch; I curl up next to Bella, and Griffin opts for the armchair. "How's Aunt Laura doing?" Bella asks us.

"She's great," I say. "Doing the same old thing, as always." The *same old thing* sounds like not much, but really, it's everything. Baking bread, loving on her kids, and holding down the fort for us.

Bella and I share a warm smile. She gets it. My mom—practically her mom too—is the cornerstone of...everything we've achieved. Bella's amazing event management career, my marshmallow business, Griff's professional hockey career, and on and on...

It's all happening because our mom held the space for us to flourish.

"She's expecting you for dinner this week," Griff adds.

"I wouldn't miss it for the world," Bella says. "I texted her when we were close to Bayshore, but I haven't heard back—"

An intense buzzing interrupts her sentence. Griffin's phone. A moment later, my own phone starts ringing from in the kitchen. I scamper to my feet to grab it.

And then Bella's phone rings as well.

Griffin's eyes are on his phone as he announces, "It's Asher."

"Dane's calling me," I inform them once I grab my phone.

"And Jett's calling me," Bella says.

Jackson's brows draw together. "Is this part of the Keegan connection, or..."

Something heavy forms in the pit of my stomach.

"This isn't exactly normal," Bella says. "They probably don't know we're all here together."

Griffin answers his phone first, and then I swipe mine on.

"Dane?"

"Piper." Dane's voice cracks, and immediately my limbs are coated in dread.

"What is it?" I croak out, watching as Griffin's face falls across the living room.

He lets out a ragged sigh. "Mom's bakery caught fire. She was inside when it happened and—"

The words land with a sonic boom. Everything goes loud inside my head, and then eerily silent. I'm not even sure he's still speaking. The world has slowed to molasses around me.

"Come to the hospital," he finishes.

I'm not aware of saying anything. Of hanging up. But the phone is in my lap a moment later and I'm pressing a hand to my mouth. Bella is looking at me, nodding, as she says into the phone, "Yeah. We're on our way."

Bella's face is grave as she turns to Jackson. "Aunt Laura was caught in a fire at her bakery. We need to go to the hospital immediately."

"I can drive," Jackson blurts. "Our car's right outside."

I don't argue. Minutes later, we're piled into their shiny black car, racing toward Bayshore Memorial while Bella instructs Jackson where to turn. In the back, I'm weak against the door, unable to stop my mind from cycling through worst-case scenarios. Dane's voice betrayed Mom's condition. I'm worried we're going to show up there and she'll be gone.

I squeeze my eyes shut, tears escaping. This can't be happening.

Griffin's jaw is clenched tight. He reaches over to squeeze my shoulder. I see all the same fears reflected in his brown eyes. "We don't know anything yet, Pipes. Let's hope for the best."

The hospital comes into view, its emergency entrance bustling with activity. Jackson drops us off so we can find out what's going on and promises to wait for us until we have news.

Inside, the ER waiting room is full of people, but I spot my dark-haired brothers immediately. Dane is pacing back and forth, running his hands through his hair. When he spots us, relief flashes across his face.

"Jett! Dane!" I call, pushing through the crowd with Griffin and Bella in tow. "Any news?"

Dane's face is tight with worry. "They're assessing her now. Smoke inhalation, some burns on her legs. Asher's trying to get more information from the doctors."

"They won't let us back there yet," Jett adds, frustration evident in his voice. "They're working to stabilize her, and they say a doctor will be out to talk to us soon."

"But...is she..." I can barely finish the sentence. My throat tightens and more tears escape.

Nobody answers me. Because nobody knows. Bella wraps her arms around me and squeezes. For now, that's the only answer I've got.

CHAPTER TWELVE

PIPER

The next few hours are the longest of my life. We wait, pacing the cramped waiting room, taking turns getting coffee no one drinks, checking our phones as if they might suddenly provide answers. Jackson eventually joins us, and of course he's recognized. He signs an autograph and poses for a picture, but mostly he stays close, offering quiet support. Bella keeps her arm linked through mine, a steady presence while everything else spins out of control.

Finally, a tired-looking doctor emerges, clipboard in hand. "Keegan family?"

We all hop to our feet and advance on her. She offers a small smile, but it doesn't last long.

"I have good news...but I also have bad news," she says. "Your mother is stable...but she needs monitoring for the next few days. She suffered severe smoke inhalation and second-degree burns on her legs from apparently trying to help others evacuate. We've got her on oxygen and pain management. She's in a coma right now. The next few days are critical."

I'm wading through the doctor's words, struggling to make sense of this. *Coma? Severe?*

"When can we see her?" Asher asks.

"She's being moved to the ICU right now. I'll have a nurse come get you when she's settled."

"Will she wake up?" I force myself to ask, dreading the answer.

The doctor's expression softens. "Given that she was found relatively quickly, I'm optimistic. But I've seen enough of these cases to know better than to say anything with certainty. Things can turn on a dime. We'll know more once we see how she progresses over the next day."

She leaves us with that cautious hope and heads back through the security door.

Asher's stern face betrays no emotion as he takes charge. Just like he did when our dad died. "We should set up a rotation for staying with her. No point in all of us camping out here."

"I'll stay tonight," Griffin blurts.

"And I'll come first thing in the morning," Jett offers.

Asher nods, though I get the sense that he and Dane were ready to fight for the honor of who stays first. "I think it would be best if the rest of us go home and try to carry on until we get some news. We should expect this to take some time. She'll have a long road ahead."

"Is anyone hungry?" Bella asks.

"Let me get dinner," Jackson suggests.

We spend some time figuring out what dinner will look like under these circumstances. We finally land on Jackson and Bella picking up some food from High-5's downtown while the rest of us wait for the nurse to give us more information. Jackson and Bella eventually return with big brown bags of food. We pass around wrapped sandwiches, and Jackson even bought extra to share with the other people in the waiting room. That earns him a few more pictures and autographs signed.

Despite the sandwich in my hands, I can't eat. I take one nibble and feel sick, somehow craving a Kru meal instead of this. Or maybe I just want the man himself. After a little longer and still no word, Asher wraps his arm around me.

"Go get some rest, Pipe Cleaner. You need to be fresh for the morning."

"You think I can rest not knowing what's happening with Mom?"

"You'll be the first to know. As soon as Griff hears something, he's calling all of us." Asher sends me a stern look.

"Are you going home?" I shoot back.

"I am. I have some work to do. To keep my mind off things."

I sigh. Wasting away in the waiting room probably isn't the best idea. Divide and conquer has always been the best approach, and I guess it works here too. I reluctantly pull myself to standing and give each brother a big hug. Bella does the same, and we all walk out to the parking lot.

"Do you want us to stay at Griff's house with you?" Bella asks.

"No, I'll be fine. Go check out your room at the hotel," I tell them as we climb back into Jackson's car. "We'll all hear something as soon as Griff does, so no need to miss out on that lake view while you've got it."

"Call me if you change your mind, okay? Family comes first. I don't give a shit about the view."

I nod, too exhausted to add anything. I rest my head against the window for the short car ride. When we pull into Griff's driveway, it's damn near eight p.m. The entire day has dissolved in the waiting room at Bayshore Memorial.

As I push open the door, Bella says, "You're sure you don't want us to stay here?"

I smile at her concern. "I promise I'll be fine. Honestly, I'm so exhausted, I'm just going to head straight to bed."

"Let me know if *anything* changes and you need me." She pops out of the car to give me one last hug and a quick peck on the cheek. "I love you, Pipe Cleaner. Aunt Laura's gonna be fine, I know it. We're all staying strong for her."

I hear her words, but they don't do much to calm that anxious buzzing behind my ribs. I wave as she and Jackson pull out of the driveway, and then I slip into the house.

I stand in the foyer, looking around for what feels like fifteen minutes. Nothing looks familiar in the wake of the bad news. The house feels too quiet, too empty without Griffin there while Mom's in the hospital. I wander from room to room, unable to settle, my mind replaying the doctor's words, imagining my mother's pale face beneath an oxygen mask.

All of my exhaustion is replaced with worry. The what-ifs. The worst-case scenarios that twist my gut and leave me breathless.

So much for heading straight to bed. I step out into the backyard, needing fresh air. The night is clear and cool, stars scattered across the velvet sky. *She'll be fine. Everything will be fine.* I sit on the edge of the lounge chair, drawing deep gulps as I repeat the words to myself. *She's alive. She's healing.* But my traitorous mind whispers the fears I've been ignoring all day: what if this is the day when everything changes? What if this week is the last time I ever spoke to her, hugged her, told her I loved her?

The tears I've been holding back all day finally fall.

I already lost my dad. I'm not ready to lose my mom, too.

That cracks me open. The tears rush hot and fast. My face falls into my hands, shoulders shaking as the emotion heaves through me. I'm fully sobbing when a soft voice breaks through the darkness.

"Piper? What's wrong?"

I look up to see Kru standing at the fence, concern etched across his face. I hastily wipe at my tears, but it's too late—he's already realized what's going on.

Without a word, he vaults over the fence in one smooth motion. He's at my side in seconds.

"What happened?" he asks, crouching down beside me.

I draw a shaky breath. I don't know if I have the strength to tell him everything. "My mom...her bakery caught fire..." My words are punctuated with hiccupping sobs. "And...she was inside..."

Suddenly his thick arms are around me, pulling me against his chest. He's all solid heat, the scent of firewood and cedar sinking deep into me. My brain weakly protests—*you don't need him, you shouldn't be relying on your rival*.

But my heart knows better. I melt into him, letting his warmth seep into my bones.

"She's going to be okay," he murmurs into my hair. "Your mom's gotta be a fighter, if she's anything like the daughter she raised."

His sweet words prompt more tears, but for a different reason altogether. I draw deep breaths, relishing the scent of Kru that laces through my senses. The sobbing subsides to mere sniffles.

"She is," I whisper. "But not knowing...I just can't stand the thought that maybe she's...she's...I can't even say it."

"I know." He rubs gentle circles on my back. "I know."

We sit like that for a long time, his arms around me, my head buried in the front of his chest. He doesn't make a move to leave...and neither do I. The comfort of his embrace is something I didn't know I needed. I burrow deeper against him. I want to stay like this for as long as possible. Before my rational mind or the real world catches up to us.

"I saw the fire trucks on my way home," he says eventually. "I had no idea..."

The simple admission—that he noticed something was wrong in town—makes me realize that he's part of Bayshore too. Which brings a fresh wave of conflicting emotions. Part of me hates that he's here, disrupting my Bayshore cocoon. Another part is starting to wonder if I even want him to leave.

"When's the last time you ate?" he asks suddenly.

I try to remember. "I had a bite of something in the ER waiting room."

"Wait here." He gently untangles himself from me.

Before I can protest, he's jogging to the fence. He launches himself over easily, and while he's gone, I finally notice how chilly it is out here. I bring my knees to my chest, wishing for his arms around me again. He returns a few minutes later with a paper baggie in one hand and a blanket over his shoulder. He sits down beside me on the lounger again, draping the blanket over both our laps. Then he peels back the brown paper and pulls out a sandwich.

"Have this," he says. "Nothing fancy, but it's protein and carbs."

The simple gesture—making me a sandwich when I'm too distraught to think about food—cracks something open inside me. This is Kru, my supposed rival, the man who's turned my life upside down. And yet here he is, taking care of me in the most basic, human way. I take a bite and my eyes flutter shut. It's a deli meat sandwich, but it's more than that too. He's got some special sort of mayo—that has to be it. And are these sprouts on here?

"Thank you," I say when I'm done chewing, my voice thick with emotion. I can't stop the next words from spilling out. "We got sandwiches earlier and all I could think about was how I wanted your food instead."

A warm smile curls his lips.

"And thank you for this. For...being here."

He wraps his arm around my back. "Nowhere else I'd rather be."

We sit side by side on the deck while I finish off the sandwich, talking softly about nothing important—a new recipe he's testing, a mishap I had with a batch of marshmallows earlier in the week, the weather forecast for tomorrow. Normal things, safe things, worlds away from hospitals and fires and fear.

When I swallow the last bit, exhaustion hits me like a semitruck. I can barely keep my eyes open.

"You should sleep," Kru says.

"I'm afraid to," I admit. "Every time I close my eyes, I imagine what she went through at the bakery."

Without a word, he repositions himself on the lounger so he's leaning all the way back and opens his arms. I hesitate only a moment before settling against his chest, my head tucked under his chin.

"Sleep," he murmurs, arranging the blanket over top of us. "I've got you. I'm here."

And somehow, despite everything, I fall asleep in his arms.

CHAPTER THIRTEEN

KRU

There's a certain point in the night when the blanket no longer cuts it. My breath comes out in little white puffs on every exhale as I slowly wake up. We've been out here for hours, my stiff limbs inform me. My gaze drifts up to the inky black sky illuminated by the perfectly round and brilliant full moon. I slip my phone out of my pocket and check the time. It's one a.m. My right arm has gone numb where Piper rests against it, but I wouldn't move for anything.

Not when she looks so peaceful. The worry tugging at her face all night has finally smoothed out, her breathing deep and even. One of her hands is curled into the fabric of my T-shirt as if she's making sure I don't slip away.

She doesn't know it, but I'm not going anywhere.

I've known this woman for barely two months, but something about her has burrowed in deep. Sure, I fell in love with her during that first night in

Cleveland, but it's everything else I've learned about her since that has me desperate for more.

She stirs, eyelashes fluttering against her cheeks before she blinks awake. For a moment, she seems confused, her gaze darting around until it settles on my face.

"You should go inside," I say softly. "It's getting cold."

Reality crashes back in. I can see it happening—the brief disorientation, then remembrance, the flash of grief tightening her features.

"I fell asleep," She pushes her tangled hair back from her face, which causes the blanket to slip off her shoulders. "I didn't mean to keep you out here all night."

"You didn't keep me anywhere I didn't want to be."

She looks like she doesn't quite believe me, but she doesn't argue. Instead, she wraps her arms around herself. I drape the blanket back around her shoulders. She blinks, still groggy for a few moments, then hurries to check her phone. She swipes through screens, nibbling on her bottom lip.

"Mom's in ICU, Griff went in to see her about two hours ago." A shaky sigh escapes her. "She's still in a coma but she's stable." She sets her phone down, drawing a deep breath. "It feels like a win. Or maybe a loss. I can't tell."

"It's too soon to tell. Which means you need to sleep while you can."

She peeks up at me through her eyelashes. "That sounds like a good idea, I guess."

"You need help making it to your bed?" I'm not making a move. I mean it honestly. Though I can't help but think about all the dishonest intentions that being in her bed would facilitate. Now is not the time.

I can be a friend to her. Even if I want so much more than that.

Her throat bobs. "Maybe."

"Say no more, Maven." I sweep her into my arms, hoisting her easily. A soft giggle escapes her, and she clutches my biceps as I pull open the sliding glass door. The house is dark inside, and I fumble around for a moment.

"Head to that hallway over there." She points with her foot.

Once my eyes adjust to the low lighting, offered solely by the full moon high in the sky outside, I realize this place looks suspiciously like mine. In the narrow hallway, there are three doors: two bedrooms and a bathroom at the end, just like my rental.

"Which one are you?" I ask.

"This one." She points to the righthand door with her foot, and I push it open with my shoulder. A chaotic bedroom greets us, shadowy clothing piles on the floor, nightstand covered with jewelry, half-open luggage strewn around. I'm the cause of this chaos, I'm aware. I gently set her down on the bed, and her eyes flutter shut for a moment.

"Sleep tight," I tell her, my voice pinched. I want to stay. I don't know why, but I do. Things just feel right with her in my arms. It makes no fucking sense, but here we are.

She blinks slowly, then reaches for my hand.

"Stay with me." She says it so quietly I wonder if I even heard it. But it has to be real, because when I slip into the bed and bury myself under the covers alongside her, she hums with pleasure.

Piper fits into my arms easily. Like she was made for the space there. It's the last thing I think about before I finally drift off to sleep beside her.

When I awake the next morning, the first thing I notice is that Piper is gone.

I wonder if I dreamt it all—until I turn over and realize I'm in her bedroom. In her bed. Water rushing from the bathroom down the hall tells me she's getting ready for the day. I squint at the bedside clock—six thirty. Shit, it's time for her to get to work.

I yawn and sit on the edge of the bed, contemplating life. Piper breezes in just as I'm stretching and rolling my neck. She casts me a sheepish grin.

"I didn't mean to wake you up."

"If you're going, I need to get going too." My voice is extra deep from sleep. I rub at my face, trying to get my brain working. I've got a long Monday ahead of me. She does too.

She tips her head toward the door. "I've got a new toothbrush in the bathroom if you want it. I know I hate waking up in a new place without any of my stuff. You can use whatever you want in there."

"Thanks, Maven." I wink at her, and she bites her bottom lip. I slip past her and get ready for the day—toothbrush included—and try to make myself resemble a chef. My hair is messy, my eyes look tired, and dammit, maybe I'll just go home and sleep some more.

When I head back into the bedroom, Piper is wearing teal leggings with an oversized cream sweater. She looks cute enough to eat.

I lean against the doorframe. "I think I'm gonna go lie down. Either I'm getting old or sleeping outside in early October isn't good for the joints."

She winces. "Sorry about that. It's totally my fault."

I roll my shoulders, wincing at the crick in my neck. "Nothing that some sleep and a hot shower won't fix."

"I could make you breakfast," she offers, then seems surprised by her own words. "I mean, if you want. Even though you just told me you wanted to sleep. Sorry, dumb idea."

There's something tentative in her voice, like she realizes she's crossing a line. I should say no. I should go back to my side of the fence, take a nap, and resume that careful distance that's supposed to exist between landlord and tenant, rivals and neighbors.

"That sounds way better than sleep, actually."

Piper's grin wakes me up more than a cup of coffee could. She moves through her brother's kitchen with familiarity, pulling out eggs and bacon, bread for toast. I sit at the counter, watching her work. There's a grace to her movements, even at this hour of the morning.

"I specialize in sweet, not savory," she warns as she cracks eggs into a bowl. "So lower your expectations accordingly."

"I'll try to restrain my professional critique. Is there anything I can do to help?" I ask.

She shakes her head. "Just sit there and relax. I'm sure managing one more kitchen is the last thing you want to do."

"All right. So you want me to just sit here and look pretty." I crack my knuckles. "I can do that."

She snorts. "Right. Look pretty."

"I'm only great at a few things, Pipes. Cooking, looking pretty, and...well..." I drag my gaze up to her. "There's another thing I'm pretty good at, do you remember what it is?"

Her cheeks flush, and I know she's remembering exactly what expertise I'm referring to—the way I made her thighs shake in Cleveland after I buried my face between her legs. But she doesn't take the bait.

"You want orange juice?" she asks instead.

"Yeah. But let me get it." I get up and pour us each a glass, comfortable in the domestic rhythm of it all. It should feel strange, this morning-after routine when nothing actually happened between us, but somehow it just feels...right.

The bacon sizzles in the pan, filling the kitchen with its mouthwatering aroma. I'm hungrier than I realized, even at this ungodly hour. Piper flips the bacon with practiced ease, then starts on the eggs.

"Scrambled okay?" she asks.

"Perfect."

She works in silence for a few minutes, lost in thought. I can tell she's not fully present, her mind probably still at the hospital with her mom.

"So did you get any sleep last night?" I ask, knocking her hip. I slide her glass of orange juice toward her on the counter and take a big gulp from mine.

"I did." She smiles up at me, her green eyes sparkling. "Thanks to you."

"I'm available for cuddling whenever you need it," I tell her. "Getting bad news; cold night on the couch; maybe you're just too lazy to go get a blanket. You can call me instead."

"Except I can't," she shoots back. "I don't have your number."

I feign confusion. "But Piper. I gave it to you once already." I touch my chest, making sure my jaw drops in spectacular, outrageous fashion. "*You mean you didn't keep it?*"

Her cheeks flush again, and she keeps her eyes on the eggs.

"Don't be embarrassed that you tried to ghost me and then I moved in next door to your business. It happens. I mean, not often, but clearly it happens."

She snorts, covering her eyes with her free hand. "Kru. This is so embarrassing. We're supposed to never talk about it."

"I know. You've been trying very hard to avoid this topic. I commend you on your agility. You've done an amazing job avoiding it even when directly confronted."

Her cheeks are fully red now, but she's shaking with silent laughter.

"I won't even ask you *why* you ghosted me. We'll save that for a rainy day when I feel like making you uncomfortable again."

She sighs, shaking her head. "There's no dramatic why, Kru. I'm focused on my business. My family. That's it."

I relate to that. But the connection we shared—*still share*—warrants some further explanation. Not to mention exploration. I'm a little frustrated she doesn't share that opinion.

"So no room for the occasional body-shaking orgasm," I confirm.

She looks up at me with wide eyes and pink cheeks. "*Kru!*"

"Just making sure we're on the same page."

She huffs, snapping off the stovetop and reaching for plates. "I can't go there. Sorry. It's nothing personal. My family would—" She stops short and shakes her head. "It's just a non-option."

Needle points prickle across my chest. I'm being rejected in real time. But I brought myself here for a reason. I need to lay this infatuation to rest, and this might be the only way to do it.

"I can't say I'm not disappointed." My eyes are on her plating the food, watching her movements. In my head I'm prepping the garnish, readying the drizzle of sauce I'd add as a finishing touch. But this is breakfast, and Piper's in control. Chef Kru needs to stand down. "So no more kisses when you start hitting chip shots at the fence again, huh?"

She dips her chin. This looks suspiciously like a pout. She wants the kisses as much as I do.

"If it makes you feel better, I won't tell anybody if you kiss me at the fence line." I bring my lips closer to her ear. My lips brush her lobe as I whisper, "It can be our dirty little secret."

Goosebumps flourish along her neckline, and I can't restrain myself. I take a tug of her earlobe with my teeth, and she sucks in a sharp breath.

"Seducing me will not make these eggs taste better," she warns me. Her eyes are hooded as she turns to me, presenting me with my plate.

"I beg to differ." My gaze washes over the plate, and my stomach immediately begins rumbling. Maybe I am a breakfast guy after all, if Piper makes it for me. "Our emotions show up in our recipes. I'm just doing my part, getting you all horny while you cook for me."

A laugh bursts out of her and she brings her plate to the small dinette along the windows overlooking the backyard. I bring my plate over and sit next to her. Our knees knock as I fit into the space beside her.

"My true goal is to get your mind off the sad stuff." I take one last sip of orange juice before I dig in. "Did it work?"

She's chewing and smiling up at me. "It did. Thank you."

"Your mom sounds amazing," I say quietly. "I want to go check out the bakery once everything is put back together."

"It's a Bayshore staple," she says, forking some more eggs. "She took it over from the previous owner and kept the legacy going. Now it's famous for her recipes and her style. And my mom is incredible. She didn't exactly have it easy in life. After Dad died, she held us all together. Four rowdy boys and then me, the unexpected girl addition...until Bella became the final unexpected girl addition when she moved in with us." She flashes a brief, sad smile. "My mom's the strongest person I know."

"Explains where you get it from."

She raises an eyebrow. "You think I'm strong?"

"You're the youngest of five *and* a business owner. Not to mention a marketing maven and pioneer. Yeah, I think you're strong. It takes strength to cut it in the business world, and you've got a solid track record already."

She blinks a few times, her throat bobbing. "Why are you so sweet?" She takes a bite of toast.

"I'm not sweet. I'm honest."

"You're both," she says as she chews. "Now eat your food and let me know how I did."

I take a bite of the eggs. They're simple but good—fluffy, seasoned well. The bacon is crisp, just how I like it. It's not haute cuisine, but it's honest food, made with care.

"Do you want me to be sweet, or honest?" I ask her.

"Let's try for both again," she says with a laugh.

"They're..." I pause, narrowing my eyes critically. "Agreeable to the palate."

She snorts out a laugh, the sound warming me more than the food. "High praise. I strive to create a breakfast that begs to be called *agreeable*."

"Hey, if there's a food critic in my restaurant and they call my menu agreeable, I'll take that compliment and run."

She tilts her head as she looks over at me, something dreamy coming over her. "Are you trying to get food critics in your place?"

"Of course. Not shooting for a Michelin star with my concept, but I want to be on the map." I take another big bite of eggs, winking her way. "For my dad."

"Is he a chef too?"

"He was, in his own way. Before he passed."

Understanding shudders through her, and we lock eyes. The more I learn about her, the more I want her. The more I realize how much she fucking complements me. She's an ingredient I never planned on finding, and I suspect she'll meld nicely in the recipe of my life.

If she wanted the same thing, that is.

"How old were you when he died?" she asks quietly.

"It was about four years ago. Cancer. He fucking loved that I had trained to be a chef and was working on food trucks. It was like the missed opportunity of his life, you know? That thing he never got to do but always wanted to try." Emotion is welling inside me. I need to tread carefully. "I wish he could have seen the reality TV show. Man, he would have lost his shit." I laugh to myself and take another bite of eggs to stop the way my throat is tightening up.

"What was his name?"

"Ray."

Her eyes widen slightly, and I can see the pieces clicking into place. "That's why you named the..."

I nod. "Yeah. It's for him. In his honor."

She touches her chest, tears welling in her eyes. She bursts into a sob and covers her face with her hands.

"Oh shit," I start, "I didn't mean—"

"That is the absolute sweetest thing I've ever heard." She cries into her hands then sniffles, looking up at me with red-rimmed eyes. "Oh my god, Kru. I'm so sorry I said Ray's was some neo-hipster chain restaurant."

A laugh bursts out of me. "That's right. What else did you tell me? That I was going to dance on the bar hourly? Brutal."

"I was mad at you." She wipes tears away from under her eyes.

"Fair." I bite into the bacon. "When did you lose your dad?"

She takes a deep breath, her gaze drifting down to her plate. "I was young. Like six. I barely remember him. He was in the wrong place at the wrong time—car accident. Not his fault." She toys with a piece of bacon as she continues. "It was hard for all of us. And my oldest brother Asher nominated himself as the honorary Dad after that. He tried so hard to fill Dad's shoes...which was an impossible task, especially for a grieving twelve or thirteen year old."

"I can't imagine." I reach out and squeeze her free hand. "Losing a parent is always hard, but I think it's hardest when you're young and you haven't gotten the hang of the world yet."

Piper nods slowly, then takes a bite of her bacon. "Yeah. Well said. Dad's still around though. We keep him in an hourglass in the family room, so he can participate in game night."

My brows draw together. "You...what?"

"His ashes," she clarifies, then pauses. "Yeah, that still sounds pretty crazy huh?"

We eat in companionable silence for a while, the weight of our conversation hanging between us. I feel closer to Piper than ever. I *want her* more than ever.

But something is in the way.

And I'm nothing if not persistent.

Once our bellies are full and I clear the plates, the sight of her bathed in the early morning sunlight has desire humming through me. Fuck, I want this woman. I know how good we are together—and she does too.

"So," I begin, coming up behind her in the chair. I squeeze the tops of her shoulders, bringing my mouth closer to her ear. "How does 'you and me' become an option?"

Her eyes flutter shut. "Kru...I...this is why I ghosted you. It's bad timing."

I grunt softly, nipping at her earlobe again. "Wrong answer."

"And now, the bad timing is even worse," she adds.

"Fine. But don't come looking for me at night," I warn her. "Now give me one last kiss for the road."

She narrows her eyes, but doesn't protest when I dip down and claim her lips with my own. She makes a small noise in the back of her throat as our tongues meet. She's warmth and honey and the tang of orange juice. Fuck, I want more of this woman. But I pull myself away.

"If you need anything other than kisses, a good fuck, or a boyfriend, I'm right next door."

She rolls her lips in, covering her pink cheeks with her hands. "I know where to find you."

I pause at the sliding glass door, looking back at her. The morning sun is climbing higher, painting her face in soft golden light. Despite the shadows under her eyes and the worry etched into her features, she's beautiful.

"Kru," she says, just as I'm stepping onto the deck. "Thank you. Again. For everything."

"Anytime, Maven."

I head back to my place, hopping the fence with now practiced ease. Everything inside me wants to stay with her, to dive deeper into the warmth that opens up between us whenever we're together for more than a minute and nobody is blocking the curb cut.

But she's drawn the line between us.

Somehow that line is supposed to keep Piper Keegan as strictly my neighbor and rival when everything between us is begging both of us to cross it.

CHAPTER FOURTEEN

PIPER

Waking up in the muscled arms of a reality TV chef inside my brother's house was not on my bingo card for this year.

I'm pedaling to Cloud Nine, mind raking through the previous twelve hours. I can't even think about how I might have accidentally decorated his shirt with my drool last night. Probably not the sexiest night he's ever had with a woman—drying my tears, propping me up, keeping me from catching hypothermia on the back patio. Then cooking an impromptu bacon-and-eggs breakfast for an actual trained chef? Nerve wracking.

And that doesn't even cover the very serious feelings I have blossoming in my chest every time I catch a glimpse of his mischievous grin or his warm, brown eyes. I've counted the kitchen-related scars on his forearms and biceps so many times I'm embarrassed to admit that I know exactly how many he has (twelve).

I shouldn't know these things about my rival and landlord.

Yet I'm collecting these details about Kru like I'm gathering a wildflower bouquet. I love the way Kru's eyes crinkle when he smiles and how his voice gets all soft and rumbly when he's being gentle. I love that his restaurant is in his dad's honor. I love the name he chose for it. I love why he does what he does.

I damn near love Kru himself.

I frown, pedaling harder, as if that might excise the thought from my head.

I can't love him. I don't have room for him in my life. My brothers would never accept him. Mom's in the hospital. *This is not the time to fall in love.*

I repeat these words like a mantra as I punish myself through cycling like I'm training for the Ironman. But it does nothing to dissolve the conflicting emotions swirling inside me.

The bike ride empties out my brain eventually. But then I get to the shop and see the façade of Ray's and I'm right back to Square Kru.

I briefly wonder what Kru is doing right now. Did he really go back to sleep? Is he still thinking about that goodbye kiss we shared? Is he plotting more ways to be both sweet and honest with me so I fall even further in love with him?

I hurry inside, eager to get things open for Jerrica to come and take over. I called her last night to take over since I wasn't sure what hospital rotations would look like, and she immediately offered to take on more hours indefinitely. Once Jerrica is all set, I'll be heading straight to Bayshore Memorial to see Mom. According to Griffin's update earlier that morning, Mom is still unconscious but her vitals are stable.

I've barely got the espresso machine warmed up when Jerrica comes bouncing in. She's perky and friendly, an excellent addition to Cloud Nine. After we've run over the morning tasks, I'm milling around the back room, trying to figure out if I've forgotten anything. Instead of going over my to-do list, my mind is wandering to that little fantasy corner of my brain where I've been stashing details for my future business expansion I don't quite know how to make a reality: the event space. Jerrica showing up reminded me that I'll need to hire more wonderful employees like her if I want to expand.

But how? Finding more people like her seems impossible. She's the daughter of a longtime family friend, so of course she's amazing.

Piper, this is not the time to be thinking about business expansion. Or hot neighbors for that matter.

Even ridiculously attractive ones with talented hands and a way of making me feel seen.

Jerrica assures me she's caught up and ready, and she practically pushes me out the door. I hop back on my bike, pedaling across town to Bayshore Memorial.

Mom needs her kids. That's priority number one.

The hospital is quieter this morning than it was last night. I find my way to the third floor, ICU room 317, and pause outside to brace myself. Hospitals put me on edge—the antiseptic smell, the beeping machines, the forced cheerfulness of the staff. But when I push the door open, what I see stops me in my tracks.

Mom's room is full of flowers. Not just any flowers—beautiful, artful arrangements of late summer and early fall blooms. Sunflowers, dahlias, chrysanthemums, all in vibrant oranges, yellows, and deep reds. They're everywhere—on the windowsill, the bedside table, even a small arrangement on the wheelie table that goes across the bed.

Griffin looks up from his chair by Mom's bed, his expression weary but relieved.

"Asher went a little overboard with the flowers," he says by way of greeting. "He bought a couple himself but also got a few other local business owners to chip in, which snowballed into, well, this."

I move closer to examine the nearest arrangement. There's a small card tucked into it. I flip it open.

"For our rock. Get better soon. We need you. Love, Asher."

My eldest brother, always the steady one, the one who stepped into dad's shoes when we needed him most. Of course he'd fill Mom's room with color and life.

"Leave it to Asher to turn the place into a botanical garden," I say, feeling a lump form in my throat.

Griffin nods. "He said the room was too depressing. Too clinical." He gestures to the largest arrangement. "That one's from all of us, technically, but Asher picked it out."

I sink into the chair next to him, my eyes on Mom's sleeping form. She looks smaller somehow, vulnerable in a way I'm not used to. But the oxygen mask has been replaced with a nasal cannula, which I take as a good sign.

"Any word on what caused the fire?" I ask, reaching for Mom's hand. Her skin is warm and soft, betraying nothing of the bandages around her legs covering the burns.

Griffin shakes his head. "Police are investigating. They think it might have started in the basement, but they're not sure if it was electrical or..." He trails off, his jaw tightening.

"Or what?"

"Or deliberate."

The word hangs in the air between us.

"Who would want to burn down the Bayshore Bakery?" I ask, my voice barely above a whisper.

Griffin shrugs. "It's prime real estate right on the waterfront. Developers have been trying to get their hands on it for years. At least that's what Dane is saying."

Almost all of downtown Bayshore features various grand old buildings, almost all of them with a lake view. They've been rehabbed and converted into a wide variety of businesses—the bakery, of course, but the other historical buildings feature a heart clinic run by Dominic Daly, The Daily Grind coffee shop, and Hazel Homes, Hazel Daly's realty outpost.

"We have to be prepared for the building to be a total loss," Griffin continues. "Jett went by this morning, and it's burned right down to the foundation. The brick walls are still standing, but barely."

A lump forms in my throat. The building that housed the Bayshore Bakery was old, built back in the early 1800s when Bayshore itself was founded. The loss stings. Not just for us, but for the community.

We sit in silence for a while, both lost in our own thoughts. Then the door opens, and a nurse walks in.

"Oh my," she says, taking in all the flowers. "Someone's popular."

She moves around the room efficiently, checking Mom's vitals and making notes on her chart. "Her oxygen levels are looking much better this morning. Doctor will be by soon to evaluate her breathing and decide if we can take her off supplemental oxygen."

"When do you think she'll wake up?" I ask.

"Hard to say. The sedatives are wearing off, so it could be anytime. Just keep talking to her—hearing familiar voices often helps."

After she leaves, Griffin stands and stretches. "Now that you're here, I'm going to grab some coffee and something to eat. Want anything?"

"No, I'm good. Thanks." I don't dare tell him that Kru was inside his kitchen this morning and that I fed my nemesis from Griff's own fridge.

When he's gone, I lean closer to Mom, taking her hand again. "Hey, Mom. It's Piper. You've got to wake up soon. You need to see all these flowers. The room looks like a botanical garden." I swallow hard, fighting back tears. "Everyone's here for you. All the boys and Bella. She brought Jackson Bedd—can you believe it? You gotta wake up so you can meet him. He's so nice and regular, just like Bella said."

I keep talking, telling her about the shop, about the Best of Bayshore competition, about anything I can think of. I leave out the part about spending the night with Kru.

The door opens again, and Griffin returns with coffee and a sad-looking hospital cafeteria sandwich.

"Nutritious," I say, eyeing the plastic-wrapped triangles dubiously.

"Beggars can't be choosers. Besides, Dane's bringing real food when he comes in for his shift. Apparently he's stopping by that new brunch place on his way."

I squint at Griff's sandwich as he unwraps it, which is somehow both dry and soggy at the same time. "Mmm. Let me know how it is."

He takes a bite and grimaces. "Like eating moist cardboard."

"Don't say that word," I hiss.

He grins evilly as he chews. "Moist."

I roll my eyes, sinking into my chair. There's no escaping brothers, even when you're all adults.

We sit in silence for a while, both of us watching Mom's chest rise and fall with each breath. The doctor stops by, confirming what the nurse told us—she's stable, but nobody is positive when she'll wake up. It's just wait and see for now.

About an hour later, Dane arrives, a takeout bag from Annie's Brunch tucked under his arm.

"How is she?" he asks, nodding toward Mom.

"Same," Griffin says. "Stable."

Dane sets the food down and goes to Mom's side, taking her hand. "Hey, Mom. Brought you some blueberry pancakes. You need to wake up and eat them before your vulture-spawn gets to them."

I snicker. "Griff's extra hungry because he only had two thousand calories for breakfast so far."

Griff narrows his eyes, leaning in close to me. *"Moist."*

I push at his arm, but he doesn't budge. Sometimes I don't understand how we came from the same parents—me so small and blonde and him so hulking and dark-haired. I pinch his skin on the bottom of his forearm and he winces. That'll count as my victory for today.

"I should head back to the shop," I say, checking the time. "Jerrica's there alone, and we've got that big order for the Hendersons."

"You still down for a night shift tonight?" Dane says.

"Of course," I tell him.

Dane nods, pulling me into a quick hug. "I'll call if anything changes."

I bend down to kiss Mom's forehead. "I'll be back tonight," I promise her.

The shop is mercifully busy when I return, forcing me to focus on something other than my tumultuous thoughts. Jerrica has kept things running smoothly, but there's always more to do. I dive into finishing the Henderson order, grateful for the mindless rhythm of measuring, mixing, piping.

I'm so focused on my work that I nearly jump out of my skin when the bells on the door jingle sharply just before noon.

"Welcome to Cloud—" I start, then break into a grin when I see who it is. "Bella! Jackson!"

I abandon my work and come out from behind the counter to give her a big hug—and Jackson too. He doesn't even resist, his leather jacket crinkling as I squeeze my arms around him. Immediately I can tell eyes are on us—well, on *Jackson*—but according to Bella and Jackson, the move is to ignore it and press on.

"How was the visit with Aunt Laura?" Bella asks as I return to my post behind the counter. There's nobody in line so they stand near the front as we chat.

"A little depressing. She looks so small and weak. But her vitals are stable. They think she'll wake up soon." I try to offer a smile, but I can feel my cheeks twitching with the effort.

"It's gonna happen any time now," Jackson reassures me.

"Did you get any sleep last night?" Bella asks me. I notice she looks a little tired.

"Some," I say. "It was hard to fall asleep thanks to my thoughts. Did you?"

"Same situation for me." She reaches over and squeezes my wrist. "I can take a shift at the hospital while we're here. I want to."

"That would be great. I'm gonna head over there after work for my overnight shift. Hopefully we won't be needing to do them for too much longer," I say. "Now what do you guys want? On the house, of course."

I point out our specials in the display case, giving Jackson a quick rundown of the marshmallow ethos and options of Cloud Nine. Once they settle on a pumpkin caramel latte and a hot chocolate with every marshmallow combination available, a loud knock from the back room distracts me.

"Hang on guys...let me go see what that was about," I tell Bella and Jackson as I rush toward the back of the shop. As soon as I step over the threshold to my storage room, a hand grabs my wrist. I spin toward the arm, a yelp escaping me. A moment later, I'm against Kru's hard, warm chest.

I laugh into the front of his black chef's coat, melting into him. "Oh, hey there." I prop my chin on his chest, looking up at him as I slide my arms around his firm torso. This is nice. *Really* nice. "Was that you making a mess back here?"

"Purely fictional mess, I promise." His lips quirk up into a smile and he tilts his head, his gaze washing over me. His thick arms encircle me, pulling me tighter against him. "How you doing? I wanted to check on you. And your mom."

I'm touched that he's thinking of me after our fraught conversation about *us* this morning.

The truth is that this doesn't feel like bad timing to me.

It feels like perfect timing...but the wrong family.

"She's still in a coma but stable. And I'm...okay."

He nods, his grin widening. "That's a win, considering the situation."

"I think so."

"And just so you know, I didn't initiate this hug. That was all you, Maven."

I open my mouth to protest, but that's when I realize I *have* been contentedly settled in his embrace of my own volition. Embarrassing, after the big stink I made that morning.

"Well, you're...comfortable," I tell him, as I slowly begin extricating myself.

He tuts, shaking his head. "I shouldn't have said anything."

My head is swirling when it comes to this man. I'm desperate for more of his kisses, but it's too complicated even think about right now. "Don't you have a lunch rush to tend to?"

"I just cranked through a bunch of orders and got Brady set up so I could disappear for ten. But I should be getting back."

"Everything okay back here?" Bella's voice cuts through the convo and I gasp, spinning on my heel.

"Oh my god, you scared the crap out of me," I hiss.

"I didn't mean to interrupt," she says, her words slowing as her gaze sweeps over Kru.

My cheeks heat up—I feel caught.

"You're the chef who opened up the new place next door, right?" she asks excitedly. Bella knows I had a hot hookup with a man in Cleveland a couple months ago *and* that my new landlord, who kicked me out of my apartment, was on a reality TV show. She doesn't know they're the same person.

"Yeah, proud owner of Ray's," he says, extending his hand. "I'm Kru. Nice to meet you. And you are?"

"Bella," she says with a sly smile, just as Jackson shows up in the back room. "I'm Piper's cousin. And this is my boyfriend—"

"Holy shit," Kru says, eyes widening. "You're Jackson Bedd."

Jackson grins in an affable way that I can only assume is practiced and holds out his hand. Kru shakes it, looking a little starstruck.

"I am. Nice to meet you…"

"Kru. Short for Krueger. It's my last name."

"You can also call him Uncle Lobster," I point out cheekily, but as soon as the words leave my mouth, I realize I made a critical error.

Bella's gaze swings my way and hardens into a point. I can practically *feel* the pieces clicking into place for her. *Shit.*

"But you need to get back to lunch service," I say, shooing him away. "And I need to get Bella and Jackson their marshmallows."

"Does he always come in through the backdoor?" Bella asks before Kru is fully out of earshot.

Kru calls over his shoulder, "Shared storage space. Fire code shit."

"That sounded really inappropriate," I inform her. "But yes, he enters through the rear. Of the building. Through the door in a building which is not my butt. We don't have butt sex. Or any sex for that matter."

Bella and Jackson are shaking with silent laughter.

"Whatever! You know what I mean."

I stomp behind the counter, intent on leaving the almost-discovery behind me. It's not like I was doing anything wrong. I simply…hugged a gorgeous man when he was in my storage room. Is that a crime?

Bella leans over the display case as I return to the half-finished drinks. "So when were you going to tell me that Cleveland Hookup is also Jerk Landlord?"

I sigh testily. "Never, because if I ignore it, it's not real."

"Do your brothers know?"

"*No.* And that's how it's going to stay."

She dips her chin. "They're going to find out."

"No they aren't. Because there's nothing to find out about. There's nothing going on between me and Kru."

Bella starts laughing, low and staccato. "Sure. That looked like nothing back there."

I finish decorating their drinks with a variety of marshmallows and push them their way on the countertop. "Order's up."

But Bella isn't fazed. "When you're ready to confess that Jerk Landlord is actually Hot Hookup Landlord, I'm all ears."

"Thanks, I'll put that on my calendar," I say dryly. "Right after 'recover from family emergency' and 'win food competition against said Hot La ndlord.'" When I see Bella's smile grow sly, I hurry to add, "I mean Jerk Landlord. I mean—ugh. Nevermind."

"What's his first name?" Jackson asks.

"I have no idea," I tell him, then turn to Bella. "See? That's how much this isn't a thing. If it were a thing, I'd know his first name, and I don't."

Bella doesn't look convinced. She and Jackson mingle in the shop for a while as Jerrica and I tend to a new wave of customers. I'm not fully able to stop thinking about the hug in the back room nor the fact that Bella now knows my dirty secret.

At least I know it's safe with her. For now.

They eventually leave and head to Bayshore Memorial to visit Mom for a bit. The rest of the workday flows uneventfully, and I'm sad that Kru doesn't come inventing another spill for me to investigate.

Once the shop is closed up, I quickly bike back to Griff's house to get ready for my overnight shift at the hospital. I take a quick shower, then I pack up a little overnight bag—my tablet, a notebook, a book, and a variety of highlighters just in case. Once I'm mostly ready in the living room, trying to think of anything I might have forgotten, I begin to drift to the back door.

I wonder if Kru is home.

Maybe he could meet me for just a few minutes by the fence.

The handle of the sliding glass door is in my hand. Just as I'm pushing it open, the front door opens and Griff comes in.

"Hey, Pipes."

I turn quickly, popping on a bright smile. "Hey, Griff! You just come from the hospital?"

He shakes his head. "Nah, I had to head into Cleveland for a bit today. What are you up to? Were you about to head out back?"

The cool night air pouring into the house reminds me the door is still open. I hurry to shut it. "No, no, I..." Nothing comes to me. And the longer I fumble around for a response, the higher Griff's brow raises.

"You're not going to spy on your landlord *again*, are you?"

The incredulity in his voice is a warning. I step away from the glass sliding door while I laugh off his suggestion.

"That is ridiculous. I've spied on him enough, thank you. I like the fresh air before I head to the hospital."

"Be real with me. Does he bother you during the day? Does he come over to your shop ever?"

My heart starts beating a little faster as I recall today in the storage room. "He keeps to himself."

"Good. I can't stand guys like him. He needs to stay the fuck away. In fact, he should go back to Cleveland." He rakes a hand through his hair and sighs testily.

"I think he's going to be in Bayshore for a while," I offer.

"Then you need to be *extra* careful around him. He's got his hooks in you big time. First the building, now this dumb reality TV show. You see it, right? I have an idea of what he's going for next."

My heart, is the first thing that comes to mind. But I clamp my mouth shut.

"Your business," Griff finishes, as though I had any interest in him continuing his tirade against Kru. "Your future."

"I promise you," I say firmly, "you don't have to worry about him wanting my business."

"I'm not worried about *him*," Griff corrects me sharply. "I'm worried about *you*. Look how much he's gotten already. Who's to say he's not angling for even more?"

"I'd never warm up to someone like him," I reassure Griff.

The words echo painfully inside me.

Because they're a lie...and I'm not sure I'll ever convince my brother of it.

CHAPTER FIFTEEN

KRU

Seven days into Ray's and I've survived the delicious, chaotic, adrenaline-fueled blur. Even better, the place is humming like a well-oiled machine already.

Being cleared for sit-down service yesterday was the final piece falling into place, that last satisfying click when you complete a puzzle that took way too fucking long to finish. Regulars who'd been surviving on takeout these past few days could finally experience the ambiance I'd worked so hard to create. The TV crew is only hanging around for another day or two—their focus was on the renovation and opening, and now that we're locked and loaded, Pat and the camera crew will be moving onto their next featured business.

On Friday night, Ray's is packed. Every table filled, the bar seats occupied, reservations stacked through closing. Even my patio is full of diners enjoying the unseasonably warm autumn night, though I have tower heaters at the ready in case it gets too cold.

"Order up! Table seven—two salmon, one steak, medium rare!"

I call out orders in rapid succession, wiping sweat from my brow with my forearm. The kitchen is hot—both literally and figuratively. We're on fire, pumping out dishes with military precision. Brady has gotten better and more in tune every shift; Rafael on expo is hitting his stride after a week, making sure every plate that leaves the kitchen is perfect before it hits the dining room. I've added a front of house manager and our new bartender is pulling in regulars already. In a way, starting with take-out service was a blessing, because it gave us all a chance to warm up together before shit hit the fan with a packed dining room.

"Yes, Chef!" Rafael responds, grabbing the plates I've just finished.

There's a rhythm to a good kitchen, a dance that happens when everyone knows their part. The sizzle of meat hitting hot pans, the clattering of plates, the shouted confirmations—it's music to me. A kitchen in the flow is a dopamine rush I'm addicted to.

My dad would be proud. The thought hits me suddenly as I'm plating a perfect lobster tail. Fuck, the grief comes out of nowhere sometimes. My throat gets tight, and I wish with my whole heart he could have made it long enough to see this place. To see me and this crew and this menu.

To meet Piper.

"Chef, special request at table twelve. They want to know if you can do the lobster tail without the risotto, extra asparagus instead."

"On it," I nod, my hands already moving to accommodate the request. "Brady, fire two more asparagus for table twelve's special."

"Yes, Chef!"

I'm so in the zone that I don't immediately notice the movement at the back of the kitchen. It's only when Brady's rhythm falters slightly that I look up and spot her.

Piper is standing in the doorway of our shared storage space, looking slightly hesitant. Her hair is piled on top of her head in that messy bun she favors, a few strands escaping to frame her face. She's still wearing her work apron, dusted with what looks like powdered sugar.

She's beautiful. And she's in my kitchen during our busiest dinner service yet.

"Keegan. What are you doing here?" I add a little bark to my voice without abandoning my post. Just so she knows that in this kitchen, there's an order to things.

"Don't mind me," she calls out over the kitchen noise. "You weren't supposed to see me."

"You didn't answer my question," I shoot back.

"I need to steal a ladder, and I didn't want you to see me."

I shake my head as I drizzle the finishing sauce over top a new order of the lobster tail. "Move fast. Don't touch anything else."

"Sir, yes sir," she teases.

"It's 'yes, chef'," I correct.

She drifts closer, gaze stuck on the work I'm doing with the plates. "Very dictatorial in here."

I grin, not looking up from my work. "It's called respect in the kitchen. Chain of command. Not that you'd understand the concept since you run a one-woman show."

"Excuse me, I have Jerrica," she retorts. "And she respects me without the militaristic call-and-response."

"I bet if you said 'jump,' she'd ask 'how high?'" I slide another plate toward the heat lamps where Rafael is readying the orders. "Order up."

She rolls her eyes, but I can see she's fighting a smile. "I need to get back."

"You forgot 'Yes, Chef'," I tease.

"In your dreams, Lobster Man."

Rafael hurries over. "Chef, table fourteen is wondering if they can meet you when they're done with their meal."

"Sure, let them know I'll stop by when things slow down."

"Yes, Chef."

Piper makes an exaggerated face at the exchange, and I can't help but laugh.

"See?" I nod toward Rafael. "Respect."

"Or you could call it hero worship," she counters.

"You worshipped me a time or two before, if I recall correctly." When her cheeks pinken, I add, "Say it once. You might like how it feels."

She cocks her head, considering. Then, with deliberate slowness, she leans in closer. "No."

Something about her defiance, the sparkle in her eyes, the closeness of her—it short-circuits my brain. Without thinking, I close the distance between us and kiss her. Right there, in the middle of my bustling kitchen, with orders piling up and staff all around.

It's brief but electric, and when I pull back, her eyes are wide with surprise. It takes a second for reality to crash back in—the realization that I just kissed her in front of my entire staff and, more importantly, the cameras currently capturing every moment of our dinner service.

"You need to get out of here," I murmur.

Piper grabs the ladder and bolts out of the kitchen just as Rafael says, "Uh, Chef? I'm missing a salmon for table six..."

Rafael's words jar something loose inside me. The hair on the back of my neck stands up as a quiet voice inside me whispers *this is what happens.*

I knew it once before. And I've forgotten already. I'm fucking up orders my opening week because I'm letting myself get swept away in a bad idea.

This shit stops now.

"My bad, Raf. Won't happen again. Coming now."

"Was that planned for the show?" Pat, the producer, asks as he sidles up next to me.

"Nope," I admit, already back to preparing the next dish. "More of an accident than anything."

"The viewers are going to eat this up," he says gleefully. "Rival business owners falling for each other? This is ratings gold."

I don't bother correcting his "falling for each other" assessment. Mostly because I'm not sure he's wrong.

The rest of the dinner service flies by, and it's nearly eleven when we finally clear the last table. My body aches from standing all day, but it's the good kind of tired, the satisfaction of a job well done.

Once the kitchen is cleaned and the staff has gone home, I take a moment to check my phone. There's a notification from the Bayshore Best page—yes, I signed up for daily updates—and I open it to check the updated standings.

My lobster tail with asparagus risotto is now up to fifth place. Fuck yes. My Bayshore dudes are loving it, despite my late start to the competition with the soft launch gone awry. Piper's strawberry s'mores torte is in second. And sitting pretty in first is The Golden Pear with their brown butter apple croissant with blue cheese and honey.

I frown at the screen. The Golden Pear's dish sounds good—really good. The kind of sweet-savory balance that people go crazy for. It's got me thinking. I'm not sure how to leverage that for my dish or if I even can.

But then something Piper told me at the fence one night comes back to me. *You'll need to add a marshmallow to make it better.*

I start mulling over that possibility. Marshmallow additions to the recipe fill my head as I shut the kitchen down. I'm itching to test some things out. Maybe Piper was right. That could be a pivot that snags me number one.

Once all my final closing tasks are completed, including pocketing one of my home knives that somehow drifted here to the restaurant, I notice a light from the Cloud Nine side. Surprising, given the hour. I don't think I've ever seen Piper here this late. I walk through our shared storage space and peek into her shop.

Piper is hunched over a table covered in papers, a laptop open in front of her, lo-fi electronica pumping through the speaker. Her brow is furrowed in concentration as she sketches something out on paper. There are paint swatches and fabric samples scattered around her. She's too absorbed in whatever she's planning to notice me walk in.

"Dang, you're here late tonight."

She startles, her hand flying to her chest. The pencil she was using flies through the air. "Kru!"

"Sorry," I say, lifting my palms. "Four older brothers, I remember." I head for the tossed pencil, picking it up and placing it gingerly on her table. As I do, I take a glance at what she's working on.

Blueprints.

She leans back, stretching her arms above her head. The movement makes her shirt ride up slightly, exposing a sliver of skin at her waist. My mouth goes dry, but I remind myself that there can be no more of this.

I know what happens.

I know better.

"I'm glad I caught you. I had an idea I wanted to ask you about," I say, my gaze drifting over the blueprints.

"Oh yeah?" She tries to stifle a yawn behind her hand. "What's that?"

"I was wondering if I could bulk order some marshmallows. I'm taking your advice to add marshmallow to my lobster dish, and I want to start experimenting tomorrow."

Her face lights up. "Hey, that's awesome. I'll drop off a set for you tomorrow morning before you get in, so they'll be ready to go when you start prepping for lunch. Any flavor preferences?"

"I'd like a variety. Surprise me."

"Consider it done."

"Thanks, Maven. So, what's all this?" I gesture to the chaos on her table. She hesitates. "Nothing."

"This looks like the opposite of nothing," I say.

"I'm planning an...event space."

When she doesn't add more, I tip my head to seek out her gaze. "Go on."

She watches me for a moment, almost like she's waiting for something. Then she lets loose. "I want to expand Cloud Nine into event catering and hosting. Weddings, corporate parties, that sort of thing. It's just a future thing, though. I've been thinking about it for almost two years now, but I have no idea where it would go, and I feel like I'd have to relocate the entire business to be wherever this place is, which would be a really big hassle and relearning for my customer base, not to mention a huge gamble in terms of rent prices and, well, how do I find another place that's affordable so close to the lake, and it's just—" She pauses, then lets out a huff. "I'm getting myself worked up into knots over something that doesn't exist yet."

I move closer, examining her sketches. "All of that aside, these are good. You've got an eye for layout."

"Thanks." She sounds surprised by the compliment. "It's just ideas right now. I'm not working with any real building yet, since I need to find the right space, figure out permits, hire more staff..." She trails off.

"You know," I say, an idea forming, "when I bought this property, it included another building I didn't expect. The barn at the far end of the parking lot."

Her eyes widen. "The barn?"

"Yeah. If I'm not mistaken, it has a view of the lake. It's old, would need a lot of work, but when I checked it out, it was solid. I haven't spent too much time inspecting it, since it was more of an add-on from the previous owner, but you're welcome to look at it and see if it might be something that could work for you. Rustic charm and all that."

"Are you serious?" She's sitting up straighter now, excitement replacing fatigue in her expression.

"Completely serious. I don't really have any plans for it. I thought maybe I'd use it for storage, like overflow..." I shrug. "But it's not even on my radar right now."

She's quiet for a long moment, wheels clearly turning behind those bright green eyes. "Would you...would you consider renting it to me?"

I laugh. "Maven, you haven't even seen it."

"I've seen it. I've looked at it every single day for the past three years."

"I mean the *inside*." I lean on the counter, watching her. "But to answer your question, I'd consider it. But that barn will need a lot of work to be event ready. You'll need to have a solid plan for renovations."

"I do!" She jumps up, suddenly energized, and starts shuffling her papers. "I mean, I will. I'll figure it out. If the space is right, I'll make it work. But I have a sneaking suspicion it'll be perfect because I've been imagining a barn in my mind the entire time I've been planning this out."

She spreads out her sketches, pointing out details, explaining her vision. It's impossible not to get caught up in her enthusiasm. She's practically glowing as she talks about fairy lights strung from rafters, a dance floor beneath exposed beams, tables arranged to maximize the view of the water. She even pulls out her phone and shows me the various inspiration boards she made on Pinterest. It's a complete step-by-step plan. One that just needs the right space to allow her vision to become reality.

"What do you think?" she asks finally. "Is it too much? Too ambitious?"

"I think," I say slowly, "that this would be yet another amazing Cloud Nine creation."

Her smile is blinding. "Really?"

"Really." I step closer to her. "If your shop looks like this, I can only imagine how incredible the event space would turn out. Besides...Cloud Nine Events. It has a nice ring to it."

"It does, doesn't it?" She's still smiling, her eyes locked on mine.

Something electric shudders between us. For me, it feels a lot like a heavy hand at my back. Pushing me forward, into Piper, the same shove I get whenever I'm near her. It's inconvenient—disorienting, even. Like earlier today during the lunch rush. I kissed her in front of my staff. In front of *cameras*.

I shouldn't be doing shit like that.

But I can't stop myself.

She must sense my hesitation because she tips her head to look up at me, those pretty green gemstone eyes zeroing in on me. "Aren't you going to kiss me?"

"Do you want me to?" I ask. Though I don't need to. I can see the answer written on her lips, which are parted and waiting for me. I can see the answer on her pebbled skin, in her dilating eyes, in the way she arches closer.

Piper's lips curl up at the corners. She fists the front of my shirt and tugs me closer. "Yes, chef."

CHAPTER SIXTEEN

KRU

If there was ever a password to open the floodgates for me, it's that. I grunt, closing the space between us in a quick swoop until her lips meet mine and we're kissing. Urgently. *Desperately.*

Piper clings to my shirt as I back her up until her thighs hit the table. My tongue plunges into her mouth, tasting her, needing more of her. She whimpers through a kiss, wriggling against me like she's impatient. I break the kiss and sweep my arm across the table, pushing the papers to the side before I pop her up onto the edge of the table.

"I would have swept the papers off the table dramatically," I tell her, "if they weren't your very special plans."

She giggles, smoothing her hands along my jawline. "You're so sweet."

"No promises next time though," I warn her as my hands trail up the sides of her legs. I tug her closer by the hips, and she inhales sharply. All the tension that's been building between us since Cleveland is finally snapping.

I dip down, capturing her lips in a heated kiss. She arches toward me again, and I can taste the hunger and fire pouring out of her. I cup her head in my hands, getting drunk on these kisses. My cock is fully hard and begging for attention by the time she breaks the kiss. Her eyes are hooded as her hands drift to my belt line.

"Kru," she whispers.

"Maven."

"I was wrong."

I lift a brow. I've barely got a foot in this world after that make-out session, so I'd be lying if I said I knew what the hell she was referring to. "Uhhh..."

"Avoiding you was wrong. I was just scared of how intense it was. And *will* be."

I brush my lips against hers. "Heard."

She grins. "Is that another kitchen thing?"

"It is." I press a soft kiss to her lips. "And I'm scared, too. But you should know that I plan to fuck your brains out the second you admit that you've been dying for it."

Her eyes flutter shut, and when she looks at me again, I can see the decision in them.

"I've been dying for it."

I can't stop the grin that comes over my face. I cup her cheeks in my hands. "I definitely heard that."

My hands are trembling as I tug her leggings off and toss them aside. She's got me unmoored and floating in outer space already, and she hasn't even touched my cock.

"You are so fucking beautiful." My voice is a rasp as I behold her, in panties and an oversized Cloud Nine t-shirt. I squeeze the tops of her thighs, parting her legs slowly so I can see that delicious V. The crotch of her panties is damp, and I grunt, tilting my head to take it all in.

She's too hot to resist. Too fiery to turn away from. And fuck, I want this woman more now than I ever realized was possible.

Piper hooks a leg around my waist, bringing me closer. "Take your jeans off," she commands.

I do as she says and push my pants down, revealing my black boxer briefs and the enormous bulge beneath. She scoots to the edge of the table so her pussy grinds up against my erection. I suck in sharply and press my palms flat into the table, matching her movement.

"Fuck, Kru." She whimpers, rocking her pussy against me, faster now.

I roll my hips, pleasure prickling across my back. This is dry humping at its finest. I bury my face in her neck, groaning. "You want me to come in my pants, don't you?"

"Is that an option?"

"If you keep humping me like this, yes."

She bursts into giggles. I take the opportunity to lift her shirt and tug it off, tossing it to the side. I scan the bakery again, double checking all the front windows are shuttered. I don't want any Peeping Toms, because now that I've got Piper's legs wrapped around me, I'm not moving an inch.

My gaze solders to the creamy mounds of her breasts tucked behind a silky pink bra. Of course her bra is on brand as well. I bite my bottom lip as I reach behind her to unfasten the damned thing. There's no fucking way. I struggle with it for a few moments before I realize a quicker solution. Time is of the essence. I reach into the pocket of my pants and bring out the sheathed paring knife I'd tucked away to take home.

Piper gapes as I toss the leather holder to the side. "What are you—"

Rrrrrip.

The bra falls limply around her.

"Sorry, couldn't wait." I drop the knife and dip down, pressing kisses to the tops of her breasts. A low moan escapes me as I relish her cleavage. "I'll buy you another one."

Her shoulders shake with repressed laughter. "Did you just cut my bra off with a paring knife?"

"Correct." I close my lips around one rose-pink nipple and then do the same to the other one. "Too delicious to wait."

"So my clothes aren't safe around you," she murmurs, running her fingers through my hair as my kisses trail between her breasts. "Will you cut off my hair if I put it in a ponytail?"

"Nope. But I'll cut your panties off if they look at me wrong," I warn with a laugh. She responds by scooping my face into her hands. Our lips smoosh together. The kiss feels like we've known each other for years, not weeks.

Her hands slide down my chest, exploring the ridges of muscle there. When her fingers dip beneath the waistband of my boxers, I have to break the kiss, sucking in a sharp breath.

"Impatient," I murmur against her lips.

"You're one to talk," she shoots back, gesturing to the remnants of her bra. "Is this a skill you learned in chef school? Cutting things that get in your way?"

I grin wickedly. "Only when there's something delicious underneath."

True to my word, I hook my fingers in her panties, dragging them down her legs. She lifts her hips to help, and I drop to my knees, pressing kisses along her inner thighs as I go.

"Kru," she breathes, her fingers tangling in my hair.

I look up at her from between her legs, taking in the sight of her—flushed, disheveled, and utterly gorgeous. I'm on cloud nine, and I'm reveling in this play on words when I say, "Yes, Maven?"

"Don't tease."

"But I'm so good at it," I reply, my breath hot against her pussy. I run my tongue along her inner thigh, so close to where she wants me but not quite there. "Tell me what you want."

Her eyes, heavy-lidded with desire, meet mine. "Your mouth. On me. Now."

Abso-fuckin-lutely. I swipe my tongue over her sweet heat, finding her swollen clit. I'm tasting her, my tongue exploring every delicious inch. She gasps, back arching, thighs trembling as I focus on the needy nub that makes her squirm.

Her hands tighten in my hair, guiding me, showing me exactly what she needs. I'm more than happy to follow her lead, alternating between flat strokes and targeted suction, adding a finger and then another, curling them inside her until I find that spot that has her crying out.

"Don't stop," she pleads, hips rocking against my face. "Please, Kru, don't stop."

I have no intention of stopping—not when she's making those sounds, not when her thighs are quivering around my head, not when I can feel her getting closer with each stroke of my tongue. I double down on my efforts, adding a third finger, stretching her gently as I suck and lick.

When she comes, it's with a shout that echoes through the empty shop, her back arching beautifully, pussy clamping around my fingers. I work her through it, easing off only when she tugs at my hair, too sensitive to continue.

I wipe off my mouth with the back of my hand before I rise to my feet, ridiculously proud of the dazed look on her face. "You came right?"

"Shut up. Like the entire town didn't hear it," she says with a laugh, then reaches for me. "Get these off." She tugs at my boxers.

I comply, kicking them aside, my cock springing free. Her eyes widen slightly, and a slow smile curves her lips.

"Just like you remember?" I murmur as she wraps a hand around my length.

"Bigger, actually." She bites her bottom lip, then swings her pretty gaze up to find mine. "Do you have a condom?"

I close my eyes briefly at the sensation. "Yeah, in my wallet."

She raises an eyebrow. "So you were hoping for a happy ending, huh?"

"Boy Scout motto," I manage to say as her thumb circles the head of my cock, capturing the precum oozing out. "Always be prepared."

"You were never a Boy Scout," she accuses, but she's already reaching for my discarded pants.

"Come on, only a Boy Scout would know how to handle an uncooperative bra," I retort, watching as she retrieves my wallet and finds the condom tucked inside.

She's shaking with silent laughter as she tears open the foil package and rolls the condom onto my cock. "So you're telling me undressing a lady is part of the Boy Scout curriculum? I'm not buying it."

I grunt, seeking out the sweet hollow of her neck. "All right, I taught myself that part. But I really was a Boy Scout."

"Boy Scout. Uncle Lobster. Reality TV show legend. Chefpreneur." She lifts a brow, hooking her ankle behind my waist as I position myself between her legs. "What else am I missing, Kru?"

I pause, searching her face. "Love of your life?"

She inhales sharply. *Fuck.* I meant it like a joke, but shit, that one landed heavy. My cock grazes her swollen folds and I swoop down to catch her lips in a kiss.

"That was supposed to be funny," I murmur against her lips. "Let me re-do. Cloud nine companion?"

In response, she wraps her legs around my waist and pulls me forward, causing my cockhead to slide partway inside her. We both gasp at the sensation.

"Fuck, Piper," I breathe, sinking deeper, inch by excruciating inch, until I'm fully buried within her. She's tight, hot, perfect. Now I really am on cloud nine. "You feel amazing."

Her nails dig into my shoulders. "Oh god, it's better than I remembered."

"You say that like it's a bad thing."

"It is," she gasps. "It's definitely a bad thing. Now move, Kru. Please."

I obey, pulling back before thrusting in again, setting a rhythm that has her moaning with each thrust. Her legs lock tighter around me, urging me deeper.

Piper is a hot, silken vice I can't get enough of. I brace one hand on the table beside her hip, the other scooped around her waist to make sure she stays soldered to me. She meets each thrust with equal fervor, her gaze locked on mine.

"God, I've wanted this," I confess, my voice rough. "Wanted you. Since Cleveland."

"Me too," she gasps, her pussy tightening around me. "I couldn't fucking stop thinking about it."

The confession pushes me closer to the edge. *She felt it too.* More than just a one-night stand. I slide my hand between us, finding her clit, circling it with my thumb as I thrust harder.

"Fuck, you feel good, Maven," I murmur, feeling my own release building.

A wispy laugh escapes her as her head drops back. "Tell me about it."

The sight of her splayed out and delirious with pleasure is too much—my orgasm rips through me and I grunt, burying myself deep inside her. I grind into her, sinking my teeth into the top of her shoulder as heat and bliss wind through me.

Her pussy begins pulsing around me and she's whimpering, clawing at my back.

Number two for her.

For a long moment, we stay joined, foreheads pressed together, struggling to catch our breath. Eventually, I ease out of her, both of us wincing slightly at the loss of connection.

I toss the condom and grab a damp cloth from behind her counter, gently cleaning her up before taking care of myself. When I return to her, she's smiling softly, looking thoroughly debauched and satisfied.

I help her gather her scattered clothes, though the bra is a lost cause. "Sorry about that," I say, holding up the severed straps. I tuck it into my pocket. "I'll take it as a souvenir."

"For your altar, no doubt," she teases.

Once we're dressed—Piper sans bra, which I find deeply distracting—I help her tidy up the shop. We work in companionable silence, stealing glances and occasional kisses.

It's after midnight by the time I finally check my phone. "Maven, it's late for you. Aren't you tired?"

"I am...but I'm too excited about the barn," she admits.

"Tomorrow. We'll check it out, I promise. Don't get your hopes up though. I don't want you to be disappointed if it's not what you imagined inside."

She nods, looking thoughtful. "Yeah. Same to you."

"What?"

She cracks a smile, but it looks sad. "Don't you go falling for me. I don't want you to be disappointed. This needs to stay a secret from my brothers."

"About the barn?" I ask, deliberately obtuse.

"That, and, you know...us."

Disappointment shivers through me. "Ah." I pull her against me, enjoying the feel of her body against mine. I hope it's not the last time she gives in to this passion between us. "They're not a fan of my food, huh?"

"It's just easier this way."

I walk her to the back door, watching as she gathers her keys and phone. Before she can leave, I pull her in for one more kiss, deep and thorough.

"Can I drive you home? I know you rode your bike. I'll toss it in the bed of my truck."

She shakes her head. "I think I need a lakeside bike ride right now. I appreciate the offer though."

"Text me when you get home?" I reach for her phone, which is unlocked, and start to input my number. "Now you can't use the excuse that you don't have my number."

She bites her bottom lip, sending me the cutest and coyest smile. I want a picture of this moment. I could look at her pretty face for years and not get tired of the view.

I can't remember the last time I felt this way about anybody.

"Night, Kru." She pushes out the back door and blows me a kiss as she leaves.

Only when the door closes behind her and I'm left with my thoughts do I feel the squeeze in my chest, the swirl in my gut.

Piper's warning came too late.

I've already fallen.

CHAPTER SEVENTEEN

PIPER

"Paprika. Are you here? Hello."

I'm rummaging through Griffin's spice cabinet for the third time, trying to determine whether I'm blind or if Griffin just truly does not have any variety of paprika. Addressing the spice cabinet directly is probably the best way to find what I'm looking for. Unfortunately, it doesn't respond.

"Fine." I shut the door and look around at the messy kitchen. I'm mid-meal prep, an emergency request from Griffin who's been too busy with hospital shifts and his hockey schedule to get his super-specific meal train in motion while his nutritionist is on vacation. I offered to help because he's been pulling so much time at the hospital, which means Jerrica is running the show for me at Cloud Nine while I get Griff's meals in order. On top of all that, I'm prepping dinner for family game night.

I'm nothing if not a Keegan servant.

I also had to postpone the barn showing with Kru, which has me practically combusting with anticipation.

Between the excitement about the barn and the residual giddiness from my late-night encounter with Kru yesterday, I'm almost useless in the kitchen. I can barely focus. If I'm not thinking about the way Kru made me come with his tongue, then I'm fantasizing about what my new barn space is going to look like when I'm done renovating it.

Piper, seriously, you need to calm down.

Except I can't. I'm horny, I'm excited, I'm halfway in love with Kru, *and* the whole package is coated with deep-seated, crippling anxiety about what happens if Mom doesn't wake up.

That's the part I'm trying to avoid thinking about too much.

So barn planning and orgasms it is.

"One last chance to reveal yourself, Smoked Paprika!" I try to say it menacingly. Smoked Paprika doesn't care.

I'm making a few healthy dishes I pulled from the list of recipes Griff sent over, this one being some Spanish-style patatas bravas. I check my phone. Who the hell can I call at this hour who would have teaspoons of smoked paprika, or any variety of paprika, for me to steal?

A smile curls at my lips as I realize who I need to text.

Perfect mid-day excuse to bother him, too.

PIPER: Krudite, you know where I could find some smoked paprika on the fly?

I wonder if he likes my bastardization of his name.

KRU: I know a guy. How much you need, Half Pipe?

I smirk. That's a new one.

PIPER: 3 tsps for my various recipes. Is there some at your house? I can go break in.

KRU: Nah, I'll deliver. I'm running errands right now anyway. See you soon.

A shiver of excitement races up my spine, and I can't stop the cheek-splitting smile. It's nice to have a lover...even if he has to be a secret.

My brothers are too uptight and closed-minded to go anywhere near even *mentioning* that I'm sleeping with my landlord and usurper. It's just a no-go all around. So I'll have my fun in the shadows until I can figure out what to do from here.

I continue with my meal prep, ignoring all things requiring paprika. About a half hour later, a knock at the front door startles me from concentration. It has to be Kru. That cheek-splitting smile is back. I rub my hands on my frilly kitchen apron and hurry to the front door. When I pull it open, Kru fills the doorway, looking every inch a working chef in his black tee and belted black pants.

He grins as soon as he sees me. I can't help but drink him in, appreciating every last detail: the way his biceps strain the edges of his sleeves, his broad shoulders, the handsome smile that reminds me how much he enjoyed last night too.

Neither of us has said a word; we're lost in each other's gaze.

"Hi," I finally breathe.

In lieu of a greeting, he dips down and coaxes a kiss from my lips. I slide my arms around his neck as he backs me inside the house. I kick the door shut behind him and suddenly I'm up against the wall, lip-locked and loving it.

"Hi," he says when we break for air. "Missed ya."

"Good thing I needed paprika then," I giggle, running my hands through his hair. "You might not have survived the day without me."

He grins, his brown eyes crinkling at the edges. "Whatcha making?"

I lead him into the kitchen by the hand, eager to share the day's chef adventure. He nods appreciatively as I show him my sliced potatoes, the marinades, the seared chicken, and more.

"Two of my five recipes call for smoked paprika," I inform him, "and apparently Griffin has never added spices to a dish in his life before. He only has the most irrelevant items in his spice cabinet."

"Irrelevant?" Kru asks with a laugh.

"Yes! Like, sesame seeds and petrified mustard powder, but not even a whiff of paprika, oregano or, I don't know, pepper? Who is this man?"

"You haven't been cooking much either, I take it," he muses.

"Well, it's easy to avoid cooking when a chef opens up shop next to you," I say. "Besides, Griff normally hires his meals out during the season, which just started."

Kru lifts his brow. "Wow. Private chef level. That's nice."

"You ever wanted to go the private chef route?" I ask as he hands over the paprika. I get to measuring.

"I thought about it. Wouldn't be a bad gig, honestly. But a restaurant was always the dream with my dad." Kru smiles and crosses his arms as he watches me finish up the dishes that were waiting on the paprika.

"Your dad would be so proud of your place," I tell him as I pass him the jar. "I know I never met him, but I just know he would be."

His eyes crinkle at the corners again. He hooks his arm around my shoulders and smashes me against him in a hug. "Aw, thanks, Pipefitter."

"No problem, Motley Kru."

The laughter that rumbles through his chest feels like a balm. I slide my arms around his thick torso and nestle against him. God, this feels good.

"I should let you get back to cooking," he says into the top of my head.

"Yeah. Don't you have a restaurant that's open right now?" I don't let go of him though.

"Brady's working on handling the slower hours solo to see how he does. That gives me a chance to take a quick break. I haven't gotten any emergency calls yet, which I'm taking as a good sign."

I squeeze my arms a little tighter around him. "Maybe you can just stay here until you get that emergency call then."

He takes my chin between his thumb and forefinger, tipping my head back until our gazes lock. His caramel brown eyes are so deep, so mesmerizing. When he cocks a grin, I almost lose it. This man is too attractive.

I need him inside me. *Again.*

And my brother isn't due home for at least another hour, so this all works out perfectly.

"Come on. What do you think?" I snake a hand between our bodies, seeking the front of his pants. I rub my hand over his bulge so he gets the message. He grunts, rocking his hips against my hand.

"Maven. You are insatiable." He coaxes a sloppy, sexy kiss from my lips and then he grabs me by the hips, popping me onto the countertop. I wriggle my hips, pushing the cutting board off to the side.

"And you aren't?" I retort.

He scans the kitchen, reaching for the butcher knife on the cutting board. He flips my apron off to the side and pins the hem to the cutting board with the knife with a loud *THWACK*. His evil grin tells me all I need to know.

"That's called *mise en place*," he says. "Everything needs to be in the correct place before beginning. All tools and ingredients within easy reach."

"And my vagina is one of the ingredients?" I ask with a laugh.

"Correct. The absolute backbone of the dish."

We both burst into laughter. My forehead drops to his shoulder as his hands snake along my waist under the apron, tugging at the waist of my leggings. His fingers skate hot and exploring along my bare waist, sending shivers along my spine.

"God, you're a dream," I murmur as his hands push up beneath my bra. "Just don't cut this bra off, okay? It's my favorite."

"Heard," he whispers, just as he covers my mouth with his. He kisses me slowly and carefully. Like he's memorizing the experience and also savoring it. Every inch of my body is tingling when the kiss ends, and I clutch at the front of his shirt, drawing deep breaths.

"You are such a good kisser," I admit.

"So are you," he whispers into my ear before nibbling at my lobe. More electricity. I squeeze my legs together. Damn, he knows how to get me riled up in no time flat.

Just as I'm about to demand he produce a condom right this second, I hear a very familiar rumble from outside.

A rumble that doesn't make sense.

I perk up, listening as the noise comes closer.

"Oh my god…" I mutter. It's a car. Griffin's car, to be precise.

Pulling into the driveway.

"Oh my *god*," I repeat as I hear the engine cut. I push at Kru's chest. "You have to leave. My brother is here. Oh my fucking god you have to get out of here now!"

His eyes widen and he nods. "All right. I'm gone."

He bolts for the front door but I bark out, "No! Back door! *HURRY!*"

My heart is in my throat as Kru corrects course and bolts for the sliding glass door. He pulls it open, slips out, and is gone a moment later over the back fence. Two seconds later, Griffin comes in the front.

He smiles amicably at me as he wanders into the kitchen.

Where I am currently pinned to the cutting board with a butcher knife.

"Hey Piper. What's uh…" His brow furrows as he spots the way my predicament. "What's going on here?"

I pop on a bright smile. "Hey! You're home early!" I'm gritting my teeth so hard I feel like my head might explode from the effort of appearing casual. I wonder if he can see how my chest is pulsating from my rapid heart rate. I might pass out, in fact.

"Yeah, I got out of my event a little early and just came straight here to help out." He blinks, his gaze glued to the cutting board. "Is this how you meal prep?"

"It's so silly," I say, tugging at the knife. It takes a couple pulls to get it dislodged—Kru has some force in those muscles. "I was up here looking through the spice cabinet and I accidentally stabbed my apron into the cutting board."

His brows are now nearly touching in the center of his face. This is a really bad excuse, and we both know it.

"Do you always use the cutting board like you're practicing for axe throwing?" he asks.

"I do," I lie.

He nods slowly. "Okaaay. Cool. You might need to take some cooking lessons. Jussayin'."

I slide off the counter top and scoff. "Not exactly the right thing to say to the woman who just whipped up five days' worth of meals for you, Griff. Not to mention dinner for family game night."

He softens, slinging an arm around my shoulders. "You're right. What I meant to say was you are an absolute angel, I could not live without you, and maybe you should take some cooking lessons to learn how to properly use a knife."

I snort. "Better...but could still use some work."

My heart is pounding as I flit back to my patatas bravas. They're ready for the oven, and I'm praying I am coming off unaffected and natural and not like I was almost spotted by my six four, 270-pound brute of a brother making out with my rival in his kitchen.

I'll be honest—if Kru and Griffin ever had to throw hands, I'm not sure who would come out on top.

Actually, I am.

My brother.

I just pray I never see the day any of my brothers find out about this little fling with my landlord. Even though he's so much more than that now.

Griffin wanders away, and I focus on finishing the cooking. It's my turn at the hospital tonight, but since it's Wednesday, we're bringing game night to Mom before I pull the all nighter. I offered to make the dinner that we'll all eat at her bedside. Asher is bringing Dad in the hourglass, Dane's got the disposable plates and silverware, Jett is bringing the cards, and Bella is bringing the rock star. I think we've collaborated nicely.

This is the type of healthy family dynamic I like to see.

There's no room for someone like Kru here.

Something painful burns hot through my chest for a brief second and then dissipates. Yes, it stings to admit, but I need to be realistic.

There is too much going on in my life for a fling, much less a boyfriend. The fact that I am scampering around trying to hide the evidence of this infatuation should be sign enough that it's a bad idea.

If it were a good idea, it would come naturally. Easily. Without so much stress.

Because the truth is I don't have the time or energy to figure it out. I just have time for my family and my business. And that's the bottom line.

Griff and I pile into his car with the food for tonight. My thoughts turn darker as Bayshore Memorial comes into view, reminding me of all the unanswered questions that await us inside. Mom has been in a coma for three days now, and while the doctors say she's stable and things are within the realm of normal, it's hard not to imagine the worst.

The hospital corridors are quieter in the evening. The fluorescent lights cast everything in a sterile glow as we make our way to Mom's room. *Maybe today will be the day she wakes up.* I repeat it to myself like a mantra as we wind through hallways en route to her room.

Asher and Dane and Lia are already there when we arrive, seated on either side of Mom's bed. She looks small and fragile against the white hospital sheets. The steady beep of the heart monitor provides a rhythmic backdrop to the quiet.

"Hey, guys," I say cheerfully, lifting the insulated bag of food. "Dinner's here. Any changes or good news?"

Asher shakes his head. "No change."

"But at least there's no *bad* news," Dane adds.

I set the food down next to Dad's hourglass then give Dane and Asher my standard-grade hugs, followed by an extra-long squeezy one for Lia. Then I move to Mom's side, carefully taking her hand in mine.

Jett breezes into the room a moment later, his handsome smile looking strained as he heads straight for the hospital bed to kiss Mom's forehead. "Hey, fam. Got the cards. Sorry I'm late."

"Where were you?" Griff asks as he pulls the crockpot of food out of the insulated bag. Dane works on setting out plates and silverware while Asher pushes together two small tables to create a sitting area.

"Out." Jett flashes a cryptic smile that tells me he was probably hooking up with a new flavor of the week or something.

"That's our sign not to pry," I remind Griff. "Because when he's *out* somewhere, it means he's usually *in* someone."

"Jesus, Piper," Asher hisses. "In front of mom? And Lia?"

I gesture to our mother. "She doesn't mind. Besides, I'm sure she agrees. And Lia doesn't understand the nuance yet."

"She doesn't," Dane confirms.

"When did you get so crude?" Jett elbows me, and I stumble from the brotherly shove. "You're not wrong, though."

A nurse pops in to check Mom's vitals as we serve plates of the beef stew I made. By the time the nurse wraps up, we've all mostly slurped down dinner. Then Bella and Jackson stroll through the door, eliciting a raucous round of hellos and even more hugging.

"I'm glad you guys could make it," I tell Bella as I squeeze her. "Maybe all of us being here together will help her wake up."

"God, that would be incredible." Bella's eyes are shimmering as she pulls back to look at me. "I never expected to be sharing game night with you guys in a hospital."

"Hopefully it's the last time," I say as she and Jackson squeeze into extra chairs that Asher rustled up from somewhere. "Because you're ready to wake up, aren't you, Mom?" I tap the end of her hospital bed, but she doesn't respond.

Lia snuggles into my lap as my brothers get things set up for euchre. I smile into her berry-scented blonde hair, thinking about how even though this evening feels like we're making the best of a bad situation, I also feel like something is missing.

Something I'm not ready to admit to myself.

Bella opts for the first game, with Asher as her teammate, playing against Dane and Jett. Griff, Jackson, and I watch as they trade shouts and barbs and groans.

"So you do you use the hourglass for euchre?" Jackson leans in to ask me, jerking his chin toward Dad on the table.

"Oh, no. You don't need an hourglass for this game. We brought it along because it has our Dad's ashes in it."

His brows shoot up and he nods slowly. "Okay."

"We like to have it on hand so he's with us when we play. And game night isn't always euchre, so we do sometimes use it. We go through seasons of games. We were stuck playing Taboo for close to a year, and you need a timer for that one. Dad liked that game."

"Like, from the hourglass or...in life?" Jackson asks just as a swell of cheers erupts from Asher and Bella to match the groans from Jett and Dane.

"Both, I guess."

"Grampa lives in there," Lia adds helpfully, reminding me she was still listening.

"Yes he does," I confirm.

Griff, Jackson, Lia, and I provide moral support as the game goes on. Asher and Bella euchre my brothers *twice*. Incredible. They pull off a ten to zero victory, looking especially smug as everyone throws the cards into the center of the table.

"Bella stacked the deck," Jett grumbles.

"I only did it once in ninth grade," she shoots back. "And never again."

"Don't be a sore loser," Asher advises as his gaze shifts to me and Griff. "You guys next?"

"Fine. Griff, let's show them what it looks like to *really* win." I strut over to the seat that Jett had been sitting in and crack my knuckles. Griff slides into the seat across from me.

The game begins. Cards fly as Lia peppers Dane with questions about why the adults are laughing and groaning so much. Mom lies unresponsive and quietly beeping. It's familiar at the same time it's so strange. Still, we make the best of it. Griff and I don't pull off the spotless victory that we imagined.

We're tied seven-seven when Jett comments, "I swear I saw Mom's hand twitch just now."

We all swing our gazes to the bed.

"Maybe game night is good for her," Griff says.

"We should do this around the clock then," Asher says in his *I-mean-business* voice.

"We could make it work," Dane says. "I'll do it if it means Mom wakes up quicker."

"Piper, you've already got an employee, you can start giving her more hours," Asher says, already planning things out. We went from game night to all of us living at the hospital in two seconds flat. My head is spinning.

"Or hire another one," Jett offers.

In my head, I'm groaning. *Here we go again.*

"I'm not going to hire another employee just so we can have endless card games at the hospital," I say.

"Even if it meant Mom woke up faster?" Griff asks, already agitated.

I can feel the boil of irritation building inside of me. Except I don't think it ever fully goes away; it must be stuck at a low simmer, ready to kick into gear whenever my brothers think they can decide what I do or how I do it.

A lightning bolt of frustration strikes through me. They don't understand my business, my profit and loss statement, or my strategy.

"I'd only hire another employee once I launch the next phase," I snap. "There's too much that goes into training and onboarding someone to get a new employee just for a few days or even a week. Come *on*."

I feel a few sets of eyes burning on me as I finish shuffling the cards. I ignore them all as I deal the next hand.

"What's the next phase?" Asher finally asks.

Fuck.

"Can we just play the game?" I ask with a sigh.

"No, I wanna hear about the next phase," Griffin says, pushing away the cards I just laid in front of him.

I dip my chin, sending him my best glare.

"When that look comes out, you know there's something good she's not telling us," Jett says as he elbows Dane.

"Guys—" I try to protest.

"Now you *have* to tell us," Jett says, elbowing his way into the table where I'm locked in alternating death stares with Asher and Griffin.

"There's nothing to tell," I begin, but the attention and pressure emanating from my older brothers is too intense. I already know the truth: I'm doomed. There's no way out of this. I have no excuse at the ready, and they won't let up until the truth pops out of me like a gross zit.

"There absolutely is," Jett confirms with a maniacal smile, because of course he's right.

I heave with a sigh, setting my own cards down. Bella has drifted closer, watching me with a worried look. My stomach is twisted, and my palms are sweating. This is a moment I've been avoiding for years.

And here we are.

"I want to expand Cloud Nine," I finally say.

"Into what?" Asher's brows are drawing closer together.

"Events—catering and planning."

Bella gasps, her face lighting up. "Piper, this is a great idea—"

"Wait." Asher lifts a hand, and Bella rolls her lips inward. "Tell us more. Because I don't think any of us know enough to say whether it's a good idea."

Bella rolls her eyes, though Asher can't see her do it. Bella's always been on my side, but it's never enough against my brothers.

"I've always wanted to get into event planning—"

"Event planning?" Dane enunciates, as if it's a foreign language.

"Yes. I think I could really kill it with private events. Weddings, corporate parties, luncheons, all sorts of things. I'd cater all the sweet stuff and probably collaborate with a different business to supply a savory menu—"

"Not your landlord, that's for damn sure," Griffin mutters.

"*Probably* collaborate?" Asher repeats my words back to me, his suspicion evident.

Some of my excitement dissipates in a puff of smoke. Maybe I could see Griffin writing off Kru as a potential collaborator as him accepting that my vision *will* become a reality. My feeble grasp at optimism doesn't last long, because Dane cuts in.

"This is like, two whole other businesses, Piper." He looks seriously concerned, as though I just told him Lia needed medical attention or something. "On top of the one you already run. That's new concept development, investment, staffing, business planning..."

"Not to mention renting or buying a whole new building just for the event stuff," Jett says.

"Do you have a place in mind for this...space?" Asher asks, crossing his arms.

I can't tell them Kru offered up his barn. I haven't even seen it yet. So I answer, "A couple that I'm looking into."

"Have you signed anything yet?" Dane asks, his brows raising.

"No," I blurt.

"Thank god. We need to approve anything before you do." Asher's jaw is flexing, his gaze heavy on me.

I scoff, crossing my arms to match his. "You don't trust me to make my own decisions?"

The heavy silence in the room is my answer.

"God, you guys." I push away from the table, coming to standing. "This is exactly why I didn't want to say anything."

"You need to focus on what's already working, and expand *that*," Asher says firmly.

"Yeah, you don't need to get into a whole new industry," Jett adds.

"We saw what happened when you started Cloud Nine. If you expand too soon..." Dane trails off, all of his doubts and hesitations ballooning in the empty space between us.

"You've got a killer business right now," Griff says. "What's wrong with it?"

"Nothing," I admit, while the tightness in my chest expands and eventually engulfs my entire body.

I'm too heavy and tired to defend myself or this idea that they haven't even truly heard.

All I know is that the crushing feeling has returned to my chest. This suffocating smallness that's been my companion since childhood, a place I so often find myself with my brothers.

So I do what I know best.

I swallow the frustration, and we get back to the game.

CHAPTER EIGHTEEN

KRU

It's seven a.m. on a Thursday, and I'm at the restaurant instead of catching up on precious sleep.

Why?

Because Piper Keegan has me wrapped around her finger.

She wants to see the barn, and this is the only time that works for her around her shop and her schedule with her brothers at the hospital. Of course I make it work, even if I get four hours of sleep as a result. I'm yawning for the hundredth time that morning as I stumble through the kitchen, struggling to brew a pot of coffee.

Once that first sip hits, I feel a semblance of clarity zip through me. Maybe I've got a shot at this day. By the end of the cup, I can think again. *Hell yes.*

The back door creaks open, and I know it's her before I even look up.

"There's my first barn tour of the day," I call out, not bothering to hide my smile.

Piper appears in the doorway to the storage room, a to-go cup of coffee in each hand and that messy bun I've come to adore perched on top of her head. She's wearing leggings and a Cloud Nine hoodie, practical for exploring a dusty old barn.

"You say it like you have other tours lined up, which is...not allowed." She pushes one of the coffees into my hand. "But you know what they say. Early bird gets the worm. Or in this case, the barn."

"They do say that," I agree before taking a sip of the coffee. "And you brought me coffee? That's dangerously close to a nice gesture."

"I'm just ensuring you're properly caffeinated before you show me my future event space."

"You're optimistic." I stand, grabbing my keys. "It could be completely rotted and decrepit inside."

"Or maybe it just needs some TLC," she says, falling into step beside me as we head out the back door. "And once it's got long wooden tables with wildflower centerpieces, and a dance floor beneath its old, exposed beams, it'll come right back to life."

The excitement in her voice is contagious. As we cross the parking lot toward the barn at the far end, I find myself seeing it through her eyes—not as the dusty storage space I initially considered it, but as something with real potential. Set against the cresting hues of dawn, the barn looks extra moody and photogenic as we approach.

"Just remember," I warn her, "it's been empty for years. It will likely have a lot of issues."

She waves a dismissive hand. "Nothing a little elbow grease and a good moss wall can't fix."

The barn itself is larger than I realized—a substantial two-story structure with weathered red wood siding and a metal roof that's held up surprisingly well. The original sliding doors are massive, though one hangs slightly off its track.

I fumble with the padlock, then slide the door open with a dramatic flourish. "Welcome to the barn I never anticipated owning."

Piper steps inside, her eyes widening as she takes in the space. Dust motes dance in the beams of light filtering through the high windows. The interior is mostly empty, save for some abandoned wagon wheels in one corner and a rickety wooden staircase tucked against the far wall, leading to a loft.

"Oh my god," she breathes, turning slowly to take it all in. "It's perfect."

"Not to mention a tetanus shot waiting to happen," I add, but I can't help smiling at her enthusiasm.

She's already pacing the length of the main floor, her arms stretched wide as if measuring the space. "Look at these beams! And the height of the ceiling! And those windows—they're filthy now, but imagine how much natural light they'll let in once they're cleaned."

I lean against the door frame, watching her. She's vibrating with enthusiasm...with *vision*. It's contagious, to be perfectly honest. She looks so at home here already. I can almost see the wheels turning behind those bright green eyes.

"Did you see that loft?" I ask, nodding toward the upper level.

Piper eyes the rickety staircase warily. "Is it safe to go up there?"

"Only one way to find out." I start toward the stairs. "I'll go first. If I crash through, consider it structurally unsound."

"My hero," she says dryly but follows me anyway.

The stairs creak ominously under my weight but hold. When we reach the top, I'm pleasantly surprised by the condition of the loft. The floor seems solid, and the pitched roof creates a cozy feeling up here.

"This could be a bridal suite," Piper says immediately, spinning around to take it all in. "Or a VIP lounge area for corporate events. Or a separate bar space for specialty cocktails..."

"Any of those would be awesome."

She nods, then moves to one of the small windows overlooking the property. "Oh my god, Kru—you can see the lake from here!"

I join her at the window, and sure enough, there's Briggs Bay visible between the trees. "Well, would you look at that."

"This changes everything," she says, turning to me with those big eyes sparkling. "Lake views add a premium to any event space."

"So what do you think?" The question seems unnecessary—she's vibrating with *give it to me now.*

"What do I think?" She cups the side of her face like she's holding in an explosion. "Kru, this place is beyond perfect. It needs work, obviously—a lot of work—but the bones are incredible. The location is amazing. The size is ideal. It's like this barn was custom built for what I want to do."

It's impossible not to get caught up in her vision. "So you want it?"

"Yes!" She bounces on her toes. "Can we make the deal? Right now?"

I laugh at her eagerness. "Slow down, Maven. I need to figure out the details first. Rent, lease terms, renovation parameters..."

"Fine, fine," she says, waving a hand impatiently. "But the answer is yes. I want it. *Immediately.*"

"I need to figure out some paperwork then," I say. "I'll draw something up and then let you take a look to see what you think."

As we make our way back down the stairs, Piper suddenly stops, turning to look at me seriously. "Kru...thank you. For showing me this. For even considering renting it to me."

The sincerity in her voice catches me off guard. "You don't have to thank me."

"I do. You agreeing to rent to me completely begins a new chapter of my life. This is huge. I've wanted to do this for so long but have been too scared to make a move...and now it's suddenly *happening*."

We come to a stop on the dusty floor in the center of the barn. The cool fall air whips in through the open barn door, scattering hay that still litters the floor. She looks up at me, her big green eyes sucking me in. She's so beautiful, in a way that makes my heart ache. I brush back a piece of her strawberry blonde hair that drifts across her forehead.

"You're welcome," I finally say. "I'm happy to help."

"Is it okay if I get started before you draw up the paperwork?" She clutches my forearms, practically bouncing in front of me. "Nothing major. I just know I won't be able to wait to get started. Sweeping and stuff like that."

"I suppose that'd be okay..." I look around, instantly overwhelmed by the amount of work this place requires. "Are you sure you want this thing though? I mean, this is gonna be months of work."

"I'm not afraid of work."

"I didn't mean that," I say. "It's just going to be *so much*. You'll have to hire a crew, it's gonna be a *lot* of money, Maven."

"I'll figure it out," she snips. I get the sense I'm raining on her parade, so I nod.

"You will. You're right."

We take one last look at the barn before stepping outside. I slide the big door shut and lock it back up, then hand her the key.

"In case you want to start sweeping later," I say.

She squeals, clutching the key to her chest. "Thank you, Kru." She pushes up onto her tiptoes and presses a kiss to my lips.

I wrap an arm around her, bringing her against my body. "It's my pleasure. I want to help however I can."

She has stars in her eyes as she beams up at me. Then something clouds her gaze, and she steps away, nibbling on her lip.

"I think this will need to stay our little secret for a while," she says, running the pad of her thumb over the key. "I still need to figure out a way to tell my brothers I'm taking the plunge on this. They won't be happy."

"There're a few things you don't want your brothers to know about, huh?" I stuff my hands into my pockets against the stiff breeze as we walk back toward the main building.

She frowns. "If you knew my brothers, you'd understand."

"Will I ever meet them?"

"Not if I can help it."

I study the ground, a knot forming in my gut. I don't like that comment one bit, but I don't feel like I have any right to object. We haven't talked about *us*. So I file it away for later.

I wish her a good work day, and we head our separate ways. Inside my office, I bury myself in invoicing and inventory orders. There's tons to do on a daily basis, so my extra early start won't be a waste. Eventually Brady comes in, followed by Rafael and the rest. Office work bleeds into prep, and then suddenly we're open for the day and serving a bustling dining room of customers. It's easy to click into the groove here, something I'm relishing as the work day melts away beneath us in an easy flow.

Before I know it, it's four o'clock, and I realize I haven't eaten since breakfast. I'm good about making sure the crew takes a break to eat after lunch service, but I don't usually follow my own guidance. Typical for a working chef. I put together a quick sandwich, pause, and then make a second one.

If I haven't eaten, I bet Piper hasn't either.

I head next door with the grilled chicken and ciabatta sandwich I whipped up for her, wrapped in foil. As I step through the back storage room door, I spot her in full Cloud Nine regalia—pink headband, frilly white apron, facing down a small crowd of marshmallow enthusiasts. Four long tables are set up at the back of the shop, three students per table, facing Piper at the front. Everyone has their own pastel pink mixer. I watch for a moment as she gives a demonstration of how to whip the marshmallows to perfection.

"The whipping is where the magic is," she says brightly, showing the crowd exactly what to do, a huge bowl on the table in front of her.

I lean against the doorframe and watch, transfixed, as she regales her students with tips and advice. I've never seen a more beautiful marshmallow maven. They all follow along with their own mixers. As she walks among the tables to inspect the progress of her students, her gaze flicks my way.

I'm happy to note her face lights up when she sees me. I'm sure mine does the same. I hold up the wrapped sandwich and mime eating a sandwich. I point to the table by the backdoor, and then give her a thumbs up. I think she gets what I'm trying to say because she nods effusively and mouths *thank you* before bending over to check out the progress of one of her marshmallow students.

My heart swells a little as I head back to my side of the building. I like taking care of Piper. And if I'm being honest, I'm crazy about her. Having her close is so nice—not just in the backyard of my rental but here at my side throughout the day.

My head is swirling with thoughts as I head back into my kitchen and snag my own sandwich to wolf down before getting back on the line. I've been mulling all day on the rental agreement for the barn. I'd be lying if I said her plans for it weren't exciting to me. I just don't like the fact that she's trying to build this thing up in the shadows.

And if I'm being honest, I don't like that she wants to keep *me* in the shadows either.

I'm chewing and stewing in my thoughts, the back of my mind analyzing the cayenne-forward seasoning combination I used on the chicken before

I grilled it while the other half of me is wondering what I truly want from Piper.

We're both busy small-business owners in the midst of expansion. I need to be logical. Ruthless.

I'm mere weeks into the launch of my own brand-new business venture. Why would I get tangled up in this pipe dream of Piper's too?

Be real, lobster man. You need to focus.

I down the final bite of my sandwich, making a mental note to add more lemon to the homemade mayo next time. I head to the sink to wash my hands, still lost in my thoughts as I scrub.

I know what happens when I get lost in a new relationship. Emphasis on the word *lost*. I damn near quit cooking after I got in deep with my ex, Vanessa. I fell too hard, too quickly. The end of our relationship was brewing right when the food truck competition reality TV show came up. She didn't want me to apply—I applied anyway. When I got accepted, she wasn't even happy for me. And I damn near turned down the offer to go on the show until my Mom talked some sense into me. Just thinking back to that time in life scares the shit out of me. Going on the TV show carved out the path to my dreams, and my ex had only seen it as a threat.

I'm terrified of being derailed like that. Of casting aside everything I've worked for in the name of love.

I tear off a paper towel to dry my hands, scanning the now-bustling kitchen as orders begin to pump through the printer.

It's not that I think Piper herself is a threat; it's that anything that is not my business is a threat. I do not have time to get lost right now. Everything about my business requires all of me. All my focus.

And I'll be damned if I get swept away and lose sight of the goal.

CHAPTER NINETEEN

PIPER

I never thought one tiny key could change my life.

But right now, the key to the barn padlock is more than just burning a hole in my pocket. It's overtaking my mind.

I can't say I mind, either. Every minute my mom remains in a coma ratchets my anxiety up a bit higher, and I just wonder when I'll reach the point where I finally crumble. The doctors are confident she'll wake up, but seeing her day in and day out in the same bed, unresponsive, unchanging...it does something to my hard-won optimism.

But Barny is here to fix it.

Or rather, I'm here to fix Barny.

The first sign that I might have jumped off the deep end was when I coined a nickname for my barn. Yes, it's mine. And its name is Barny. It's not terribly creative, but he likes it. So we're sticking with it.

Is it insane? Yes. Is it what I'm called to do? Also yes.

The barn key feels weighty in my pocket as I make my final preparations at Cloud Nine on Friday morning. I've ensured the shop is covered with

Jerrica handling the front counter for the entire day, all bulk orders are ready, and the Bayshore Best special is stocked and ready to go. This frees me up to spend every spare second at the barn, armed with industrial-strength cleaning supplies and pure determination. Now that Kru and I have signed a basic rental agreement, with a heavily discounted rent due to the renovations I plan to do on the building, I'm ready to rumble.

"Are you sure you don't need help?" Jerrica asks, eyeing the collection of cleaning supplies I've amassed in the back room. "That's a lot of bleach for one person."

"I've got this," I assure her. "Besides, you're already winning Employee of the Year by taking on more hours for me."

"I'm your only employee," she reminds me.

"And the best damn one there is!" I load up my caddy of cleaning supplies, adding another roll of paper towels on top. "If anyone asks for me, just tell them I'm in a meeting. And if any of my brothers show up, tell them I'm gone. Say nothing about the barn to any of my relatives. We don't speak of the barn to blood relatives. And if anyone has a genuine emergency, come get me."

"O...kay." She laughs, but I can see the curiosity in her eyes. She knows I'm heading out to the barn on the property, but not why. The fewer people who know about my barn project before my brothers, the better.

I slip out the back door, hurrying around the building and off to the barn. It stands at the far end of the parking lot, looking both intimidating and inspiring in the afternoon light. It's a building I've basically ignored for the past five years—and now, I can't see anything *but* this barn. I glance around to make sure none of my brothers are magically materializing to question my activities. Who knows—they might receive an emergency notification as soon as I put the key into the padlock for the first time: *PIPER HAS MADE A DECISION WITHOUT CONSULTING HER*

BROTHERS! THE NEAREST KEEGAN MUST REPORT FOR IM-
MEDIATE INTERVENTION!

The key Kru gave me turns smoothly in the padlock, and better yet, none of my brothers pop out from behind the bushes. I slide the heavy barn door open just enough to slip inside with my supplies, then close it behind me.

Even though it's almost one o'clock, the interior of the barn is dim thanks to the grimed-over windows. I flip on the industrial work light I purchased and dropped off yesterday, casting the cavernous space in a harsh glow that highlights every cobweb, dust bunny, and questionable stain. It's overwhelming if I look at it all at once, so I focus on one section at a time.

"Windows first," I mutter to myself, setting up my supplies. "Let some actual light into this place."

The first window takes me nearly twenty minutes, inside and out, to clean properly. Years of grime have created a film that requires serious elbow grease to remove. But the satisfaction when I finally finish and step back to see sunlight streaming through the clear glass is worth every aching muscle. It's just one window, but it feels like a portal to the future.

"One down, eleven to go."

Three windows later, I take a break to check my phone. There's a notification from the Bayshore Best page, and I open it eagerly to check the updated standings.

My strawberry s'mores torte is holding strong in second. Kru's lobster tail with asparagus risotto has moved up to third. And The Golden Pear still has first place with their fancy schmancy croissant.

I frown at the screen, my competitive spirit flaring. The Golden Pear has been around for a few years longer than I have, and one of their owners is incredibly well connected in town. I'm sure that's helping them retain that number one spot. But aside from begging complete strangers to vote for me daily, which I'm not afraid to do, maybe I need to rethink my strategy. Add something unexpected to my s'mores torte to give it that extra edge.

"Focus on that later, Piper," I scold myself, tucking the phone away. "One project at a time."

I return to the windows with renewed vigor, determined to finish at least half of them today. The physical labor is therapeutic—each swipe of the cloth revealing more of the barn's potential. With clean windows, I can better see the sturdy wooden beams overhead, the surprisingly intact plank flooring, and the way the afternoon light creates a warm-honey glow throughout the space.

Just when I'm about to start on the next window, I hear the barn door slide open. Thanks to my perch in the loft, I can't see who it is.

"Making progress, I see." The deep voice sends shivers down my spine.

I climb on my hands and knees to the edge of the loft, peering down. Kru stands in the doorway, leaning against the frame with an amused smile. He's wearing a gray henley, the sleeves rolled up to expose those forearms that immediately make me remember when he pinned my apron to the cutting board.

"I'm on a mission," I explain, gesturing to the half-cleaned windows. "Operation Let There Be Light."

He chuckles, moving closer to inspect my work. "It's crazy how much a clean window can change a place."

I come to my feet and carefully descend the stairs. "You taking a break?"

"Lunch service calmed down so I figured I'd see how you were doing. You want any help?"

I hesitate, torn between my stubborn independence and the practical reality that this job would go much faster with an extra set of hands.

"You don't have a restaurant to run?" I ask instead of answering directly.

"Brady's handling things for the next hour." He picks up a clean cloth from my supply pile. "So, which window am I tackling?"

I point to one at the base of the loft stairs. "That one's next on my list."

"On it." He rolls up his sleeves another notch and gets to work. I try to bite back the smile that threatens to take over my face as I go back up to the loft and my half-clean window.

This is nice. *Really* nice.

We clean in companionable silence for a while, the only sounds our scrubbing and the occasional satisfied sigh when a particularly stubborn spot finally gives way.

"So," Kru says eventually, "you checked the Bayshore Best standings today?"

I glance down from my perch, surprised. "How did you know?"

"Just assuming you check as compulsively as I do. Congrats on holding on to second place."

"For now," I sigh. "That Golden Pear dish is killing it."

"It's the blue cheese," Kru says thoughtfully. "The surprise savory element with the sweet apple. People go crazy for that contrast."

"I know." I attack a particularly dirty spot on my window. "It makes me want to think outside the box and beat them."

"Your s'mores torte is incredible as is."

"Thanks for the vote of confidence, but it won't make me forget that you're still trying to beat me," I remind him.

He shrugs, a mischievous glint in his eye. "All's fair in love and Bayshore Best."

The casual mention of love makes my stomach do a little flip that I resolutely ignore.

After a moment, Kru adds, "I toyed around with the marshmallow delivery you dropped off the other day. They were all amazing but I think the nutmeg one was next-level. I'm officially adding your nutmeg-infused marshmallow to the lobster dish."

I gasp. "That sounds wonderful. Now I need to try it again."

"Anytime, Maven. You're gonna love it," Kru says. "Though I'm nervous your brothers will come after me if I beat you in the competition. Or if they find out I'm your landlord twice over."

I wince, unable to entirely dismiss the possibility. "They'll come around," I say, though I'm not convinced myself. "Probably."

"After they break my kneecaps, maybe," he mutters.

"They wouldn't—" I start, then reconsider. "Okay, Griffin might. But the others would just threaten to."

"Very reassuring." He finishes his window and moves to the next. "Have you thought about when you're going to tell them about this place?"

I focus very intently on a spot of dirt. "I'm working on it."

"Which means 'not yet,'" he translates.

"I'm waiting for the right moment," I explain. "Preferably when they're all in really good moods. Maybe after Mom wakes up and is back to normal."

Kru's expression softens at the mention of Mom. "How is she doing?"

"Still stable. No change yet." I swallow around the lump that forms in my throat whenever I think about Mom in that hospital bed. "But the doctors say they expect her to wake up within a few days, so that's something. And hey, I've got this big huge dirty barn to take my mind off things."

"I'm available to take your mind off things too, you know." He winks up at me.

My cheeks heat up, which causes a big grin to blossom on his lips. He drops his cleaning supplies and starts up the stairs at the same time I thump down them toward him. We meet in the middle and he presses a kiss to my lips.

"I love it when you blush."

The comment just makes me blush harder. I fist the front of his shirt, bringing him in for another kiss. "I love it when you make me blush."

He searches my face for a moment, looking like he wants to add something else. Instead, he covers my mouth with his, pressing me against the wall. I smile through our kisses, the abandoned, woody scent of the barn mingling with the manly, cedar scent of Kru. A lightning bolt of happiness strikes me, splitting me down the center. This man. This project. This future.

Even while there are so many things that aren't quite right, somehow Kru overrides it all.

When we break from the kiss, we're breathless. My chest heaves as I search his face, wondering if he felt the intensity I did.

"Those were some of the best kisses I've ever had," I admit weakly.

He nuzzles my neck. "Absolute same. You need to spend the night at my house tonight."

He drags his drugged gaze up to find mine. Something heavy shudders between us. I can feel the steel of his cock pressed against my belly and I move against him slightly. He looks like he wants to say more, but before he can, the barn door slides open again.

"Piper? Are you in here?"

Bella's voice echoes through the barn. For a moment, I can't understand what I'm hearing. *Bella? In the barn?* Kru and I exchange a panicked look and he steps down, away from me. Across the barn, both Bella and Jackson are inside the threshold. Bella's watching me with eyes the size of saucers.

"Bella!" I call out cheerily. "What are you doing here?"

Kru waves. "Hey, guys."

Bella's surprise morphs into understanding. "Well, if it isn't Piper and Hot Cleveland Hookup Landlord." She crosses her arms over her chest, looking immensely pleased with herself. "This certainly looks like 'nothing going on' here."

I groan and stomp down the stairs, Kru following me. "Bella! I really don't need your shit right now."

"Is that what you call me?" Kru asks with a half-smile, looking a little smug.

"It was once. Well, a few times." To Bella and Jackson, I say, "What brings you guys to Barny?"

"Barny?" Jackson asks, Kru echoing him.

"It's the barn's name," I say.

"You named it," Bella says slowly.

"Yes. Because it's deserving of a name." I gesture around us, as though this explains everything. "Listen, I told Jerrica to turn everyone away unless it was an emergency, so I need to know how you made it out here. Did something happen?"

Bella dips her chin. "Nothing happened. I was just curious. The way she answered my questions made me think you were somewhere around here. And then she said she could only summon you in the event of an emergency. So I told her it was an emergency because I wanted to snoop. Jackson and I are going back to LA soon, I can't have mysteries like this hanging in the air before I leave."

I groan. "I should have given Jerrica clearer instructions when it came to the Keegan family."

Jackson's head is tipped back, looking into the rafters and all around. "Can I ask what you're doing in Barny? Or is that an inappropriate question?"

"We're in Barny because...I'm working on Barny," I say.

Bella's eyes round once more. "Oh my god. Is this for the business expansion you were talking about the other night?"

I nod. She squeals, grabbing my forearm.

"Is this the place?" she asks in a shriek-whisper.

"It is," I say, unable to contain my smile.

"Holy shit, Pipe Cleaner! This is incredible! This is gonna be an *amazing* event space." Now she's looking around like she's seeing into the future alongside me. Jackson is nodding as well, a grin overtaking his face.

"I know Piper's going to turn it into something epic," Kru says, squeezing my arm.

"Thank you. There's a long road ahead, but it'll come together. I've cleaned nine windows so far, so, you know, I'm basically at the finish line."

Bella snort laughs, then her gaze returns to me and Kru. "So is this, like...official?"

"Barny?" I ask.

"No, *you two*," she clarifies.

"Oh," I blurt.

"Well," Kru says at the same time.

"We're—" I look over at Kru. "It's..."

Bella and Jackson are both laughing as we fumble to answer.

"Just don't say anything to my brothers, please," I finally spit out.

"I'm her dirty little secret," Kru says, though I can hear a note of unhappiness there.

"Just like Barny here," Bella says. "I take it your brothers don't know about either of your secret men."

"Hell no," I say. "And it needs to stay that way. For now."

She sighs. "Piper, you know they're going to find out eventually."

"I know," I acknowledge. "I'm just waiting for the right time to tell them."

"And when will that be? The grand opening?"

I roll my eyes. "Very funny. I'm just trying to avoid another lecture about taking on too much, not doing things the right way, not doing things *their* way..."

"Well, I'll say it since Aunt Laura isn't here to say it herself: they mean well." Bella's tone suggests she understands my frustration all too well.

"I know they do." I sigh. "But this is important to me, and I don't want them getting in the way."

"You really paint your brothers to be lovely people," Kru cracks, crossing his arms.

"They *are* lovely. And intense. And overbearing. And…" Before I can add too many more adjectives, my phone rings in my apron pocket. I pull it out, expecting to see Griffin's name and preparing my excuse for why I'm not at the shop. Instead, it's Dane. "I gotta take this, guys. Hang on."

"Hey," I answer, turning away from Bella's knowing gaze. "What's up?"

"Mom's awake," Dane says without preamble, his voice tight with emotion.

My heart skips a beat. "What?"

"She just woke up like three minutes ago. She's groggy but she knows who we are. The doctor's on his way now."

"Oh my god." My free hand flies to my mouth. "I'll be right there. Bella and Jackson are with me, so I'll bring them, too."

I hang up, turning to the others with wide eyes. "Mom's awake."

Bella screams, covering her mouth with her hands. "Are you serious? That's amazing!" She immediately wraps me in a hug. "Let's go!"

"Yes. Let's fucking go," I tell her, already gathering my things. "I'll meet you there."

Bella and Jackson hurry out, promising to see me at the hospital. I turn to Kru, who's watching me with a huge smile.

"That's incredible news," he says. "I'm so fucking happy to hear it."

"It really is." I'm practically vibrating with a mixture of relief and excitement. "I need to get to the hospital."

"Of course." He helps me gather my cleaning supplies. "Do you want me to drive you? You seem a little wobbly."

I consider it for a moment, tempted by the offer, but shake my head. "Thanks, but I should go on my own. My brothers will all be there and..." I trail off, not needing to finish the thought.

"Right." His face falls slightly. "Text me later, okay? Let me know how she's doing. How *you're* doing."

"I will." I hesitate, then impulsively rise on tiptoes to press a quick kiss to his lips. "Thank you. For everything."

His hands catch my waist, holding me there for a moment longer. "Anytime, Maven."

It's still nice enough this time of year to be biking instead of driving, so I race outside to hop on my bike. The ride to the hospital is a blur of stop signs and my own racing thoughts. Mom's awake. After five days of uncertainty and fear, she's finally awake. The relief is so overwhelming, I'm streaming tears for the second half of the ride to the hospital.

I find Asher, Dane, Jett, and Bella already clustered around Mom's bed when I arrive. Griffin is apparently on his way. Mom herself is sitting up slightly, looking pale and tired but undeniably awake.

"Piper," she says when she spots me, her voice hoarse.

"Mom!" I rush to the bed, carefully embracing her. "Oh my god, this is the best day of my life. You're awake!"

"So they tell me," she says with a weak attempt at a smile. "Though I feel like I've been hit by a truck. On the inside."

"Smoke inhalation and burns will do that to you," Dane says.

We're all crowded at her bedside, beaming down at her. I'm holding one of her hands; Asher is holding another. Dane, Jett, and Bella are gathered around the foot of the bed.

The doctor comes in shortly after I arrive, gently shooing us out so he can do a quick exam. We huddle in the hallway, all of us too keyed up to sit quietly in the waiting room.

"This is good, right?" I ask, seeking reassurance. "She seems like herself."

"She knew exactly who she was and who we were when she woke up," Asher confirms. "But she was surprised to hear how long she's been out. They'll know more soon."

Relief floods through me, exhaustion on its heels. I lean against the wall, suddenly aware of how tired I am. Between the shop, the barn cleaning, and the emotional rollercoaster of Mom's condition, I'm running on fumes.

"Where were you when Dane called?" Jett asks, eyeing my dusty clothes. "You look like you've been rolling around in an attic."

I tense slightly. "Just...cleaning the storage room at the shop. It was overdue."

Jett raises an eyebrow but doesn't press, which I appreciate. The last thing we all need right now is to talk about the barn.

Griffin arrives, slightly out of breath, having clearly rushed from whatever he was doing. "How is she?" he demands.

"Awake, alert, and knows who we all are," Asher reports.

Griffin's relief is palpable as the tension visibly drains from his shoulders.

The doctor emerges after what feels like an eternity, clipboard in hand. "She's doing remarkably well," he tells us. "We'll need to keep her for observation for a few more days, but barring any complications, she should be able to go home by early next week."

The collective sigh of relief from the Keegan siblings is probably audible three floors down.

"Can we go back in?" I ask.

"Of course. But be aware she does need rest. Try not to overload her with conversations. She's been through a lot, and rest is very important right now." The doctor offers a warm smile before striding away.

We file back into the room, where Mom is looking more tired than before, but still alert.

"The doctor says you're getting out of here soon," Jett tells her, perching on the edge of the bed.

"Not soon enough," she says with a weak smile.

We laugh, the sound both relieved and a little tearful. For the first time in days, the knot of fear in my chest begins to loosen.

"Next game night will be at home," I tell her.

"Mmm. Did we miss one?" she asks softly.

"No, Mom. We brought it to you." Jett smiles down at her, taking her hand in his. "Could you feel us here?"

She mumbles something, but it's clear she's getting ready to conk out. We all take turns pressing kisses to her forehead, getting ready to clear out.

"I'll stay until Asher comes for the night shift," Dane whispers once Mom's eyes have drifted shut. "I'll let you know when she wakes up again."

After saying our goodbyes, we head to the parking lot, all of us walking a little lighter than when we arrived. Before I hop onto my bike, I pull out my phone and type a quick message to Kru.

PIPER: *We talked to her, she's groggy but things are looking up. Should be home by Monday.*

His reply comes almost immediately.

KRU: *That's great, Maven. I'm so happy for you.*

I smile at the screen, warmth spreading through me at his words. A second message follows.

KRU: *You coming over tonight?*

I bite my lip, fighting a smile.

PIPER: *That sounds like a good idea.*

KRU: *I'll make it a great idea.*

PIPER: *I'll try my best to stay up that late. Text me when you're done at the restaurant.*

KRU: *I could always come to you...*

PIPER: *Not with Griffin there!!!!*

KRU: *When are you gonna be real with them? Not gonna lie...I'm sick of hiding this.*

PIPER: Well…what is this?

My phone rings immediately. My stomach is in all sort of fluttery knots as I answer. I can't believe we're about to have this talk.

"No more texting," his deep voice rumbles. Pinpricks of desire skate through me, and suddenly I'm desperate for him to be in front of me, wrapped around me, *inside me.*

"I didn't mean to make it all serious," I tell him.

"Will you just be my girlfriend already?"

I gnaw on the inside of my cheek, fighting a grin that I know will split me in two. "I could arrange that. But I'll be honest…I can't date someone if I don't know his first name."

"Herman."

"Oh, wow. I wasn't expecting that. Now is your formal name Uncle Herman Lobster Krueger, then?"

"If you want. I'll respond to whatever you call me. I happen to like the names you come up with, Pipesqueak."

My entire body feels warm and buzzy now. I'm covering my mouth with the back of my hand, I'm smiling so hard.

"That's a new one," I tell him.

"Come over tonight," he says again, his voice gritty. "So we can celebrate the Pipe Crew. And if it doesn't happen tonight, then I'm absolutely getting my hands on you tomorrow."

"That sounds like a threat," I tease.

"A promise," he clarifies. "Because I don't break my promises to my girlfriend."

The way he says it sends me into the clouds. I didn't realize something so forbidden—*prohibited*—could feel so damn right.

CHAPTER TWENTY

PIPER

I wake up the next morning horny, confused, and extremely well-rested. The last thing I remember is lying in my bed, waiting for a text from Kru to hear how his night was going.

"Shit." I fumble to grab my phone, which spent the whole night unplugged on the bedspread beside me. I swipe to see all my missed notifications. There's one from Bella, who confirmed she and Jackson made it to LA from the Cleveland airport last night. All the rest are from Kru throughout the night.

KRU: Whatcha doin, girlfriend?

KRU: I don't mean that in the sassy side character way. I mean that in the "I am your boyfriend" sort of way.

KRU: Last customer is almost out and I'm getting ready to come home.

KRU: Don't tell me you're ghosting me a second time.

KRU: You awake? I bet you fell asleep already...

KRU: Sleepy Pipesqueak? You there?

I hurry to tap out a message, my stomach sinking. This is not a great start to our brand-new relationship.

PIPER: OMG. Fell asleep at nine last night and just woke up.

It's six a.m. I don't expect a response this early. I roll out of bed and get my bearings on the day. After freshening up in the bathroom, I get dressed to open Cloud Nine—bright leggings, a fluffy sweater, and a wide pink headband to complement my high ponytail. Once I'm ready to head to the shop, I check my phone. Nothing from Kru. I need to make this up to him, and I think about how I might do it as I hop on my bike and head to work.

I get the shop turned on and humming. I start with a latte, of course, followed by arranging my early orders and getting things prepped for Jerrica to take over. She's been helping out a lot more lately, and I have to say I like it. It's been a huge relief to know I can hand the reins over to someone who is here frequently and can keep up with the tiny details. I've scheduled some downtime at the house today to get more meal prep done, this time for Mom for when she comes home, so it'll be a lot easier than meal prepping for Griffin. My brothers and I spent a lot of time yesterday figuring out what would make the most sense once Mom is home, and I jumped on the chance to make the meals after so many years of having meals made for me by her.

Kru finally responds around nine.

KRU: Damn. Sure wish I'd woken up with you in my bed.

PIPER: Can you take a lunch break today? After your lunch rush is done, of course. I want to make it up to you.

KRU: What time? And where?

PIPER: I'm stuck in the kitchen at Griff's house all day. Just go there whenever you're done feeding the masses.

KRU: You sure it's safe?

PIPER: Positive. There's some team function he's attending in Cleveland today so he won't be back until at least five.

KRU: You got it, Piperdelle.

I'm elbows deep in attempting to recreate Mom's famous lasagna when I hear the knock on the front door. I squeal—*it's my boyfriend!*—and hurry over to the front door. Except I forgot to take my oven mitts off, so there's a bit of an awkward struggle with the doorknob before I finally just whip the mitts off and pull the door open.

"Hey." Kru's effortless smile immediately woos me. He's in his standard dark Henley and black cargo work pants, the attire he wears when he's not in his black chef's coat.

"Kiss me," I say, and he's closing the distance between us before I'm even done saying the words. He scoops me up into his strong arms, hoisting me so that my legs close around him. I giggle through the kiss. I feel so safe and secure in his arms, I never want to leave them. The door swings shut behind us as he walks into the house. He props me on the kitchen island, taking a step back to admire me, squeezing my thighs.

"Mmm. Now this is the best lunch break." He dives back in for another kiss, our tongues meeting in the middle. We make out, hot and heavy, until my timer goes off. The lasagna is done. I gasp, sidling out from underneath him to open the oven. I slip on the mitts before I pull the big casserole dish out of the oven. It looks perfect. Kru lets out a low whistle as I place it on the stovetop.

"So that's how you wanted to make it up to me?" he asks.

I swat his arm. "This is for my mom when she gets home. I want her to have all her meals taken care of for the next week."

"Sweet of you." He presses a kiss to my temple.

"*Your* gift is right here." I sling my arms around his neck, pressing my body to his. "I realize now that this may be slightly underwhelming, but my body is yours."

"Mmm. I've never heard sexier words." His lips are on mine again, and we're kissing long, slow, deep. These kisses have my head spinning and my pulse racing. I'm back on the countertop, his body filling the space between my legs. The thick ridge of his arousal presses against my inner thigh, sending desire skating beneath my skin.

"You done cooking for now?" he asks, sounding drugged. His gaze is stuck on my lips. "We need to take this party elsewhere."

"Mm-hmm." I can't form words. "Mmm."

He hoists me into his arms again, carrying me out of the kitchen and deeper into the house. When we pass through the living room, I wriggle my hips.

"Here," I gasp out. "I can't wait."

Kru gently lowers me onto the couch and then tears his Henley off. My gaze trips over his muscled chest, the dark hair scattered across his pecs and down the center of his belly. I reach for him, bringing him down on top of me. The warmth of his body is a welcome balm; every cell inside me sighs with relief.

Shit. Is that normal for a new relationship? To feel this head-spinny? I'll think about that later—right now, this chef god is showering me with kisses, head moving lower to lavish attention over the pink lace of my bra, which he exposed by pushing my sweater up.

I grind up against him, desperate for more friction, more contact. A rough groan erupts from him as he matches my movements.

"Fuck, Piper. You weren't kidding."

"I need you inside me," I whisper into his ear. "Please, Kru. Now."

He pulls the lace bra down, covering my nipple with his tongue then closing his lips around the rosy bud. I squirm against him as he does it again and then moves to the other side. He sits back, pulling me up so he can gently remove the sweater and then my bra, no knives needed this time since it's a front clasp. He revisits each nipple and then kisses his way down my belly to the waistband of my leggings. He nuzzles in between my legs, looking up at me with heat in his gaze.

"Late lunch," he says with a cocksure smile.

I'm so focused on him I barely notice the slam.

The heavy thuds across the floor, followed by three words that slice through my body from head to toe:

"*What the fuck?*"

It's Griffin.

But that doesn't make sense. I can't even begin to pair his voice with the fact that Kru is on top of me until I see a huge hand fly through the air.

Everything happens in a blur after that. One moment Kru's between my thighs, the next he's being hauled off me by a furious Griffin. I scramble to cover myself, grabbing my discarded sweater as Kru is pushed to the floor.

Griff heads for Kru, who scrambles to his feet.

"Get the fuck off of my sister!" he bellows. I've never heard him so angry. I'm struggling to get my bra fastened as I watch Griffin close the gap between them in two powerful steps.

Kru holds up his hands. "It's not what you think—"

But Griffin doesn't care. He swings anyway, primal mode activated. His fist connects with the side of Kru's face. Kru stumbles backward, clutching at his cheek while a string of curse words fall from his lips.

"Griffin, stop!" I shout.

But he's not listening.

"It's exactly what I think!" Griffin lunges forward, but Kru sidesteps him, hands lifted again. I can tell my brother is ready to punch again. My bra snaps into place and I race forward, inserting myself between Griffin's fist and Kru.

"Stop!" I scream. "I invited him."

Griffin freezes, fist still in the air. His chest is heaving, face full of confusion. "No fucking way."

"Let him go. He did nothing wrong," I plead, my voice shaking. Kru is keeping is cool remarkably well, despite being attacked by my rhinoceros of a brother. "Put this down." I guide his fist lower, out of punching range of Kru's face.

"Why the fuck would you invite this piece of shit into my house?" Griffin spits.

His words land like the punch his hand couldn't inflict. To both me and Kru. I can see him wince.

"He's not a piece of shit," I correct him. "We're *together*."

Griffin blinks slowly, like he's processing information in a foreign language. "Together?"

"Yes. He's my boyfriend."

Griff's eyes go wide, which make me think I could have improved the transition a bit better. "No fucking way."

Kru offers a helpful smile. The side of his face is already red from where Griff landed a punch.

"There's no way in hell you'd be with someone like him," Griff tells me. "He's the enemy."

"I prefer the term 'friendly neighborhood chef,'" Kru offers.

"Nobody asked you," Griffin warns, sliding his forearm across Kru's throat. To me, he says, "Are you punking me right now? This is the guy who kicked you out of your apartment."

"I did give her notice," Kru adds. "Politely."

"Shut up," Griffin growls at him.

"Griffin," I start.

"This shit isn't funny, Piper. Snap out of it! You're dating your landlord? Do you know how many horror stories start this way?"

"We could consider this more of a rom-com," Kru says helpfully.

Griffin brings his face extra close to Kru. "I was not asking you, Chef Boyardee."

"Guys, stop it. Griffin, let him go. We all need to take a deep breath." Including me, because right now, my heart is pounding so hard I think I'm going to pass out.

Griffin gives Kru an extra-spicy death stare before removing his forearm from Kru's throat. Kru takes a tentative step away, as though testing that Griffin won't pounce at the movement. And then another.

Griffin turns his angry gaze toward me. "I can't believe this. You actually let him on top of you? In my *living room?* On my fucking *couch?*"

"You weren't supposed to be home for, like, three more hours," I explain.

"Get dressed," Griff snaps. He turns back to Kru, who takes a defensive step backwards. "And you! Get the fuck out of my house."

"Griffin—" I begin, but he cuts me off with a raised hand.

"I don't want to hear it."

And there it is. The shut-down I was worried about from day one. Kru looks at me, conflict in his gaze. My shoulders sag, my stomach a thorny mess.

"You should go," I say to him quietly.

"I'll call you later," he promises, slipping his shirt back on. He leaves the house without fanfare, and I hurry to slide my sweater back on. My legs are jelly, every inch of my body on high alert as I cautiously follow Griffin into the kitchen.

Silence settles between us like a lead blanket.

"So your event ended early?" I say, because I have no idea where to even begin with this.

Griffin spins on his heels, eyes blazing. "Don't even act like everything is normal after that."

"I don't know what to say!"

"I feel like I don't even know who you are anymore," Griffin spits. "You've been sitting here, lying to my face, for god knows how long. I don't know what's even real anymore, Piper. This is the guy who kicked you out of your apartment, remember? The one who's been battling you in the competition? Breaking through your storage room wall, harassing your customers, impacting your sales?"

"They were all temporary inconveniences due to construction—"

"Oh my god." Griffin drags a hand down his face. "Listen to yourself! He's brainwashed you!"

"He has not brainwashed me!" I snap, my own anger rising to match his. "I like him, Griffin. A lot. I've gotten to know him over the past few weeks and he's a good guy. I promise you. I just never told you because I knew you wouldn't accept it."

"He's using you, Piper. Can't you see that? First he gets you to do that reality show, then he gets you into bed. What's next? Taking over your business too?"

"It's not like that," I insist.

Griffin paces the length of the kitchen, shaking his head. "I can't believe this. After everything that's happened with Mom, with the shop, you decide now is the time to hook up with the enemy?"

"It's my choice. Mine."

"And it's a stupid one," Griffin shouts. "What happens when he gets bored and moves on, huh? He's not just some random guy you can avoid after it falls apart. He's your landlord. Your neighbor. The guy who has all the power in this situation."

A seed of doubt begins to root. Hadn't I worried about the same thing myself?

"It's not going to fall apart," I say, with more conviction than I feel.

Griffin snorts. "Right. Because you know so much about long-term relationships."

The barb stings more than it should. It's true that I haven't had many serious relationships—always too busy with the shop, with family, with everything else—but hearing Griffin throw it in my face makes me want to curl into myself.

He's reminding me yet again that my entire family sees me as the young, dumb one who can't be trusted with her own decisions.

"That's not fair," I say quietly.

Griffin leans against the countertop, his mouth a thin, angry line. "I expected better from you, Piper. You're smarter than this."

The disappointment in his voice cuts deeper than his anger.

"I'm sorry you found out this way," I tell him. "And I'm sorry I didn't clue you in earlier. But I'm not sorry about *him*."

Griffin looks over at me, his eyes hard. "Does Mom know? Or our brothers?"

I shake my head. "Only Bella."

"Well, I'm done keeping your secrets," Griffin bites out. "And I'm done talking to you. You're the only one who can't see what's really going on: power hungry guy buys up the property, has his way with the tenant, gets what he wants, leaves her broken. And probably broke at the end of it."

His words hit me like a brick. What if he's right? What happens when Kru moves on?

"You don't know him," I say weakly.

"And neither do you," Griffin counters. "A few weeks of sneaking around doesn't equal knowing someone."

"I didn't meet him when he bought the building," I blurt, my cheeks going hot. "I knew him from before. We met up in Cleveland once and connected. But then I ghosted him."

"Oh. Great. So he's your stalker now, too."

I groan. "*Griffin*! You are impossible! I'm going back to the shop. Maybe someday we can all talk about this like adults, do you think? Can you possibly imagine a world where I know what I'm doing and can be trusted?"

Griffin just stares at me, saying nothing.

"Great. Well that sure makes me feel like a capable adult." My throat is pinching and the tears are near. I can feel them coming. I stalk off to my bedroom, feeling a lot like the little girl who's gotten in trouble yet again.

I angrily change clothes in my bedroom, putting on barn-appropriate clothes since I plan to spend as much time in there cleaning up as I can. While I'm washing my face to help myself cool down, I hear the front door slam shut.

A sigh escapes me, and I take a moment to let the afternoon-gone-awry sink into me.

I can't believe it happened. And I can't help but wonder if there's some truth to what Griffin says. His warning feel like stones in my shoes. Uncomfortable, grating, but not painful enough to make me stop.

But there's nothing left to do from here but move forward.

And pray that my brothers don't all take turns punching Kru in the face.

CHAPTER TWENTY-ONE

KRU

"Somehow, it looks worse than it did ten minutes ago."

Brady's grim assessment of my face makes me wince. I've stopped looking in the mirror. The black eye just reminds me of the piss-poor introduction I got to one of the Keegan Keepers, which is absolutely the hockey team Griffin should start playing for if his professional contract with the Cleveland Crushers ever ends. Because Piper wasn't kidding – her brothers mean business, and I can't believe there's three more of them I have to get through.

"If anyone wants to meet the chef tonight, I'm gonna have to send you out, okay?" I say it like a joke, but I'm kind of serious. I don't want anyone meeting me like this, thinking I'm some sort of back-alley street fighter. I don't think the real reason—getting hazed by my girlfriend's older brother—will sound like an acceptable excuse either. I'm just glad the camera crew is gone. This would have been too embarrassing to immortalize in a new season of reality TV.

"You want any ice yet?" Rafael asks. I've been too busy to use any, but I made sure to use an ice pack before I went to bed last night. Not that it helped.

"I'm fine," I say, wiping down my station even though it's already sparkling clean after the lunch rush. "Let's just focus on pumping out dinner."

Since it's Sunday, Piper's not open, but she's out in the barn working. I've gone out there to check on her a couple times today, but each time she's been mysteriously missing. She's apologized no fewer than twenty times since yesterday's unfortunate ambush—I mean, family introduction.

She doesn't know that I'd happily let all her brothers rough me up. She's worth it. But the aftermath *does* sting a bit.

Work sweeps us up and away as usual. Today's dinner service is brutal—quickly spiraling into three large parties and one particularly demanding table that sends back their lobster twice before finally accepting that it is, in fact, cooked perfectly. But one of my later tables sends a note with Jackie that his lobster and marshmallow dish was so delicious he needs to speak with me urgently. He sent his business card, which lists his company as Midwestern Restaurant Group.

Overall it's a lucrative evening—one on top of many before it. My business model is working. And the marshmallow touch to the dish has helped me slide into first place in the Bayshore Best competition—and probably helped keep the dining room full tonight. I'm not sure how long I'll retain it, but I've got my staff reminding our customers at every turn to go vote for us in the competition, so maybe we've got a shot.

As my crew and I work through the closing checklist, exhaustion sets in. These long days are getting to me. All I want is to go home, ice my face, and call Piper to see how she's handling the fallout with Griffin.

When I finally lock up and step into the cool October night, my breath is visible in small puffs. The parking lot is entirely empty except for my truck. That's when I notice the light spilling out of the barn on the far end of the lot.

I walk across the lot, my footsteps echoing in the quiet. As I get closer, I can hear music—some sort of upbeat pop song. It's nearly eleven. It can't still be Piper in there...can it?

I already know the answer before I slide open the barn door.

Piper is perched on a ladder in the middle of the space, a paint roller in her hand, working on one of the massive support beams. She's set up some industrial lighting, illuminating the entire barn in harsh white light. Paint cans, brushes, and drop cloths are scattered across the floor. She's wearing paint-splattered overalls over a Cloud Nine hoodie, her hair pulled back in a messy bun with what appears to be white paint streaks in it.

She's also swaying slightly on the ladder, which makes my heart skip a beat.

"Piper? What the hell are you doing?"

She startles, nearly dropping the paint roller. "Kru! You scared me!"

"It's eleven o'clock," I say, stepping into the barn and looking around at the chaos. "Why are you up here painting? It's freezing, it's dark, and you've probably been up since six a.m."

She waves a dismissive hand, which makes the ladder wobble again. "I'm fine. Just trying to get some stuff done. I had all this energy after dinner, so I thought why not be productive?"

"Have you been working in here all day? I came out to check on you earlier and didn't see you."

"Not *all* day," she clarifies. She dips the roller in the paint tray balanced precariously on the ladder's shelf.

"Don't you want a break? Come home with me, Maven. I'll make sure you relax."

She sends me a coy look which has my cock jumping. I know that look.

"What kind of relaxation are we talking about?"

"The kind where I get you out of those paint-covered overalls and spend an hour making you forget all about this barn."

Her breath catches. "Just an hour?"

"To start." I reach up and steady the ladder with one hand, my other hand trailing up her calf. "Come down here, Piper."

She sets the paint roller aside and climbs down slowly, deliberately, her body brushing against mine as she reaches the bottom rung. I don't step back, trapping her between the ladder and my chest.

"You're covered in paint," I murmur, brushing a streak of white from her cheek.

"So are you now," she whispers, her hands fisting in my shirt.

I dip my head, capturing her lips in a kiss that's anything but gentle. She melts against me immediately, all that manic energy transforming into something hotter, more desperate. Her paint-stained fingers work at the buttons of my shirt.

"Kru," she gasps when I move to her neck, finding that spot that makes her knees weak. "Someone could—"

"Nobody's coming out here now," I say against her skin, my hands making quick work of her overall straps. "It's just us, Maven. Let me take care of you."

The overalls pool at her feet, leaving her in just her hoodie and under-wear. I lift her easily, settling her on one of the ladder rungs so we're at eye level.

"Better?" I ask, my hands spanning her waist.

Her answer is to pull my mouth back to hers, and I lose myself in the taste of her, in the way she wraps her legs around my hips and pulls me closer. I know I promised an hour, but it's late, and we're both tired, and fuck if I'm not hard as a rock already.

"Help me bless the barn," she murmurs, bucking her hips toward me. "I need it."

She doesn't need to ask twice. I fish my cock out of my pants and guide myself toward her slick center. She's gripping my shoulders like she's afraid I'll drift away, her fingernails digging into my skin. I scoop her closer by the small of her back.

She's sugary and warm. Pure velvet and juice. A grunt escapes me as I sink into her, our kisses turning desperate, hungrier.

"Jesus, Piper," I bite out. "You feel so incredible. Like you're made for me."

"Maybe I am," she breathes, clenching around me. I thrust into her, wanting to go slow and relish this, but a desperate need overtakes me. She's clawing at me, urging me deeper, faster. I can only obey. The ladder creaks as I push into her, her soft, girlish moans sending me higher.

"Best barn ever," I grunt out just as my fingers find her swollen clit. I pinch and prod her, loving the way her moans get louder and she arches even harder against me. "That's it. Come on, Piper. Give it to me."

I massage her clit until she breaks. Her whole body goes rigid and her head rolls back. As her pussy turns into a vice grip around my cock, my own release bursts through. I bury my gruff cry into the hollow of her neck, and we sit there for a few moments, relishing the sticky aftermath.

"I think we can consider this barn blessed," she says with a sleepy smile. She's blinking slowly, and I can't tell if it's from sexual satisfaction or sleepiness.

"Happy to do my part." I press a quick kiss to her lips as I adjust myself. I help her get cleaned up with a fresh rag nearby, then I pull her overalls back up. "You ready to go?"

Some of the fire returns to her gaze. "Go? How can I go when I'm on a roll? Look at all this progress! I got three beams done already."

I survey the barn, and she's right—there's definitely been progress. More than should be possible for one person working alone. Which means...

"Be real with me," I say. "How many hours did you put into this barn today?"

"I ran a bunch of errands," she says quickly, climbing the ladder again. "I was in and out. So like, eight hours. Nine, maybe. Well, more like ten."

"Ten hours? Piper, this is supposed to be your day off."

She looks down at me with confusion. "Huh. I guess you're right."

That's when I know she's hit the wall. I've been there myself—so focused on a project, so driven by adrenaline and caffeine, that you lose track of time entirely. It's not sustainable, and it usually ends badly.

"Let's call it a night," I say gently.

"I can't," she says, already turning back to her painting. "I have so much to do. Jerrica's going to open the shop tomorrow, so I can work a late night. Now's my time. The whole space needs to be painted before I can move on to flooring, and then there's the electrical work and the plumbing and—"

"And you think you're going to be able to do all that?" I ask with a laugh.

Her face hardens. "Excuse me?"

I need to reconfigure my approach. "Just come down. Please."

"I'm fine!" she insists, but her voice has a manic edge to it. "I can handle this. I can do it all."

"I know you can. But not in one night."

She finally looks down at me, and I can see the exhaustion beneath the frenetic energy. Dark circles under her eyes, a slight tremor in her hands that could be from cold or fatigue or both.

"Actually," I say, struck by sudden inspiration, "Maverick's coming over to my place tonight to celebrate the restaurant's first two weeks down. You should join us, especially if you don't have an early morning tomorrow. Take a break, have a drink, relax for real."

She considers this, setting down her paint roller and climbing down the ladder with careful, deliberate movements. I can see she's trying to hide how unsteady she is.

"That sounds nice," she says when she reaches the bottom. "But I should finish this beam first. I'm on such a roll, and if I stop now—"

"The beam will still be here tomorrow," I interrupt.

"But I'm in the zone! This is when the best work happens!"

"The best work happens when you're well-rested and thinking clearly," I counter. "What you're doing right now is dangerous. You're exhausted, you're alone, and you've been using power tools."

"I'm not using power tools right now," she argues, gesturing to the paint roller.

"Even a paint roller is dangerous when you're sleep deprived. Look, why don't you just come have one drink with us? Then you can get some actual rest."

Her expression shifts, and I can see something defensive creeping in. "I don't need you to manage my schedule, Kru. I'm perfectly capable of deciding when I need rest."

"I'm not trying to manage anything. I'm worried about you."

"Why?" She crosses her arms. "Because I'm working hard? Because I'm dedicated to my project? You do the exact same thing! How many times have you worked until closing and then gone home just to get up again at dawn?"

She has a point, but this feels different somehow. More desperate. More manic.

"That's different," I say. "I'm launching a new business. It's expected that the first few months will be crazy."

"And I'm launching a new business too!" she exclaims, gesturing around the barn. "So why is it okay for you to work yourself into the ground but not me?"

"Because you're—" I stop myself before I can say something I'll regret.

"Because I'm what?" Her voice has a sharp edge now. "Because I'm a woman? Because I'm smaller than you? Because you think I can't handle it?"

"That's not what I was going to say."

"Then what? Because it sure sounds like you think I'm incapable of managing my own project."

I can see Griffin's words echoing in her defensiveness, the way she's interpreting my concern as doubt in her abilities. "Piper, that's not—"

"You know what? Forget it." She turns away from me, starting to gather her painting supplies. "Thanks for the invitation, but I think I'll pass. I have work to do."

"Come on, don't be like this."

"Like what? Like someone who doesn't appreciate being told what to do?" She's shoving brushes into a bucket with more force than necessary. "I'm fine, Kru. I can take care of myself."

"I know you can. I'm just saying—"

"You're just saying I should stop working and come hang out instead. Because apparently my priorities are wrong."

"That's not what I meant."

"Isn't it?" She spins around to face me, paint-streaked and exhausted but still blazing with determination. "Everyone has an opinion about what I should be doing. My brothers think I'm taking on too much. You think I'm working too hard. Well, guess what? This is my project, my timeline, my decision."

I hold up my hands in surrender. "Okay. You're right. I'm sorry."

Some of the fight goes out of her, but she's still tense. "I just...I need to do this my way, at my pace. Can you understand that?"

"I can," I say, even though every instinct is telling me she needs to rest. "But promise me you'll go home soon? It's late, and it's cold out here."

"I will," she says, which isn't quite a promise but is better than an argument. "Go have fun with Maverick. Tell him I'm sorry I couldn't make it."

I want to argue more, to insist she come with me or at least let me drive her home. But I can see she's reached her limit for being managed today, and pushing further will only make things worse.

"Text me when you get home?" I ask.

"Yes, chef," she says with a tired smile that doesn't quite reach her eyes.

I hesitate at the barn door, looking back at her as she climbs back up the ladder. Everything in me wants to stay, to make sure she's okay, but I force myself to leave.

The drive back to my place is short. Maverick's truck is already in my driveway when I pull up, and I can see him through the front window, making himself at home on my couch with a beer. I told him the code to get in so he wouldn't have to wait in his car.

"There you are," he says when I walk in. "I was starting to think you'd forgotten about me. Where's the girlfriend? I was looking forward to hanging with her."

"She had to work," I say, grabbing a beer from the fridge and joining him on the couch. "Rain check."

Maverick takes one look at my face and whistles low. "Damn, what happened to your eye?"

"I met Piper's brother," I say dryly.

His grin is immediate and wide. "And I'm guessing he didn't approve of the relationship?"

"That's one way to put it."

"You're lucky it's just a black eye. I was expecting broken bones when you told me you were dating Griff Keegan's little sister."

We settle into easy conversation, Maverick regaling me with stories from his latest food truck adventures while I try not to think about Piper alone in that barn. But my phone stays silent—no texts, no calls.

"You're distracted," Maverick observes after I miss the punchline of his story entirely.

"Sorry. Just thinking about work stuff."

"Work stuff or girlfriend stuff?"

I take a long pull of my beer. "Both, maybe."

"Want to talk about it?"

Part of me wants to say no. There's nothing to talk about—at least, I want that to be true. But Maverick's been through his own relationship drama with Scarlett, and he's got a good head for business. Maybe an outside perspective would help.

"She's working herself into the ground," I finally say. "But nobody can tell her anything because she's been micromanaged her entire life by her brothers. This barn renovation project—she's obsessed with it. Working until midnight, forgetting to eat, pushing herself past exhaustion."

"Sounds familiar," Maverick says pointedly.

"It's different."

"How?"

"It just is." I know I sound defensive, but I can't quite articulate why Piper's work habits worry me more than my own.

"Maybe it's different because you care about her," Maverick suggests. "Makes it harder to watch someone else make the same mistakes as you."

That hits closer to home than I'd like to admit. I frown and then take a pull of my beer, letting his words sink in. "Maybe."

"Or maybe," Maverick continues, "you're seeing what it looks like from the outside when someone you care about disappears into their work."

I lift a brow. "What do you mean?"

"When's the last time you took a real day off? When's the last time you did something that wasn't related to the restaurant?"

"That's different. I'm launching a business."

"And she's launching a business too." Maverick shrugs. "Maybe you're both workaholics, and you just don't like seeing your reflection."

The observation stings. How many nights have I worked until closing then gone home to do inventory or work on menu planning? How many meals have I skipped because I was too focused on perfecting a recipe?

"Speaking of work," Maverick says, either sensing my discomfort or genuinely changing the subject, "what's next for you? You've got this place running smooth already. Most restaurants take months to hit their stride."

"I've got good staff," I say. "And I'm loving it. I think it's what I was born to do."

"So what's the next move? Expansion? Franchise opportunities?"

I laugh, but there's something in his tone that makes me pause. "Slow down there, entrepreneur. I've been open for two weeks."

"I'm serious. Have you thought about it? You're already hitting the top of the charts in the Bayshore competition. That marshmallow addition to the lobster is *fantastic*. It's the kind of recipe that can carry this location for decades. You could probably get backing for a second location pretty easily, especially with the TV show exposure."

The idea has been percolating in the back of my head. "Maybe," I admit, then I remember the business card Jackie passed along. I fish it out of my pocket, rereading the name. "This restaurant group wants to chat with me about something. Maybe they're interested in helping me expand."

"You should look into it," Maverick says. "Strike while the iron's hot, you know? Build an empire."

An empire. The word has a nice ring to it. Multiple restaurants, a recognizable brand, the kind of success that would make my dad proud. I laugh and shake my head.

"What's holding you back?" Maverick asks, noticing my hesitation.

I almost say "nothing," but that would be a lie. What's holding me back is the woman currently painting beams in a barn at midnight. Which is ridiculous. This is a brand-new relationship. Hardly a reason to limit my business growth.

But as I sit there with Maverick, thinking about expansion and empire building, I can't shake the image of Piper swaying on that ladder, exhausted but determined. And I realize that somewhere along the way, her dreams have become tangled up with mine.

"Nothing's holding me back," I finally say. "Just want to make sure this place is solid first."

"Fair enough."

"Also, it's not lost on me that your suggestion will put me deep into the throes of the workaholic life that I just got on Piper's case about."

He cocks a grin and shrugs. "Maybe we're looking into a three-way mirror here, who knows?"

We laugh, and conversation eventually turns to lighter things. Menu ideas, customer stories, ideas for the future. After he leaves, I sit alone in my living room, nursing my drink and thinking more about the idea of expansion.

Expanding wasn't necessarily the plan, but romance was never part of the plan either. I came to Bayshore to build something, to honor my father's memory, to establish myself as a serious chef and make a living.

But somehow, without meaning to, I've fallen headfirst into Piper Keegan. And the truth is that if I start expanding restaurants, I won't have time for anything, much less a girlfriend.

Is that what I want? To be at the start of my career and so invested in someone else's life that it affects my own decisions?

My phone buzzes with a text, and I grab it eagerly, hoping it's Piper saying she's finally headed home.

PIPER: *I'm back at Griff's and falling asleep. I hope you and Maverick had fun.*

KRU: *We did but I missed you. Get some sleep, Piperton.*

I finish my beer and head to bed, but sleep doesn't come easily. Every time I close my eyes, I see Piper on that ladder, paint in her hair, determined to prove herself to people who weren't even there.

And fuck if I'm not doing the same thing myself.

CHAPTER TWENTY-TWO

PIPER

The cat is officially out of the Keegan bag.

No, no. It's more than that. The panther has officially escaped the high security Keegan zoo.

My entire family now knows that I've been secretly dating my usurper, and the texts just will not stop pouring in.

DANE: Are you fucking serious?

ASHER: Tell me this is a joke.

JETT: This is the guy that lives behind you right? Confirm the address because I don't wanna fuck up the wrong guy.

Griffin was true to his word. He did not keep my secret for me, and good on him. I'm tired of the secrets. I'm tired of it all. I just want to live my life without having to explain myself every thirty seconds to four grown men who still see me as an eleven-year-old girl who can barely run a lemonade stand.

I spend all of Monday morning at the barn, ignoring my phone except for a few sweet messages to Kru. When he shows up to help me, wordlessly getting to work, I fall in love with him on the spot. No comments, no questions. Just support.

Then Monday afternoon, Mom is released from the hospital. I see all of my brothers for the first time since the bombshell revelation, and nobody exactly knows how to act. Thankfully we have Mom to distract us. She's looking so much better than a few days ago, and she walks on her own to Asher's car.

We all meet back at her house, helping her get things situated after the unexpected hospital stay. Luckily the burns on her legs won't require much more than changing dressings and time. I bring out the first meal that I prepped, a breakfast casserole, and start warming it up.

"You've been awfully quiet, Pipes," Mom says softly. Her voice is still a little scratchier than usual.

"Just trying to be helpful," I say with a shrug.

"She's probably still mad about what happened last week," Jett mutters.

I expect confusion from my Mom. We haven't told her about Kru or the beatdown or anything. But she turns to me with compassion and says, "Honey, your brothers will get over it. They'll accept him."

A chill runs down my spine, and I slowly turn to face Mom. Tears are in my eyes for some reason. My brothers are looking at each other, confused.

"Wh-what do you mean?"

"Your man. The love of your life," she says with a soft smile. "Herman."

I stare at my mom with wide eyes. There's no way in hell she could know his first name. I am so stunned I can't form a response. Luckily, I have four very opinionated brothers to step in.

"Mom, what the hell are you talking about?" Griffin asks.

Mom turns to Griff, her brows knitting together. "Her boyfriend! Why are you guys acting like I'm speaking nonsense?"

"But…*Mom*. I haven't even told you about him yet," I say slowly.

"None of us have," Dane adds.

Mom's smile stretches wide, almost conspiratorially, as she drifts my way and pats the side of my face. "You didn't have to. Bring him on Wednesday for game night."

****

Kru is understandably hesitant to be in the same room as all four brothers on Wednesday.

"That's eight fists," he says, "all of which will likely land on my face."

"They won't touch you…in front of my mom," I promise.

He smiles down at me, smoothing his hand along the curve of my neck. This is the first dinner service he's leaving in the hands of his team, and it's a big deal for him. A big deal for *us*. I recognize that sacrifice, as a small business owner.

"That's not very reassuring. But you know what? I'll risk it. Because you're worth it."

He bends down and we share a long, passionate kiss. When we're together, it's perfect. I'm falling for him more with every passing second. Meeting the full Keegan clan is the last step to really making this a thing.

"I appreciate you putting yourself in harm's way for our relationship," I tease. "Not to mention leaving the fate of your restaurant with Brady for a full two hours."

"I think he can handle it. And if not, I'm just a short drive away." He smiles, but I can see the tension in his face. It makes me nervous, too.

"Well, luckily they won't expect you to be here every week. But making an appearance once in a while would be nice," I add softly.

"You're thinking long term," he murmurs, brushing his lips against mine.

"I am. Are you?" I look up hopefully into his eyes.

"One hundred percent, Sandpiper."

Kru drives me to game night, a gesture that seems so small but no one has ever done before in my family. The only boyfriends I ever had were so short-term that they never made it home to meet my family. And all of them were while I studied at Ohio University, hours from here, far from my brothers' controlling gazes.

As soon as we get to the house, anxiety really sets in. My belly is tingling. I'm gnawing on my lip as we walk up the sidewalk.

"Listen, they're probably going to be a little...unfriendly," I warn him.

"I can handle it," Kru assures me. "I could always tell them a food joke to break the ice."

"Yeah," I say, trying to imagine how my brothers might receive one of his jokes. "That could help."

Asher opens the door before I can reach the handle. His dark gaze sweeps over the both of us. He sniffs.

Let the hazing begin.

"Hey, Asher," I say brightly.

Kru waves. "Hi. I'm Kru."

Asher stares at Kru for an uncomfortably long time. Then he holds the door open for us to pass through. "Asher."

No *nice to meet you* or general pleasantries. Internally, I'm rolling my eyes. I guess I should be grateful we've made it this far.

"Can you not be a creep?" I hiss to Asher as we pass him by. Inside the house, Mom is seated at the dining room table, and all my brothers are there beside her. The air is tense.

Mom sends us a warm smile—aside from Lia's sweet perma-grin, it's the only smile to be found in the room. She stands, holding her arms out for Kru.

"There's the chef I've heard so much about," she oozes, like she been waiting to meet him for years instead of days. "It's so nice to finally meet you."

Kru looks surprised but pleased as she pulls him into a hug. "Nice to meet you too, Mrs. Keegan. I'm so glad you're feeling better."

"Please call me Laura. And thank you." She pats his arm maternally. "Piper's told me wonderful things about your restaurant."

"I try to feed her every chance I get," he says with a grin. "I think she's tried the whole menu by now." The comment makes my brothers scoff. I shoot them all a collective glare.

"Kru, I'd like you to meet my *brothers*," I say through gritted teeth. "You've already met Asher and Griffin—"

Griffin jerks his head into a nod, still sizing up Kru.

"That's Dane, and Jett next to him. And this here is Lia, Dane's daughter." I ruffle her hair. "She's three, and the cutest Keegan there is. Everybody, meet Kru."

I wait for groans, scoffs, or backtalk. There is none. Instead, there's something worse.

Four sets of eyes boring a hole into Kru.

Kru doesn't let it faze him. "It's really nice to meet you all. And to not be getting punched by Griffin again."

My mom pales, turning to her youngest son. "Griffin! Are you the one that gave Kru that shiner?" Kru's black eye looks better than it did, but there are still swirls of purple and yellow visible.

"I did," Griffin confirms. "And I'd do it again."

"*Griffin*," I say while my brothers snicker.

"I'm sure it was a love tap," Jett says.

"I didn't have to go to the hospital," Kru says as he eases into the chair my mom pulls out for him. "So that was a bonus."

"Are we ready to eat?" I ask, eager to get the focus off of Kru and onto something resembling an easygoing rhythm. I know it will take time for my brothers to warm up to him.

"Let me help," Kru says.

"You left your kitchen to be here. I don't want you serving more people," I say, playfully swatting at him.

"I can do it," Mom says.

"Mom, you need to sit your butt in that chair," Jett says. "We'll take care of it."

"Not you," I warn Kru, gliding past him and heading into the kitchen to start serving food. Dane and Jett join me. Tension crackles between us. I can tell they're dying to needle me about my new boyfriend.

"I don't want to hear it," I warn them in a low voice as we pull plates and collect silverware.

"I didn't say a thing," Jett says wryly.

"You didn't have to. Just please, both of you—*be nice.*" I send them a warning look before I begin plating tonight's dinner, pork chops and mashed potatoes. I carry two plates out, setting one down in front of Kru and the other for Mom. Jett and Dane bring out the rest of the plates for the family, and soon we're all digging in.

"Tastes pretty good, Pipe Cleaner," Dane says.

"Thanks. I've gotten pretty good at mimicking Mom's recipes." I grin over at her, leaning in to kiss her cheek. "But never quite as good as when you do it."

"What do you think, Kru?" Jett asks, something glinting in his gaze.

Kru sweeps his gaze between my brothers, then over to me as though double checking he heard correctly. "I think it's great."

"Probably a little too plain for you, huh?" Jett goes on.

"Not at all," Kru says, clearing his throat. "Piper's an awesome cook. She's got her own style."

"You guys should see how he runs his kitchen," I add, trying to keep the conversation light and interesting. "He's a trained chef, so it runs like clockwork. They even do the 'yes, chef' stuff."

My brothers look mildly impressed.

"You guys should come eat sometime," Kru says. "On the house."

"That's very generous of you," Mom says. "With how expensive it is to run a restaurant, especially."

"A restaurant you had to renovate half of the building for, too," Asher adds before taking a bite of pork chop.

"It was expensive, but necessary," Kru says with a smile. I wonder if he can feel the air crackling. My brothers are gearing up for an attack. "The building is older, and everything was outdated. The reno will get us another twenty years out of it, easily. So that's something to be happy about."

"So the restaurant's going good, huh?" Griffin asks, sawing at his pork chop.

"Extremely well," Kru confirms.

"You're probably gonna need to expand your footprint." Griff has a hard glint in his eye as he takes a sip of water. "Might want more tables, a bigger kitchen, stuff like that. Since it's going so well."

"I'm not ready to think about that," Kru says with a laugh. "I'm just on week two."

"Still, it might make sense someday to want to...grow the dining room," Griffin goes on. I dip my chin, staring hard at him. I know where he's going with this.

"I'm really happy with the size," Kru says. "I think too many more tables would diminish the intimate environment I created."

Griffin deflates slightly.

"So why'd you rope Piper into that reality TV stuff?" Dane asks before he sips at his water. "Are they gonna make her look bad when it airs?"

"You guys, I explained all of this already," I mutter, immediately annoyed.

"I don't think they *could* make her look bad," Kru says with a laugh. "Have you seen her shop? It's like something out of a movie. Piper is the picture-perfect definition of cute neighborhood business owner."

"You're very sweet," I inform Kru. To my brothers, I say, "And I can tell none of you learned listening comprehension skills at any point in your lives."

"It's a valid question," Dane insists. "Reality TV shows hinge on drama. I just want to make sure there won't be any pitchforks coming for you once it airs."

"This was a really tame reality TV show," Kru says affably. He tastes the mashed potatoes, then nods. "These are amazing, Piper. I can tell you did the cayenne trick."

"Cayenne trick?" Jett arches a brow.

"Just chef secrets," I say with a grin before scooping some mashed potatoes into my mouth.

"So you'll be sticking around Bayshore for a while then," Mom says, reaching out to pat Kru's wrist. He smiles warmly at her.

"That's the plan. Bayshore feels like home now," he confirms.

"So you think you're a pretty smart businessman then?" Asher asks.

I sigh, pressing two fingers to the middle of my forehead. "*Asher*."

"I'm just curious about his business plan," Asher says. "Solvency. Longevity. Things like that."

"I don't know if I'm the smartest one out there, but I think I have a pretty solid plan," Kru says with a laugh, ripping off a piece of bread. "Honestly it's been great to swap ideas with your sister. She's really smart."

"Yeah, I bet you used her smarts to get ahead of her in the Best of Bayshore competition," Griffin mutters.

This time, I can't keep my groan inside. "*Griffin*."

"My sons are a bit, well…" Mom begins.

"Rude," I supply for her.

"You're the rude one," Griffin shoots back under his breath.

"Kids," Mom says, in the same voice she used when we were in elementary school. "We have a guest. Let's behave."

"She's saying that to all of you." I gesture with my fork at all four of my brothers.

Silverware clinks against plates for a few tense moments as we continue eating. Finally, Mom turns to Kru. "So tell me again where you're living."

"Right behind Griffin," Kru says.

"Oh! How convenient," Mom enthuses.

"Not convenient," Griffin mutters.

"So you already bought a home here in Bayshore," Mom says.

"No, it's short-term rental. I'm in the middle of renovating the space above the restaurant and plan to move in there." Kru pauses, and I can almost feel the doubt creep through him before he continues. "Where Piper used to live."

The words take a few moments to settle, and each passing second feels like an hour. Griffin knows the truth about what happened there, but I don't know if he's spilled the beans to the rest of the family yet. Curious glances bounce around the table. My entire body is tense.

"So you decided to renovate the apartment after Piper moved in with Griffin?" Asher asks.

Kru glances between me and Asher, like checking with me on how to move forward. But I have no idea how to move forward. I just need us to move through it, and be done with it.

"No, I uh...well, my plans for the business included me living above it and so I, uh..." Kru's throat bobs and he sets his silverware down. "I had to ask her to move out."

The silverware stops clinking. Now all eyes are on me again.

"You kicked her out?" Jett asks.

Kru pauses. "Not *kicked*—"

"So *that's* why you moved in with Griffin!" Jett says it with an ah-ha tone.

"Yes, that's why I moved in with Griffin," I say, trying to keep my voice neutral. But really, my limbs are buzzing and I feel caught somehow.

"And you seriously brought him here for dinner?" Dane asks.

"It was an unfortunate situation," I concede, "but not one that Kru designed to hurt me or anything."

"I didn't know she was my neighbor when I bought the building," Kru adds.

"Did you know about this?" Asher asks Griff.

He nods glumly. "Sure did."

"Why didn't you tell us?" Asher asks.

"She asked me not to," Griff explains.

"Okay, can we talk about something else?" I move my hands through the air like expelling a bad smell. "Please. Anything else. Kru, what should we talk about?"

"Have you told them about the progress—?" He stops short at the same time I see the realization flash through his eyes.

He's trying. I'll give him that. I deflate slightly as I cut off another bite of pork. The questions are immediate.

"What progress?" Griffin asks.

Kru grimaces. "Maybe we should talk about something else—"

"*What progress?*" Griffin repeats.

"No progress," Kru says, waving it off. I know he's trying to backpedal for my sake. He probably didn't mean to bring it up. But we're in this mess because of me. My secrecy. I'm ready to jump headfirst into the hullabaloo.

"You can tell them," I say softly.

"Yeah. *Tell them,*" Asher urges Kru.

"There's a barn on the same property as our businesses," Kru supplies coolly. But I can tell he's straining at the edges. "Piper's been gung-ho on cleaning it up and getting it ready for her business expansion."

"Expansion?" Asher asks carefully, his gaze sliding toward me. "Is this what you were talking about the other night in the hospital?"

"As a matter of fact, yes." I clear my throat, picking at invisible fibers on my leggings. "I'm moving forward with it."

Jett lets out a low whistle.

"Oh my god," Griffin mutters, stabbing his food with his fork.

"What is this idea you're moving forward with, honey?" Mom asks.

"Oh, sorry. I forgot you were in a coma when I brought it up." I clear my throat, readying myself to dive into this again.

"How could you forget mom was in a coma?" Griffin snaps. I can tell he's agitated, which just exhausts me further.

"I didn't—ugh, never mind. Long story short, Mom, I've been wanting to expand my business for a while and now I'm finally going to do it. Even though every male at this table thinks it's a bad idea. Except for you, Kru."

"I didn't realize you were talking about a *barn*. That's a horrible idea," Asher says ominously. "The renovation costs alone are going to kill you. Do you want to jump head first into a money pit?"

His words land like a spear to the chest. "It's not going to *kill* me," I say, but then the frustration overwhelms me and I snap. "Listen, I'm not talking about the barn after all. Can we talk about something else altogether? Something that isn't about me or my business."

"Fine. Let's talk about Kru." Asher's smile goes thin, and I know this isn't the right direction either.

"Have we convinced you yet that we're a normal family?" I say dryly, looking over at Kru.

He offers a smile but it doesn't last long.

"What sort of cuisine do you serve?" Dane asks.

"American."

"So you never learned about other types of cuisine other than our own?" Dane goes on. "Like, French food or something?"

"I learned about them," Kru replies. "But I had a particular vision I wanted to bring to life." He swallows his bite then glances over at me as though saying *here we go*. "And speaking of French food, do you know why the French like snails?"

My brothers all share concerned looks.

"Uh..." Dane says.

Kru grins. "Because they hate fast food."

Silence settles over the table like a punishment. Griffin blinks. Asher furrows his brow. My mom covers her mouth with her napkin as she politely titters.

Not even a fucking consolation laugh from my brothers.

"I don't think they liked my food joke," Kru whispers to me.

"It was a good one," I reassure him, patting his forearm.

"Are you looking into franchising?" Asher asks, blowing past the failed joke entirely.

Kru laughs softly and shakes his head. Maybe now he understands what I'm dealing with here. "I don't know about franchising. But there's definitely a market for expansion in other ways."

"Like what ways?" Asher asks, sounding like he might actually be simply curious, instead of calculating.

"Well, I've actually had some interest from investors," Kru says, cutting into his pork chop. "There's a group in Columbus that's been following me from the reality show. They think my concept would translate well to a bigger market. One of the investors came to eat at my restaurant the other night and asked me to call him. We had a pretty long talk about his offer."

My fork freezes halfway to my mouth. Columbus. He's never mentioned Columbus before...or this investor. "You got an offer?"

"Columbus is a great market," Dane cuts in, perking up with interest. "Lots of young professionals, good restaurant scene."

"That's what they tell me," Kru agrees, ignoring my question. "They want to meet next week to discuss possibilities."

"Next week?" The question comes out sharper than I intended, and everyone looks at me.

"Tuesday," Kru says, his eyes flicking to mine briefly before looking away. "I'd drive down Monday night and meet with them Tuesday morning to look at a space."

"And you're just mentioning this now?" I can't keep the hurt out of my voice. Going to Columbus to look at a new space for a restaurant is *huge*.

"I was going to tell you," he says quickly. "I just wanted to have more details before I said anything. Didn't want to worry you over something that might not even happen."

"But it might happen," I say quietly.

"It might," he admits.

The room has gone silent except for the soft clink of silverware. My brothers are all watching this exchange with barely concealed interest.

"That's smart," Asher says finally. "You should always explore your options, especially in the restaurant business. High failure rate."

"It's just a meeting," Kru says, but he's looking at my brothers, not me. "Nothing's decided."

"Of course," Mom says gently. "But it's exciting to have options."

"When would this happen?" I ask, my voice sounding hollow. "If they made you an offer?"

Kru shifts uncomfortably in his chair. "I don't know. Soon, I guess."

This detail sinks like a lead weight in my gut. The fact that I'm hearing about this at the table, at the same time as my brothers, puts me on edge.

Maybe they're right to be cautious. Maybe I should be a little more cautious too.

But that's something to think about later. More than anything, I want to make it through this disaster of a game night. Maybe there's a chance we can turn this ship around. I do my best to rally, to put on a smiling face. We steer the conversation back to calmer topics; plates are cleared; cards are dealt; the hourglass is brought closer to watch and so Kru can say hi. Kru opts to watch the first round since he's never played euchre, and I stick close to his side so I can explain the rules as he watches Dane play. Despite the raucous rounds of cards, I can't stop thinking about his news about the Columbus investor.

Why didn't he tell me?

After a full game, I realize I don't have the energy to be here anymore. My mood is sinking the longer we stay, and I want to avoid any additional interrogation from my brothers. If I hear one more comment about my poor business decisions, I'm going to snap. Once we finish the first round, I stand.

"All right, guys, we better get going."

"Hey, come on Pipe Cleaner, don't be a sore loser," Jett goads me, since he just won the first round with Griffin as his partner.

"Not being a sore loser; just being a responsible business owner." I point to the wall clock. "It's time for Kru to get back to the kitchen."

I get the sense that Kru is relieved. If I've been eager to go since we set foot inside, I'm sure his own discomfort has been even worse. While my brothers grumble, Kru thanks everyone for the invitation.

"Maybe I'll catch on to euchre the next time around," he says sweetly. But deep inside my heart, I'm worried he's just trying to be nice. Because he'll never come back after the way he was treated tonight. In fact, I'm positive that everything he saw and everything he heard has pushed him in the opposite direction.

After all, he's already opening a side door. There are bigger things waiting for him, away from Bayshore. I ignore the wrench in my chest and push through goodbyes. But there's something heavy on my heart, and I can't keep it inside much longer.

"Kru, go on outside. I'll be out in a second," I tell him softly. He nods and heads out the front door. Once the door clicks shut, I turn to my brothers.

"I hope you're all happy with yourselves," I bite out. Four pairs of eyes in varying shades of blue look back at me, each Keegan brother his own version of cocky satisfaction.

"Quite happy," Asher confirms, "to be thinking ahead and protecting you."

"Thanks so much for the *protection*." I use exaggerated air quotes around the word. "I don't think I'll be coming back to game night for a while. I need some time to think, because whatever you guys think you're doing to help me isn't working."

Mom tuts, coming to standing. "Piper—"

"I'll come visit you soon, Mom," I promise her, wrapping her in a quick hug. "I need to go."

I hurry out of the house before I can hear any dissent or complaints. My throat is tight as I hurry to the truck, which is running and warm as I slip inside.

I look over at Kru, unsure where to begin. He's shrouded in darkness, but still I can see the weight of the evening hanging between us.

"I'm so sorry," I begin.

He offers a smile, but it looks sad. He doesn't say anything as he puts the truck in reverse. Once he's backed out of the driveway, he finally says, "You warned me. No need to apologize."

I cover my face with my hands, sinking back into the seat. "They're just...ridiculous."

He clears his throat. "You keep a lot of things from them, huh?"

"You see how they get whenever I do *anything*," I reply. "It's been like this my entire life."

"But hiding from it doesn't help, either," he says.

"Yeah, I know that. But..." There's a frightening cocktail of frustration building up inside my chest. It's effervescent. Explosive. It feels like I could both dissolve and turn into a firework. "Sometimes it's just not worth the effort. It's not productive. They're so *judgmental*. They think they're helping but they're just...squashing."

Kru is quiet as we drive through the streets of Bayshore. I take a few deep breaths, trying to put the botched game night behind us.

"I hope they haven't scared you off," I finally say. "They'll laugh at a food joke of yours someday, I bet."

Kru remains quiet, which makes my doubts and fears spiral even harder. I'm finally ready to address the knot that's been in my gut all night.

"So...I didn't realize you were planning on leaving Bayshore soon," I say. As soon as the words leave my mouth I regret them.

"I never said that was the plan, Piper." There's no humor in his voice.

"Sounded like it's a possibility though."

"Everything is a possibility," he says as he pulls onto my brother's street. "We're small business owners. You know this as well as I do."

I mull over his words. "Opening up new location takes a lot of time and attention. If it's a good deal, though...you'll take it?"

He pauses before he says, "Probably."

"Then you'd have to be in Columbus," I finish for him.

He sighs. "Piper, I don't know. It's too soon to say. It's why I didn't say anything."

"But you'll tell my brothers the vultures before you even give me a heads up." I'm focusing on the neighborhood flashing beyond the window, trying to stave off the tears threatening to spill. The truck slows as he approaches Griff's house and then pulls into the driveway. My heart is throbbing—I feel like I've been broken up with somehow. Like he's done it without saying the words.

Maybe this is my brothers' suspicion rubbing off. Or maybe I'm just finally seeing the reality of the situation.

"It just happened to come up," Kru says. "What do you want me to say? I don't think there's any sense in worrying you when you've got so much going on."

With those words, something stony slides over me.

I'm so tired of being the last one to know. The last one anyone thinks can take care of something or understand. "Yeah. I probably can't handle it, huh?"

Kru shoots me a dark look. "That's not what I said."

The tears are coming fast now. I need to get out of here and inside, where I can unravel completely.

"Hope Brady was okay without you," I say quickly, pushing open the door. "I'll see you later, Kru."

I slam the truck door shut and race inside before he can respond.

And in my head all I can hear are my brothers saying *I told you so.*

CHAPTER TWENTY-THREE

KRU

It's been three days since the Keegan brother gauntlet, and I haven't seen Piper once.

Not that I haven't tried. I've made excuses to check the shared storage room at least a dozen times, hoping to catch her coming or going. I've lingered by the front windows of my restaurant during her busy morning rush, telling myself I'm just observing foot traffic patterns. I even walked past Cloud Nine on my way to the bank yesterday, but Jerrica was working the counter and Piper was nowhere to be seen. I'm ready to make a surprise visit to Griffin's house, or even her Mom's house, but I think that might earn me another black eye if I try.

Still worth it to figure out what the hell is going on with Piper.

The barn has been dark every night. No late-night renovation sessions, no industrial work lights casting shadows across the parking lot. Either she's taking a break from the project, or she's avoiding the one place she knows I might look for her.

I'm betting on the latter.

"Chef, table six is asking about wine pairings for the lobster special," Jackie says, pulling me out of my brooding.

"Tell them the Chardonnay," I say absently, plating another order. "The one from Oregon."

"Already did. They want something different."

I look up from the plate I'm working on, realizing I've been on autopilot for the past hour. The lunch service has been steady but not overwhelming, which means I have too much time to think. Too much time to replay Wednesday night over and over in my head.

The way Piper's face shuttered when I mentioned Columbus. The hurt in her voice when she asked if my plan was to leave Bayshore. The careful distance that had blossomed between us, polite but rooted.

I fucked up. I knew it the moment the words left my mouth, but I'd been so focused on not making things worse with her brothers that I'd made things worse with her instead.

"The Sauvignon Blanc then," I tell Jackie. "The one with the citrus notes."

She nods and heads back to the dining room. I finish plating the order and slide it toward Rafael, then check my phone for the hundredth time today. No messages from Piper.

I texted her Thursday morning, a simple *Hope you're doing okay*, but got no response. Friday I tried calling, but it went straight to voicemail. By now, I've gotten the message loud and clear: she needs space.

The problem is, I don't know if that space is temporary or permanent.

"Order up," I call, sliding two more plates toward Rafael.

Jackie appears at my elbow. "Hey, chef? That investor guy is here again. Table twelve."

I glance through the kitchen doors toward the dining room. Sure enough, Tyler Webb is sitting at table twelve, the same table he'd occupied last week when he'd first approached me about Columbus. Tall, silver-haired, expensive suit that screams success.

"He's not supposed to meet with me until Tuesday," I mutter.

"He said he was just grabbing lunch." Jackie shrugs. "But it seems like he wants to talk."

I wipe my hands on my apron, considering how this conversation might go. Part of me wants to ignore him, to focus on the lunch service and pretend Columbus doesn't exist. But another part—the practical, business-minded part—knows I should at least hear what he has to say. The truth is that I feel like I have my hands full right now. I'm happy with what's happening in Bayshore. But maybe I need to be more aggressive while I'm young.

Maybe I need to leave my comfort zone.

"Take over for a few minutes," I tell Brady. "I'll be right back."

I hang up my apron then make my way through the dining room, nodding at familiar customers as I pass. Tyler looks up as I approach, his face breaking into that practiced investor smile.

"Kru! Hope you don't mind me dropping by unannounced. I was in the area and couldn't resist trying that lobster special again."

"A lover of food is always welcome here," I say, sliding into the chair across from him. "How is it?"

"Perfection, as always. The nutmeg marshmallow is to die for." He takes another bite, then sets down his fork. "Actually, I'm glad I caught you. I wanted to give you a heads up about Tuesday's meeting."

"Oh?"

"The group is very excited about this opportunity. Very excited." His eyes gleam with the fervor of someone who smells money. "We're prepared to make you an offer that I think you'll find difficult to refuse."

My stomach does a weird flip. "What kind of offer?"

"Your reputation precedes you. Between this menu, the quality of the food you create, and the fame you've built in the restaurant world from the reality TV show, a few of my partners have agreed to fast track this endeavor."

"Fast track?"

"Full funding for the Columbus location buildout. We're talking about a flagship restaurant in the Short North district—prime real estate, built-in customer base. We're taking away the risk so you can get up and profitable practically instantly."

It's everything I should want. Everything I came to Bayshore to build toward, happening faster than I'd dreamed.

So why does it feel like a trap?

"That's...generous," I say carefully.

"We believe in your concept. And frankly, we think you're wasted in a small town like this." Tyler gestures around the dining room, which is nearly full even on a Monday afternoon. "Don't get me wrong, you're doing well here. But Columbus? That's where you could really make your mark."

Make your mark. The phrase echoes in my head. Isn't that what I came here to do? Honor my dad's memory by building something significant?

"What would the timeline look like?" I ask.

"Fast. We'd want you in Columbus by the new year, ready to open by March. We've already identified the perfect space; it just needs your touch. That's the place we'll look at on Tuesday."

Less than three months. Was that enough time to train up a full crew that could operate without me? Besides, that means I'd have to leave Bayshore.

Leave the restaurant I've just opened. Leave the community that's starting to feel like home.

Leave Piper.

"I know it seems quick," Tyler continues. "But in this business, you have to move fast. Your reality show buzz won't last forever, and that's the best time to have your restaurant open in the capital of Ohio, coinciding with the reality show premiere."

He's right about that. The show is set to air in a few months, and there's no better buzz than at the beginning. This could be my one shot at real expansion, real success. Everything he's saying is so reasonable and exciting.

So why am I not jumping at the chance?

"I'll need to think about it," I say finally.

"Of course. But don't think too long." Tyler's smile turns slightly predatory. "Opportunities like this don't come around often."

He finishes his lunch and leaves, promising to see me Tuesday. I head back to the kitchen, pausing to peer through the window into the dining room. A few customers are taking pictures of their food, probably posting to social media. A couple at the corner table is sharing Piper's s'mores dessert, which I've started ordering weekly from her.

This is what I built. This warmth, this community feeling. It's exactly what I wanted when I came to Bayshore.

But it's also small. Limited. Columbus would be bigger in every way—more customers, more revenue, more recognition.

More distance from the complications of dating your tenant.

I shake my head, standing up. I'm not making this decision because of Piper. I can't. This has to be about business, about my future, about honoring my dad's legacy in the best way possible.

Even if the thought of leaving makes my chest feel tight.

I catch a glimpse of strawberry blonde hair through the front window. My heart does a stupid leap before I realize it's not Piper—just a customer with similar coloring.

I've been looking for her in every face, listening for her laugh in every conversation. Wednesday night had created distance between us, but it hadn't erased the connection. Not for me.

The question is whether it has for her.

Back in the kitchen, Brady updates me on the orders that came in while I was gone. We fall into the familiar rhythm of lunch service, and my mind returns to wandering. To Columbus, to the choice I'm going to have to make.

And to Piper, working alone in her shop just a few hundred feet away, probably wondering if I've already made up my mind to leave.

The truth is, a month ago my path seemed clear: build the restaurant, honor Dad's memory, expand when the right opportunity came along.

Now everything feels muddled, complicated by feelings I wasn't supposed to develop and a relationship that was supposed to stay simple.

Maybe Tyler is right. Maybe I need to get back to basics, focus on the business, make the smart choice rather than the emotional one.

But as I plate another order and call out "Order up," I can't shake the feeling that the smart choice and the right choice might be two different things.

And I have no idea how to tell the difference.

As the day goes on, I'm stuck in a constant Piper loop in my head. It's killing me that she's gone radio silent. I poke my head into Cloud Nine two more times, but no Piper to be seen – just Jerrica. After a pummeling dinner service, I'm more than ready to head home and relax for the next day or two. As much as a small business owner *can* relax on off days, at least.

After saying goodbye to the crew, I lock up the restaurant and step into the cool October night. At the other end of the lot, the barn is glowing.

My heart twists in my chest. It's damn near midnight, and I'm a little worried about what I might find in there.

As I get closer, I hear music again—this time, a thumping electronic beat. I slide the door open just enough to peer inside.

Piper is on her hands and knees in the middle of the space, scrubbing the worn wooden floor with an enormous scrub brush. The place is flooded with bright light, even more lights installed than the last time I saw her in here working. She's wearing the same paint-splattered overalls over a Cloud Nine hoodie, her hair pulled back in two French braids.

She pauses, sits back on her haunches, and lets out a deep sigh. Her shoulders slump, and she buries her face in her hands. The sight of her makes my heart wrench.

"Piper?"

She startles, twisting to look back toward the door. When she spots me, her expression is guarded. Not hostile, exactly, but not welcoming either.

"Oh. It's you."

The coolness in her voice stings more than I expected. "Yeah, it's me. The guy you've been ignoring for three days."

She turns back to the bucket at her side, dipping the scrub brush in. "I haven't been ignoring you."

"Really? Because I've texted, called, and even stopped by your shop enough times to probably make Jerrica think I'm a stalker. And you're always 'unavailable.'" I step further into the barn, taking in the changes since the last time I stopped in. Despite how much progress she's made, it still seems like the road ahead is endless. "I was starting to wonder if you'd ghosted me again."

That gets a reaction. She pauses mid-scrub, her shoulders tensing.

"I wasn't ghosting you," she says quietly. "I was trying to get my head straight."

"Away from me, apparently."

"Away from all the self-righteous opinions of the men in my life," she snaps, finally looking at me. "I need space to think. To figure out what I actually want and how I'm going to do it alone."

The words hit harder than they should. "You don't have to do it alone."

"Don't I?" She tosses the scrub brush into the bucket and folds her arms across her chest. "My brothers don't support me. And I know you say it's a maybe, but I see the writing on the wall. Kru, you're not gonna stay here."

I open my mouth to argue, then close it.

"Look, I get it," she continues, her voice softening slightly. "My brothers are unhinged. You got punched once already. They'll probably never accept you. Besides, the reality show wrapped up, and you've got investors interested in Columbus. Why tie yourself down to this small town and my ogre brothers?"

"That's not—" I start, but she cuts me off.

"It's fine, Kru. Really. I'll come to terms with it eventually. I've been keeping busy anyway." She gestures around the barn. "I've been getting quotes from construction companies, applying for small business loans, really getting the road map nailed down so this thing can be ready by spring. I told you I'd figure out a way, and I will. Somehow."

I step closer, noting the exhaustion in her movements, the dark circles under her eyes. "How many hours have you been out here today?"

She pauses, seeming to calculate. "I don't know. I did other things. But I started around five a.m."

"Five a.m.? Jesus, Piper. It's after midnight."

She waves a dismissive hand, which makes her sway slightly. "I'm fine. Just trying to advance while I figure out the financing. If I can get more stuff done on my own, then the construction company quotes might be more affordable. I'm doing this on a tight budget."

But as she gestures toward her work, I can see she's not fine at all. She almost looks drunk, a slight tremor in her hands that could be from cold or exhaustion or both. She's running on fumes and sheer stubborn determination.

"When's the last time you ate something?" I ask.

"I had a sandwich earlier. Or maybe that was yesterday." She reaches for the scrub brush again, but she's sluggish. Uncoordinated.

"Piper, you need to stop. It's freezing out here, it's late, and I'm certain you've pulled multiple twenty-hour days in row."

"I need to get this done for the last construction quote," she insists, but her words trail off. Her eyes flutter closed for a moment, and I see her body start to go limp.

"Piper!"

I lunge forward just as she begins to fall backwards, catching her in my arms as the scrub brush clatters to the floor. My heart is pounding so hard I can hear it in my ears. *What the fuck?* I look down at her, arranging her in my arms carefully.

Her eyes snap open a moment later, confusion clouding her features. "What...what happened?"

"You fell asleep sitting up," I say, my voice tight with worry. "Or maybe fainted. I caught you before you cracked your skull on the floor."

She blinks slowly, like she's trying to process this information. "Thank you. I'm awake now. I just need a minute." But she doesn't move to leave my embrace.

"No, you need sleep. And food." I slowly get to my feet, hoisting her in my arms. I start to carry her toward the barn door. "I'm taking you to my place."

"No." She struggles weakly in my arms. "I can handle this on my own. Just drop me off at Griffin's. I'm fine."

"You're not fine. You just collapsed."

"I can take care of myself."

That's when something inside me finally snaps.

"Piper. *Please.* Why won't you just let me help you?" The words come out louder than I intended, echoing in the barn. "It doesn't have to be like this. You don't have to do everything on your own."

She looks up at me, startled by the intensity in my voice.

"You'll get more done if you take care of yourself," I continue, my voice softening but no less passionate. "Let me help you. Let me show you how much I love you."

The words hang in the air between us. I hadn't meant to say it like that, but there it is. The truth I've been dancing around for weeks.

I love her. I'm in love with her. And I can't stand watching her kill herself trying to prove she doesn't need anyone.

I carry her out of the barn and across the parking lot to my truck, ignoring her weak protests. The drive to Griffin's house is short, but she relaxes into the front seat, eyes closed, exhaustion finally winning over stubbornness.

Griffin's living room light is on when we pull into the driveway. I carry Piper to the front door and kick the door.

Griffin opens the door, takes one look at us, and his expression shifts from confusion to concern. "What happened? Is she okay?"

"She's fine," I say, stepping inside. "But she needs sleep. She pushed herself way too hard today."

I carry Piper down the hallway to her bedroom, setting her gently on the bed. She's half-asleep, but she manages to mumble, "I can take care of myself."

"I know you can," I say softly, brushing a paint-streaked strand of hair from her face. "But wouldn't it be better if we take care of each other?"

I pop off her shoes, take off her socks, and get her down to bra and panties so she's more comfortable in bed. Once she's tucked in, I press a kiss to her forehead.

"Sleep in tomorrow, or I'm going to chain you to this bed next time, and not in the sexy way."

That earns me a weak smile before her eyes flutter closed.

Griffin is waiting in the living room when I emerge, his arms crossed and his expression unreadable. The man looks like a guard dog—he's truly a huge athlete, and I can't help but think about the last time he and I were in this living room together. My left eye starts throbbing from the memory.

"What the fuck is going on?" Griffin asks gruffly.

"She's been working on the barn," I explain. "Nonstop. Waking up at five a.m. and doing nothing else, not even eating."

"Why are you letting her do that?"

There's something in his tone that instantly grates on me. Thank god Piper wasn't here to hear it.

"Are you fucking serious right now?" It's too late and I'm too tired for cordiality. After the day I had, after what I just went through with Piper, I can't school my voice in the slightest. "I don't control her. And neither do you."

"Don't you care about her?" Griffin steps closer.

"More than you even fucking know." I match his step until we're in the center of the living room, staring each other down. "I caught her tonight when she fell asleep sitting up and almost cracked her head on the floor."

Griffin's face darkens. "Jesus."

My frustration with the situation spills out of me. "She's going to kill herself trying to prove she doesn't need anybody. Because she thinks she has to do this alone."

"What do you mean *alone*?" Griffin asks. "She has her brothers and...*you*, I guess."

"But she doesn't see that," I say. "And you and your brothers aren't helping. In fact, you're making it so much fucking worse, and you don't even realize it. She's so desperate to show you guys she's capable that she's pushing herself past the breaking point. And all you guys do is tell her why she's making the wrong decisions."

"We're just trying to look out for her—"

"By making her feel like she has to prove herself every damn day, about every damn thing?" I shake my head. "Is that what you want? For her to work herself into the ground just to earn your respect?"

Griffin is quiet for a long moment. "No," he says finally. "That's not what we want."

"Then you need to ease up on her. Stop questioning every decision she makes. Stop treating her like she doesn't know what she's doing."

Griffin's jaw ticks and I begin bracing myself for another punch. I don't make it a habit to come into another man's house and tell him how to treat his baby sister, but this is an important exception.

"I don't think you have the right to comment on my family." He steps closer again, energy crackling between us.

"I get it," I tell him. "I'm the new boyfriend. You all can shit on me if you want. But Piper is my girlfriend, and I'm going to support every last fucking thing she wants to do. I believe in *her*. Her vision, her dreams, her future. And the shit I heard you guys saying to her this week was really fucking disappointing."

Griffin is looming over me now. I wonder if he's weighing his options: punch, or maybe just throw me out of his house by the collar.

But I can't stop now. I'm not going to watch her shrink and fidget through another game night, terrified of what her brothers are going to say to her.

"You're gonna lose her if you don't back off," I add, not breaking eye contact. I don't flinch; I don't retreat. I just hold my ground. Griffin might be like the attack dog who can smell fear, and if that's the case, he's not going to smell it on me.

Silence throbs between us, and finally Griffin says, "You think we're too hard on her?"

A sarcastic laugh escapes me. "Absolutely."

He props his hands on his hips, gaze dropping to the floor. "She hasn't said a word to me since game night."

"You might have a lot more of that to look forward to if you guys don't start getting on her level. She's brilliant. She's built something incredible with the shop. And now she's going to make something equally as amazing with the barn. She needs support and recognition. Not well-meaning criticism."

Griffin nods slowly, and I can see him processing what I've said. I head to the door. I'm probably out of face-punching danger, but one can never be too sure.

"You and your brothers can do what you want," I tell him, my hand on the doorknob. "But I think you all want a big happy family. And Piper hasn't been happy. She's been telling you all along, but none of you have been listening."

"Oh, come on," Griff says, following me. "You're in her life for like five minutes and think you have something to say?"

I turn to face him. "I didn't even need five minutes. I saw it after ten seconds. And yeah, I do have something to say, especially when it comes to making sure Piper feels supported and heard."

Griff scowls at me. "Gonna be hard to see and hear her from Columbus, buddy."

I take issue with the way he calls me *buddy*. But now's not the time to invite a fistfight with this brute of a brother. "Good thing I'll be right here in Bayshore then."

"Oh. You backing out of the deal already?"

I laugh, but there's no humor in it. "Man. You just can't pass up a chance to make somebody second guess their plans, huh? Sometimes, I can't tell if you're her brother or her bully."

His scowl deepens. "It's time for you leave before I make you leave."

He doesn't have to tell me twice. I let myself out of the house, my mind churning with thoughts. Maybe I went too far. Maybe I didn't go far enough. Maybe Piper's going to flip her shit when she finds out I talked about any of it with her brother.

As I walk back to my truck, something settles into place inside me.

Columbus is a non-option.

Not because it's too much, too soon. Not because of what Griffin said.

But because I'm all in with Piper. With Bayshore. With the business I chose and built and am loving, right next to the woman I found and fell for and am crazier about every day.

This is not the time to walk away.

This is the time to dive deeper into my dream...and hers.

Because I'm not going to lose myself in it. I'm going to grow right alongside her.

Columbus can wait. Because I *am* expanding, just in a different way than I expected.

I was drawn to Bayshore for a reason. And now I'm staying for a reason.

CHAPTER TWENTY-FOUR

PIPER

I wake up to sunlight streaming through my bedroom window. I jolt upright. What time is it? Why is it daytime and I'm still in bed? How late am I to open the shop?

Then I realize it's Sunday. I'm off today. And hell, I feel rested. A sigh of relief escapes me just as the events of last night come flooding back. The barn. Collapsing. Kru carrying me home like I was made of spun glass.

Let me show you how much I love you.

The words echo in my head as warmth coats my limbs. He loves me. I can't fight the smile. He actually spoke the words that I'd been feeling inside me too.

And then there was the conversation I'd overheard after he tucked me into bed. I'd been almost back to sleep when I heard the sharp undertones of Griff and Kru's conversation. Their voices had been clear through the thin walls and my curiosity—and shock—kept me awake long enough to eavesdrop before I finally passed out for good.

She's going to kill herself trying to prove she doesn't need anybody.

I grab my phone from the nightstand and dial Bella before I can second-guess myself. She answers on the second ring, her voice bright.

"Pipe Cleaner! Everything okay? You're lucky I'm up this early."

"Oh my god." I slap my forehead. "I totally forgot you and Jackson are back in LA!"

"It's fine. I was just about to start stretching while Jackson goes for a run. I'm still on eastern time for now. What's up?"

"I need to tell you something." I take a deep breath, wondering where to begin. "Kru told me he loves me last night."

She gasps. "Kru? You mean the guy you told me it wasn't serious with?"

"Yes, him."

"The one who's first name you didn't know because that's how not-serious it was?" she goes on.

"*Yes*, Bella. And I know his first name now, just so you understand how serious it is."

"Once you know your boyfriend's first name, it's only a hop, skip, and a jump to marriage," she cracks.

I tell her everything—the barn, the exhaustion, nearly hitting my head on the floor. And then I tell her about the conversation afterward, the one I wasn't supposed to hear.

"He stood up to Griffin," I finish. "He defended me. He said he couldn't tell if Griffin was my brother or my bully. I can't believe it. I was just waiting for Griffin to get mad and start punching him but I...I think he listened."

"Piper." Bella's voice is soft with amazement. "Do you realize what this means?"

"That I fell in love with a man who's about to move away?"

"No, silly. It means you hit the jackpot. Kru is a perfect match for you. He's an entrepreneur, motivated, and down to go along with big ideas like the barn. He'll take a punch from your brother *and* put them in their place. I'd say you need to find out this man's middle name and marry him immediately." She laughs, and then her voice softens. "This just reminded me of something."

My body is buzzing with feels. "What is it?"

"Do you remember when you called me after the Cleveland night?" She sounds breathless. "The night when you first met Kru."

I think back. Bella was the first person I'd called after that whirlwind hookup. I'd been floating, soaring, and blissed out, completely high on the life-changing hookup that I knew had to stay only that.

"Vaguely," I say. "I was completely high on Uncle Lobster so my memory is a little fuzzy."

"The first thing you said when I picked up the phone was that you had met your soul mate," she said. "And look at what's happened since then, even when you tried to stop it. Three-months-ago you would have never brought a man to game night. The old Piper would have kept him a secret forever instead of risking your brothers' judgment."

The truth of her words hits me like a gentle slap. She's right. Kru coming into my life started a chain reaction of change.

"You're on the cusp of something big," Bella continues. "And it's exciting, isn't it? Scary as hell, but exciting."

"Yeah," I whisper. "It is. But what if he leaves? I would never stop him from chasing his own dreams and his own changes."

"You support him. And you love him. And you trust that your paths will unfold exactly as they're meant to. Look at how you two have come together already. I don't think this is the end of the road. Bayshore is only a few hours away from Columbus and besides..." She laughs. "Even if he tries to walk away from what's growing, like I did with Jackson, I'm pretty sure he'll coming running back in a month because he realizes what a mistake he made."

A few tears escape my eyes. My heart feels so full. "Yeah. You did leave a famous rock star behind so you could move to Australia, didn't you?"

"Luckily he didn't hold it against me. Because he didn't want to hold me back. Jackson wants me to soar. Like Kru wants you to."

After we hang up, I find myself smiling as I get dressed. The house is quiet—too quiet for a Sunday morning with Griffin home. I pad to the kitchen and find a note on the counter in his messy handwriting:

Had to run some errands. Left you some coffee & hoping you will talk to me someday soon. -G

Before I can wonder what errands require leaving this early on a Sunday, my phone buzzes with a text from Kru.

KRU: Hey BagPiper. You have an appointment at Serenity Spa at noon. My treat. You need a self-care day after all that hard work.

PIPER: I don't know how to feel about BagPiper. Feeling very good about the spa day though.

KRU: That's your nickname of the day. I can't change it.

PIPER: OK, Kroupon.

KRU: Not really a fan of that one either.

KRU: Oh and it's your choice at the spa. Massage, facial, whatever you want.

My throat gets tight with emotion. After everything that's happened between us, after the distance and misunderstandings, he's still taking care of me.

PIPER: Thank you. This is incredibly sweet.

KRU: It's what boyfriends do. You deserve to be taken care of, Maven. Even if you don't always let people do it.

Serenity Spa is tucked into a converted Victorian house on the edge of downtown Bayshore, all soft lighting and essential oil diffusers. I'm checking in at the front desk when I hear a familiar voice behind me.

"There's my beautiful daughter."

I turn to find Mom walking through the front door, looking more vibrant than she has since before the fire. She's wearing a soft blue sweater that brings out her eyes, and her smile is radiant.

"Mom! What are you doing here?"

"Your sweet lover boy called me this morning. Said you had a spa day planned and wondered if I'd like to join you." She links her arm through mine. "I hope you don't mind that I joined."

My eyes well up with tears. "I don't mind at all. In fact, this is even better. How did he get your number?"

"I think he got it from Griffin."

That news has my head spinning. Talk about change. My boyfriend is conspiring with my brother—and my mom—behind my back to pull off sweet gestures?

We spend the next four hours being pampered. Side-by-side massages where we giggle like teenagers. Facials that leave our skin glowing. Manicures where Mom chooses a bold red polish, even though I haven't seen her with painted nails in over two decades. She'd never have gotten her nails painted before the fire. It's just one of many little changes since she woke up from the coma that have me scratching my head.

During lunch at the spa's café, she reaches across the table and takes my hand.

"I heard what happened last night," she says softly.

My cheeks heat up. "Griffin told you?"

"No. Kru mentioned it when we spoke this morning, saying that was why he wanted to send you to get pampered. He told me about the barn. And how exhausted you were." She sends me a stern, motherly look, which softens before she adds, "And he told me he had a...*conversation* with Griffin when he dropped you off."

"Yes. Which I overheard. Did he tell you the details?"

"He didn't. But I can imagine what it was about." She squeezes my hand. "Piper, I need to say something. I know I always say that your brothers mean well. Because they do. They love you fiercely, but sometimes that love comes out as fear. They've already lost their father, and they all saw how much Dad doted on you. You were his precious, protected angel, and I think they adopted that mindset when it came to you. The thought of losing you—to exhaustion, to a broken heart, to anything—terrifies them."

"I know," I say quietly.

"But fear isn't a good reason to stop living. Or stop dreaming." Her eyes get distant for a moment. "After your father died, I chose to play it safe. Keeping all of you close, never taking risks, never allowing any of us to get hurt again."

"I can understand why," I say. "As a suddenly single mom with five little kids, I would have done the same."

"But I think I took it too far. Maybe I fed too much into the overprotection," she says with a sigh. "So I'm sorry for that. I know your father would have wanted all of us to live fully, love deeply, and chase our dreams no matter the cost." She smiles, reaching for my hand. "We never know what tomorrow will be our last, sweetheart. I've been thinking about this a lot since the fire. I was granted a second chance, and I want to see all of my children going after what they truly want. Barns included."

My throat tightens as I look into her warm, smiling face. "Thanks, Mom."

After our spa day, as Mom and I are walking to our cars, I pull out my phone to text Kru.

PIPER: *Thank you for today. It was perfect. Can I see you tonight?*

His response comes quickly.

KRU: I can't tonight, but will see you ASAP. I miss you.

His answer stings, even though it's probably legitimate. I want to know more, but I'm also a little scared it's because he's on his way to Columbus. I don't feel ready to confront that yet. Mom must see something in my expression because she pats my arm.

"Give him time, honey. Sometimes the best gifts take a while to unwrap."

"What do you mean?" I ask, studying her face. "Is he planning something?"

She just gives me the same mysterious smile she's been wearing since she woke up from the coma, then leans in and kisses my cheek.

Monday morning arrives crisp and clear. For the first time in a while, I'm not running on pure caffeine and determination.

The spa day worked its magic—my shoulders don't ache, my mind feels clear. I am ready to run myself into the ground again.

No, wait. I'm supposed to be taking better care of myself. I'll figure that out as I go, I suppose.

Once I'm dressed and ready for the day, I pop my head out the back door, temping the air. It's pretty chilly, but still biking weather. I'm out the door and cruising up to Cloud Nine by seven. Jerrica is scheduled to open again for me today so I can focus on Barny.

As soon as I pull into the lot, I pump my brakes and stop short. There are vehicles in the parking lot. Plural. All parked and gathered near the barn.

My stomach dips. I didn't have anything planned for today other than visiting the barn and taking in all my progress. I don't think it's customary for construction companies to come unbidden for a quote, either.

So what the hell is going on over there?

My heart starts thumping as I pedal over. I park my bike next to an unfamiliar silver truck. And that's when I notice a *very* familiar black truck a few cars down. Next to Griffin's black sedan.

The barn doors are closed, but deep, male voices are spilling out. I slide the big door open, completely unprepared for what I see inside.

Kru is there, sleeves rolled up, conferring with another man while holding unfurled blueprints. Griffin is carrying lumber with Dane. Asher and Jett are clearing debris from one corner. A few other men I don't recognize are walking around the barn taking measurements. And then I realize who's standing at Kru's side—Hazel's husband, Grayson Daly.

They all turn when they hear the door rattle open.

"There she is," Kru says, his smile soft and warm. "Honestly I was worried we wouldn't make it here before you this morning."

"What...what is this?" I manage to ask.

Grayson steps forward, hand extended. "Hey there, Piper. Long time no see. Kru called me yesterday, said you had a vision that needed some professional input."

I shake his hand numbly, looking around at my brothers, who are all watching me with expressions I can't quite read.

"I don't understand," I say. "You guys don't want me to be doing this."

"Your boyfriend here laid it out pretty clearly," Asher says, leaning against a support beam. "You've got a solid business plan, you're willing to put in the work, and we've been idiots for not supporting you or listening to you from the beginning."

"You're awesome, Piper," Jett adds. "We shouldn't have needed a near stranger to make us really see you."

"And as I saw with my own two eyes, you've been killing yourself trying to do this alone," Griffin adds. "Which stops today."

"But I don't have the money yet for a full crew—"

"Friends and family discount," Grayson interrupts with a grin. "Plus, you've got plenty of free labor right here." He gestures to my brothers. "If you're willing for the project to take a tad longer, we can make this happen really affordably, especially with your brothers stepping up. I'll be able to fit this project into the margins of my current schedule. Kru walked me through your Pinterest boards this morning and he gave me all the outlines and blueprints you've drawn up. Your vision is incredible, Piper. Let's make it happen."

I look at Kru, who's watching me with an expression so tender it makes my chest ache.

"You did this," I whisper.

"*You* did this," he corrects. "I just made some phone calls."

I'm unable to keep myself away from Kru any longer, brothers be damned. I leap into his arms, wrapping my legs around him as I shriek with laughter.

"I can't believe this," I gush, wrapping my arms around him. "I feel like I'm dreaming. I never thought a sight like this would even be possible."

Kru's arms squeeze around my waist. The solid heat of him against me is so welcome and reassuring I could burst into tears.

"We all love you, Piper."

Tears are in my eyes as I pull back to look at him. "Even Grayson?"

We both burst into laughter. I love this man. I love how he shows up for his loved ones. I love his vision and his journey and his heart. I press my lips to his in a deep, hungry kiss.

When we break apart, I look into his soulful brown eyes and say, "I love you too, Kru."

"Um, excuse me, we're all still here," Griffin whines.

I wriggle in Kru's arms, letting out another peal of laughter. "This is the best day of my life!"

Once I'm out of Kru's arms, I walk over to my brothers. This still feels like a dream—all four of them under the roof of the place I was afraid to even mention to them weeks ago.

"Thank you guys," I say softly. "This means a lot to me."

Asher ruffles my hair the way he used to when I was little. "Anything for you, Pipe Cleaner."

"Literally anything," Dane adds. "Up to and including remodeling a barn you just started renting."

"And backing down on the helpful life guidance," Jett adds.

"And, I guess, not punching your boyfriend anymore," Griffin rounds out.

The tears are back, streaming down my face through the laughter. It feels so right...and so wild. My brothers crowd around me in an awkward, hot group hug.

"Ok, I'm sweating in here!" I exclaim after a few moments.

"No, Pipe Cleaner, we're not done hugging," Jett goads.

"Heat exhaustion, happening now!" I warn.

They crowd me a little tighter until I burst into giggles. Then they finally break apart, and I can breathe again.

The next few hours pass in a blur of sawdust, laughter, and future planning. My brothers, who I've never seen work together without arguing, function like a well-oiled machine under Grayson's direction. Kru moves between helping with the physical prep work and consulting with me on design decisions as we all get on the same page from day one.

"The electrical will need to be installed completely from scratch," Grayson explains as we stand in what will become the kitchen area. "And we'll need to reinforce this section for the commercial appliances. But the bones are solid."

"So how long do you think it will take? Any chance it could be done by next summer?"

"You'll be up and ready by summer for sure. I mean come on—look at this crew." He grins at my brothers. "Might even be spring."

"And I can definitely help out on occasion," Kru says. "Fill in any gaps in the schedule."

I dip my chin, seeing my opportunity to finally broach the question I've been content to avoid. "Aren't you going to Columbus tonight?"

He pinches my chin gently, so much tenderness in his gaze that I almost have to look away. "No, Maven. I'm not. I decided I'm going to wait on anything that isn't in Bayshore. I'll be right here with you."

After only a few hours of prep work, the transformation from one-woman show to professional construction project is visible. The space feels bigger, organized, more purposeful. Grayson's laid the framework and taken the reins. I'm so thankful to have a professional at the helm—and someone who can tell my brothers what to do. Once noon hits, all the men are grumbling about being hungry.

"Lunch is on me," Kru announces. "I'll start getting our plates ready. You guys come into the restaurant, okay?" He winks at me before heading out of the barn.

"I've gotta head out to my other project soon," Grayson says, tugging off his work gloves, "but I won't say no to whatever that man is cooking up."

"I haven't tried any of his food yet," Dane admits.

"I've heard good things," Asher mutters, though it sounds grudging.

"He's number one in the Best of Bayshore competition right now," Griffin says, and it's *clearly* grudging.

"You guys are going to love whatever he makes you," I promise. Grayson and his crew get their things packed up. We settle on a construction plan—basically part-time, based on when at least two of my brothers can help out at the same time—which feels like a major relief. I don't have to sacrifice my every waking moment to make this become a reality.

I have a plan. I have support. I have the best family. And boyfriend.

We all slowly trickle toward Ray's. Inside, it's totally empty, since today is Kru's off day. However, he called in help just for us. Brady waves at us as we come inside, taking our orders quickly since Grayson and his guys need to move on to their main project of the day. Kru and Brady disappear into the back. As we wait for the food, I'm taking in the restaurant alongside my brothers. They look impressed, if not a bit in awe.

"Did he build that bar himself?" Jett asks, nodding toward the pennies.

"He had help," I say with a grin, "but it was modeled after his dad's idea. Kru lost his father about five years ago, and this restaurant is in his honor."

Dane smiles softly at me. "He's a good dude, huh?"

"The best," I say.

Soon, Kru and Brady are coming out of the kitchen with our meals. Plates of braised short rib tacos, pistachio crusted salmon, tuna salad wraps and more are set down for our hungry table. Kru slips into the chair at my side. Everyone is oohing and aahing, but I stop short when I notice Asher has ordered the lobster with the brown butter sauce and nutmeg marshmallow.

"I had to see for myself what the number one dish in Bayshore is like," he says.

"We know Piper has the true number one dish though," Jett clarifies.

Kru just smiles, taking it in stride. "She's not just the true number one dish in Bayshore. She is also part of *that* number one dish in Bayshore." He gestures to Asher's plate. "Those are her marshmallows. And I think that's *why* I slid into first place, because of her addition."

I reach for his hand under the table. He winks at me, giving me a squeeze.

"We're better together," I say in a singsong voice.

"Lobsters and marshmallows are a perfect match," he says, before dipping down to give me a kiss. My brothers groan, even though it's barely a peck. I love that we're at kissing-in-front-of-my-brothers status already.

Everybody digs in, and soon our table is a raucous chorus of contented murmurs and delicious exclamations. As they eat, my brothers offer their feedback, which Kru laps up. Asher is notably silent, until I realize it's because he's been *inhaling* his food. He doesn't utter a word until the plate is totally cleared, minus the shell. Then he pushes it aside, looking over at Kru.

"Phenomenal," he says. "The marshmallow mixed with the sauce…"

"It's great, isn't it?" Kru winks over at me.

Grayson and his crew are the first to head out after a big round of compliments to the chef. It's just us Keegans and Kru at the table when Dane's phone buzzes. He frowns down at the screen.

"Mom just texted. She said they found a safe in the rubble at the bakery."

"Is it hers?" I ask.

"She says it's not, but it has our last name inscribed in it." Dane frowns at his phone for a moment longer then looks up at us. "There's a combination lock and she's tried to open it but can't."

"Okay. Mysterious gift from the fire," Griffin mutters.

"We have to figure out how to open it," I say.

"I guess we'll start trying combinations," Jett adds. "Starting with all zeroes."

We chat about what a mysterious safe might contain, especially one with our last name on it *and* one that Mom doesn't already know about. After some spirited discussion, Dane, Asher, and Jett head out, claiming they need to get back to work.

I let out a contented sigh. "I think that was the best lunch I've ever had. Both from a flavor standpoint *and* a personal standpoint."

"That's what we shoot for here at Ray's," Kru jokes.

"It was great," Griffin concedes. "Even if I'm salty about you getting the glory on Best of Bayshore when you used my sister's business to snag first place…"

"Trust me, there will be no doubt that this was a collaboration," Kru says. "Once the final results are published, Bayshore will know that this was not just my creation, but *ours*."

I wrap my arm around his, resting my head against his bicep. "You're the best."

Griffin sighs and shakes his head. "All right. I'm out. This whole boyfriend thing is gonna take some getting used to."

"You could work on finding a girlfriend, you know," I remind him.

Griff shakes his head. "There's no time. I'm remodeling this barn, I'm going to physical therapy, the season is in full swing..."

I grin over at him. "You're the best big brother out there, you know that?"

Griffin cracks a heartbreaker smile, one that looks just like an old picture of our dad. "I won't tell the others you said that. And you're the best little sis out there."

"I'm your *only* little sis."

"Point still stands." He pushes to standing, jerking his chin toward Kru. "Thanks again for the meal. We'll see you on Wednesday, right?"

Kru looks stunned as Griff heads for the front door. "So they want me back at game night?"

"I think this means you're part of the family now," I tell him. "All you had to do was yell at my brother a little, rope them into renovating a barn, feed them, send my mom to a spa day, and...what else was there?"

"Fall head over heels for the Keegan sister," he adds.

"Oh yes, that." I laugh before I press a kiss to his lips. I nuzzle against him, buzzing with happiness. The restaurant is a dull roar around us as we sit in our little cocoon, bellies full and hearts warm.

There's nowhere I'd rather be than right here: sitting in his thriving business, only feet away from my own thriving business, wrapped up in the arms of my perfect match.

EPILOGUE

PIPER

ABOUT SIX MONTHS LATER

Spring in Bayshore is nothing short of magical. It's early May, full of blossoming flowers and fresh lake air and all manner of springtime glory. Today feels like the culmination of everything I've dreamed of.

The ribbon cutting ceremony for Cloud Nine Events is in full swing, and I can hardly believe this barn—my Barny—has been transformed into something so beautiful. Exposed beams painted in soft white stretch toward the vaulted ceiling, where string lights create a canopy of stars. The windows overlooking Briggs Bay are thrown open, letting in the warm May breeze and the sound of water lapping against the shore. Through the windows, the stone path that we laid is visible, leading to a little bench and garden area near the shore. Round tables draped in cream linens are scattered throughout the space, each one topped with wildflower centerpieces.

"This is absolutely stunning, Piper," gushes Mayor Thompson as city officials prepare the oversized scissors for photos. "Bayshore has needed a space like this for years. Truly unique and built with love."

I beam at her, smoothing my hands over the dusty rose dress I chose for today. "Thank you. That means so much to me. We're so excited to serve the community."

The "we" isn't lost on anyone. Kru and I have officially partnered for Cloud Nine Events. Ray's provides all the savory catering, while Cloud Nine handles desserts. We thought we'd start small with a soft opening in May, but our books are completely full through the end of the year, thanks largely to the reality show buzz.

I spot a familiar camera crew wandering the barn, capturing every moment. When the original episodes aired this winter, our romance kinda sorta took over the entire storyline of the show. We became America's favorite small-town couple practically overnight—viral memes and all—which led to this follow-up episode they're filming today.

"Ready for the big moment?" Bella appears at my side, radiant in a flowing yellow sundress. She and Jackson flew in from LA just for this.

"More than ready," I say, grinning as I spot Kru across the crowd. He's talking to his family, who came from Wisconsin—his mom, his sister, and the two adorable nieces who still call him Uncle Lobster and have been charming everyone at the party.

Mom joins us, looking more vibrant than ever. Her rebuilt bakery is slated to open later this month. It's going to be an amazing May for everyone. "Look at this turnout! The whole town is here."

She's not exaggerating. I see familiar faces everywhere—my brothers and Lia, a few members of the Daly family, customers from both our businesses.

"Ladies and gentlemen!" Mayor Thompson's voice carries across the crowd. "If I could have your attention!"

I take my place next to the mayor, Kru at my side. His hand finds mine and squeezes.

"Today marks a special milestone for Bayshore," the mayor continues. "We're celebrating the official opening of Cloud Nine Events, born from the partnership between two of our most beloved local businesses."

After Kru and I operate the awkwardly large and not-very-effective scissors with some grunting and plenty of laughter, we're swept away in a rush of congratulations and conversations with guests. Everyone has something they want to tell us, whether it's just a quick burst of appreciation or a detailed plan for a party they'd like to host here. The space feels alive with possibility, exactly what I'd envisioned since the very beginning.

I'm showing an engaged couple the lake view from the loft when I notice Griffin across the room, standing stock still by the catering table that Kru's servers are occasionally refilling. Griff's gone completely pale, staring at something—or someone—near the entrance.

"Excuse me," I tell the couple, heading for the stairs. "I need to go chat with my brother real quick, but you guys keep looking around. I'll be here if you have any questions!" My feet thump down the stairs, and I make my way over to him. "Griff? You look like you've seen a ghost."

He doesn't respond, just keeps staring. I follow his gaze and see a woman with long golden-brown hair in a simple green dress, talking to one of the catering staff.

"Earth to Griffin," I tease, poking his arm. "Who are you gawking at?"

"That's...that's Casey," he says quietly, narrowing his eyes. "At least, I think."

"Casey?" I squint at the woman, trying to place her. "Casey Hart? From high school?"

Griffin nods, his throat bobbing. I remember now—Casey was one of Griffin's closest friends from high school. I always suspected he had a crush on her, but he never worked up the courage to ask her out, and she moved away for college. I've never seen my confident, professional-athlete brother look so rattled.

"Go talk to her," I urge.

"I can't. What would I even say? 'Hey, remember we used to be best friends and then never spoke for the next ten years'?"

"Old friends usually start with 'hello' and then go from there."

Before Griffin can respond, Mom appears at our side, patting his back with a knowing smile that's become familiar since she woke up from the coma.

"I see your girlfriend has arrived," she says mysteriously.

Griffin's brows draw together as his gaze shifts to our mother. "How do you—do you even know who we're looking at?"

Mom's smile widens, and then she pauses, tilting her head like she's listening to something we can't hear.

"Oh! That reminds me. We need to try this code: 47-83-47," she says suddenly.

"What?" I ask.

"Have you tried that combination yet?" Mom asks casually, as if random six-digit sequences are perfectly normal conversation topics.

A chill runs down my spine. Ever since the fire, we've been trying to open that old safe they found in the bakery ruins. We've tried every significant date we could think of—birthdays, anniversaries, the date the bakery opened. Nothing has worked.

"Mom," I say slowly, "how does a code that random just *occur* to you?"

She just smiles that mysterious smile again. "Let's try it soon. I have a feeling it'll work."

Before either Griffin or I can question her further, she drifts away to chat with Jackson and Bella, leaving us staring after her.

"So mom is mildly psychic, right?" Griffin asks.

"Absolutely, and especially when it comes to our love interests." I look over at Casey, who is now examining the wildflower arrangements. "She seems to think your girlfriend is in the barn, though. You ready to go say hi to her?"

Griffin straightens his shoulders, running a hand through his hair. "Yeah. I'm going over there."

I watch my normally smooth brother stumble slightly on his way over to Casey. I bite back a laugh just as Kru appears at my side, sliding his arms around my waist from behind. "What's happening over here?"

"Just watching Griffin try to go talk to an old friend who I'm pretty sure he had a major crush on back in the day." I lean back against his chest. "Think we looked that ridiculous when we were figuring things out?"

"Probably worse," he says, pressing a kiss to my temple. "At least they don't have TV cameras documenting their every awkward moment."

I laugh, turning in his arms to face him. The party continues around us. His nieces are teaching Lia some elaborate hand-clapping game, Asher is deep in conversation with one of the camera operators about technical equipment, and Mom is holding court near the dessert table, charming everyone within a ten-foot radius.

"How does it feel?" Kru asks softly. "Seeing it all come together like this?"

I look around the space—our space—filled with everyone we love, celebrating something we built together. The planning and dreaming, the late-night renovation sessions, the moments of doubt and the breakthrough victories. All of it led to this.

"Perfect," I say simply. "It feels perfect."

Because it's not just our business.

It's a love letter in brush strokes.

Our future in cedar beams.

Less than a year ago, I was hiding my business dreams and my relationship from my family. Now I'm running a thriving event space with the man I love, surrounded by people who believe in us.

Sometimes the best things in life really do come from the biggest risks.

Those risks led me here.

The only place I want to be.

THE END

But wait! Is that really the end? Catch a little bit more time with Kru & Piper in this bonus epilogue here: https://geni.us/apm-bonus-epilogue

Are you ready for Griffin's friends-to-lovers, roommate, fake-dating, hockey romance? Check out <u>A PERFECT MESS</u>, the next book in the Bayshore (Keegan family) series.

We love Hazel & Gray — but they weren't always Bayshore's dream couple! Have you read their enemies-to-lovers, second chance romance yet? Catch up in <u>MAKE ME LOSE</u>, book 1 in the Bayshore (Daly brothers) series.

Did you know Kru's bestie, Maverick, has his own book? Mav was the eternal playboy until he fell for his closest friend, Scarlett. Read their sizzling hot friends-to-lovers road trip romance in <u>MAKE ME HOT</u>, book #5 of Bayshore (Daly brothers)!

LET'S STAY CONNECTED!

Stay connected with me via <u>my newsletter</u>, where I share teasers, sales, and other exciting news.

Or join my reader group, <u>EMBER'S BLOSSOMS</u>, to hang out up-close and personal! Early looks at new covers, exclusive access to ARC sign-ups, and more.

FACEBOOK

INSTAGRAM

GOODREADS

BOOKBUB

TIKTOK

Website for general book info:

http://www.emberleighromance.com/

Store for all the discounts, bundles, and deals:

http://www.emberleighstore.com

And before you go...
Please consider leaving an honest review about this book! Even just a few words or a line mean so much to us authors.

ALSO BY EMBER LEIGH

THE NIGHTINGALES OF WALL STREET

Broken Bodyguard

Bossy Billionaire

THE BAD BOYS OF WALL STREET

The Price of a Promise

The Price of Revenge

The Price of Passion

The Price of Infamy

The Price of Forever

WINTER HARBOR

(co-written with Whitley Cox)

The Bastard Heir

The Asshole Heir

The Rebel Heir

The Matchmaking Heirs